Parker was taken aback by the intensity in Emma's face.

So much was going on inside her and she'd revealed so little. She could talk about Mike and Ruby and the resort in detail, but he knew nothing about how she spent her days. He knew nothing about her deceased husband except his name.

"Are you ready? I thought I'd move the birds to a separate part of the nature center now," he said.

Emma's face brightened. "Let me get my camera out."

"A real camera," Parker teased.

"Absolutely." Emma shrugged off her backpack and dug inside. "Phones are fine, but I like the real thing, too, especially since I'm creating my slideshow for the open-house weekend."

"You can wait here and I'll get the cart. I can move both birds together."

The walk to the boardwalk gave him a chance to settle down—his thinking, anyway. His heart wasn't listening to logic. Earlier, seeing Emma walking toward him, the early-morning sun shining behind her, his heart had skittered.

Dear Reader,

Welcome back to Bluestone River, a prairie community in Illinois. The new mayor and others who want the best for Bluestone River have announced exciting holiday events to bring the town back to life. In this book, a treasured landmark is also the place where love ambushes Parker Davis and Emma O'Connell—just in time for the festive season.

With the arrival of Parker Davis, a wildlife expert hired to fix up the nearly defunct nature center, the plan is to officially reopen on Christmas Eve. As Parker's teenage daughter points out, he's way overqualified for this job. That's okay. After a painful divorce he's grateful for a fresh start in Bluestone River. Emma O'Connell, a local and a big town donor, comes with a few surprises. She's healing from wounds of her own, but that doesn't stop the connection blooming between the two of them.

As Parker discovers the magic of the Hidden Lake bird sanctuary and Emma finds the new direction she's been looking for, can they learn to trust each other and believe in love again? At its heart, this is a story of healing and the joy of new beginnings.

Please visit me on Facebook or Twitter, or on my website, virginiamccullough.com.

To happy endings,

Virginia

HEARTWARMING

The Christmas Kiss

—

Virginia McCullough

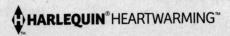

Recycling programs for this product may not exist in your area.

ISBN-13: 978-1-335-51096-9

The Christmas Kiss

Copyright © 2019 by Virginia McCullough

This edition published by arrangement with Harlequin Books S.A.

For questions and comments about the quality of this book, please contact us at CustomerService@Harlequin.com.

® and TM are trademarks of Harlequin Enterprises Limited or its corporate affiliates. Trademarks indicated with ® are registered in the United States Patent and Trademark Office, the Canadian Intellectual Property Office and in other countries.

Printed in U.S.A.

Virginia McCullough grew up in Chicago, but she's enjoyed living in many places, including the coast of Maine, western North Carolina and now northeastern Wisconsin. She started her career writing magazine articles but soon turned to coauthoring and ghostwriting nonfiction books. When fictional characters started whispering in her ear, she tried her hand at writing their stories. Now, many books later, Back to Bluestone River is her second series for Harlequin Heartwarming readers. When she's not writing, Virginia eagerly reads other authors' books, hangs out with family and friends and plans another road trip.

Books by Virginia McCullough

Harlequin Heartwarming

Girl in the Spotlight
Something to Treasure
Love, Unexpected
A Family for Jason

Visit the Author Profile page
at Harlequin.com for more titles.

To Cynthia—Cyndy—Williams, not only a wonderful friend, but a person who cares deeply for the birds who bring their colors and music to her yard all year round. Cyndy happily extends that love to every living thing.

CHAPTER ONE

THE PHOTO OF Parker Davis in the Bluestone River Weekly didn't do him justice. Not even close. The headshot of the newly hired director of the Hidden Lake Bird Sanctuary had appeared with the article announcing his arrival in town. Emma O'Connell guessed the man with a wide mouth and an appealing cleft in his chin to be around forty or so. If he were a corporate type, his wavy blond hair would need a trim, but the unruly look suited his outdoorsy appearance.

Now, seeing him standing maybe thirty feet away, Emma was drawn to what the photo didn't show. Like the muscular arms filling the sleeves of his snug black T-shirt. No baggy work pants, either. His sawdust-flecked jeans were a perfect fit, along with the tool belt.

Parker's hands were braced on a plywood sheet balanced on two sawhorses positioned on the gravel patch at the edge of the woods.

He was studying what looked like a blueprint spread out on top of the plywood and anchored with rocks on the four corners.

"Good morning," Emma called out, surprised he was so deep in concentration he hadn't already noticed her heading his way.

Seemingly startled, he snapped his head up. "Uh, same to you," he returned in a flat voice.

She checked the uneven ground in front of her and tightened her grip on her cane as she stepped toward him. When she was almost close enough to extend her arm to shake his hand, she casually tossed the cane a few inches in the air and caught it at the bottom end. She gave it a quick twirl under her arm so the handle pointed toward him. "Appropriate for a visit to a bird sanctuary, don't you think?"

Carved in the shape of a duck's head with other birds etched into the stick, her cane always brought some kind of reaction. This time it caused the corners of Parker's mouth to turn up in a closemouthed smile. Emma preferred photographing landscapes to aiming her camera at people, but she'd have enjoyed catching Parker's expression in that moment. Much better than the picture in the paper.

"Emma O'Connell. Nice to meet you." She freed her right hand and held it out to him. He quickly brushed his palm back and forth across his jeans before he shook her hand in a quick, formal way.

"I've, uh, heard so much about you," Parker mumbled.

Not quite enough, Emma thought, or she wouldn't see such frank surprise in his dark blue eyes looking at her through glasses, also dark blue.

Suddenly aware of how intently she was staring at him, Emma shifted her gaze over his shoulder and waved to two carpenters, a father-son team whose truck she'd noticed in the sanctuary's parking lot. She knew them from other construction projects, including one on her land. At the moment, Bill and Will Rivera were attaching a railing to supporting slats for the boardwalk-in-progress, the sanctuary's newest feature. The smell of freshly cut wood mingled with the typical earthy scents of fall after a day of rain. "You got the boardwalk project underway fast. You haven't been here all that long."

Parker gestured behind him. "We're just

getting started. A few people from the sanctuary board have dropped by to see what we're up to, so I've got my spiel down pretty well by now. Other people in town hadn't heard about the boardwalk so I've filled in a lot of detail about it, mostly why it's being added." He paused. "In your case, I guess I can skip those basics."

From his low tone, Emma wasn't sure if Parker thought that was good news or bad. But being a major donor to various Bluestone River projects almost always brought a mix of responses. Long ago, Emma learned it was possible for people who did the hard work of running programs and projects to appreciate her financial contribution, but still be a little apprehensive around her, too. She could almost see people's guard rising the minute they saw her coming. Like Parker.

She cleared her throat. "The board gave me a set of drawings for the additions to the sanctuary, but that was a formality. They keep me in the loop, even though I'm not involved in running this place."

Emma wanted—*needed*—to make it clear she wasn't there to check up on him. She had nothing to do with hiring him, and certainly had no intention of overseeing the boardwalk construction or any of the work going into reimagining the bird sanctuary. She leaned closer and stage-whispered, "I just throw money at stuff."

Parker responded with a short but hearty laugh that came from deep in his chest.

Mission accomplished.

Emma walked around him and pointed deeper into the woods. "So beautiful this time of year, huh? Perfect setting for this boardwalk. I'm sure it will attract lots of visitors."

Parker planted his hands on his hips and nodded. "That's the idea."

The deepening creases in his forehead didn't match the words, but Emma let it go. She sensed the frown was part of Parker covertly studying her. Too bad covert wasn't his strong suit, because now she had to try to pretend she didn't notice.

Parker pointed to the carved duck's head. "That's a beautiful walking stick, by the way. And like you said, it fits this setting."

Skipping any explanation of why she needed it, she said, "Matter of fact, it's made by a local wood carver."

Indicating the worktable, Parker said, "Come

closer, have a look. I'll show you what we've done so far."

It was only a couple steps to the worktable he'd set up, but she moved carefully and kept her eyes on the natural dips and rises in the ground. The need to consider each movement frustrated her, especially when getting around on flat terrain posed no problem at all.

"We'll be smoothing out this ground. Filling the holes and creating a gravel walk here. Maybe even a paved one eventually." Parker twisted halfway around and pointed to the already cleared path snaking through the woods. "The committee covered everything in the design. The boardwalk itself will be wide enough for wheelchairs."

"I'd heard that," Emma said.

"And we're adding lots of turnouts and bridges to crisscross back and forth, so people can double back to the nature center building without having to walk the whole thing."

"Oh, yes. That's good." Very good in fact, but it still pained her to be reassured that way. Happy that *everyone* would have a chance to enjoy the sanctuary, she hadn't fully accepted that she was one of the people whose limitations had to be considered. She squared her shoulders and looked directly into his eyes. "I usually walk more easily. I can cover fairly long distances, too. I used to be sort of a girl jock." *Girl jock?* Where had that come from? What was she defending, anyway?

Apparently not inclined to delve into her athletic past, Parker tapped his long index finger on a spot on the colorful drawing in front of him. "So, this is where we are. We've already got about a quarter mile of board-walk planked. As you can see, the guys are attaching the railings for this section. They're quite an assembly line. They cut the wood at their shop and then assemble it all here."

"The Bill and Will Rivera father-son team did the construction work on another project I was involved with last spring," Emma said. "They're good. I'm glad they got this contract." They'd put up arbors and installed benches for the butterfly garden the conservancy built on the edge of her land.

She plunked her finger on the depiction of the small pier that was part of the original resort. "So that's called the observation point now, huh?" She turned to get a glimpse of the real pier jutting out in the lake. "A bunch of us here in town spent a lot of summer days jumping off that pier and racing each other to a raft that used to be out in the middle." She might have added that she usually beat everyone, even most of the boys. "Naturally, Mike Abbot was one of the kids I used to swim with. I'm sure you were filled in on the history of his family's resort."

Parker nodded and adjusted his glasses with his thumb and index finger. "Big picture, but not a lot of detail."

"Have you met Mike yet? And Ruby?" Emma asked, taking note that Parker's thick frames were the latest style. She liked that subtle hint of healthy vanity.

The wide smile came back. "We have. The morning after Nicole—she's my teenage daughter—and I got here. Mike and Ruby and their little boy came by with their arms loaded with food." He let out a little laugh and smiled. "Not just any food, but fresh bread and donuts and apple pie. That was a big hit with Nicole."

"So what did you think when you saw the place?"

Parker tilted his head and offered a lopsided smile. "Seriously? I know a trick question when I hear one. But I'm a step ahead of you. I was warned. The hiring committee filled me in. I know the Hidden Lake Resort was a big deal around here way, way back. So I wasn't shocked to see the condition of the buildings. Besides, you can hardly find any of these old-style housekeeping cabins these days. Nic's imagination took off on a wild ride picturing what this place must have been like back in the day."

"To someone her age that must seem like eons ago," Emma mused. "But even when Mike and Ruby and I were kids this place was already out of style."

"I'll bet. Those boxy wooden cabins remind me of something out of my grandparents' era—or even earlier."

Emma recognized the little ripples of nostalgia that always came up when she thought about Mike's family's old resort and working for his folks. Her parents placed high value on impeccable—their word—behavior, good grades and fulfilling one's duty, whatever that was. Fun with friends and the pure joy of something as mundane as a challenging swim across the lake were eyed with suspicion. That's why Emma had always counted her summers of goofing around on this lake as some of the few times she felt like a carefree kid.

"Working here for the Abbots was the best summer gig for us kids in town. Mike's mom was our real boss. We all scrubbed those cabins to a shine and scooped hundreds of ice cream cones." Emma paused and tapped her thumb on her chest. A little theatrics to add a flirtatious tone. "I don't want to *brag* or anything, but I was one of the star gardeners… well, amateur groundskeepers."

Parker rewarded her light tone with his friendliest smile yet. "You can joke, but you have the same faraway look that I saw in Mike and Ruby when they mentioned those summers." He waved toward the woods. "How about a walk on the new boardwalk? It should be safe."

"Lead the way," Emma said, aware of her rising enthusiasm. "I haven't been back in these woods since I was a kid."

Parker waved to Bill and Will as they came off the boardwalk and said they were going to their shop to reload the truck. Emma called out her greeting to the two as they went on their way.

When they reached the slight incline onto the first planks, Parker raised his hand. "Stop right there."

"I'll be fine on it, Parker."

"I can see that," he said. "But I'm going to give this baby a performance test." He took a few long strides ahead and widened his stance. He bounced in place, took a couple more steps ahead and jumped high enough to come down hard. "See? The right amount of give, but no sagging. I'm calling it safe." Smiling smugly, he waited for her to catch up.

The air was cooler under the trees sheltering the boardwalk. And damper. Emma was glad she'd worn a heavy wool sweater over her turtleneck. With every puff of wind, the trees dropped more leaves and sent them floating down to the forest floor. "All these trees will be almost bare in a few days. Halloween marks the real end of fall around here," she said, hearing the sadness in her voice.

They walked along in awkward silence. At least it was awkward for her—and annoying. She didn't need more evidence of how narrow her life had become. Being alone on a simple walk with a man her age—and single, too, from what she'd heard—was a novel experience. The faint sound of a vibrating phone grabbed Parker's attention. He took the phone out of his pocket and gave it a glance.

"Go ahead and take that if you need to," Emma said. "Don't mind me."

"Nah, it can wait." He chuckled. "I thought maybe it was another update from Stacey Schwartz. They contacted me yesterday about a new plan that changes the work we're doing some."

"Oh? What's up?"

"Seems the committee has decided to host an open house over Thanksgiving weekend. Kind of like a warm-up act for the big Christmas Eve celebration," he explained. "It means fixing up the office and finishing the boardwalk are our priorities. The plan is based on luring people to wander in on the long weekend and have a look. Maybe become sanctuary members." Frowning, he stared out into the woods. "It's okay. I don't mind rearranging the work schedule."

She forced a neutral expression. An open house on an otherwise busy shopping weekend struck her as a huge waste of time. But that was just her gut reaction. Now and then, something took her by surprise and challenged her hands-off stance toward the sanctuary and the people who ran it. This was one of those times.

"You're surprised?"

She offered a coy smile. "And I thought I hid it. But then, I haven't talked to Ruby about things going on in town lately."

Parker's frown was back.

Her fault. He'd still be in the dark about who was linked to who and why. "Sorry, I sometimes forget all these local connections might confuse you at first. Ruby's my best pal—since grade school. If Ruby and I aren't talking on the phone, we're texting. She keeps me up-to-date on most everything going on these days, mainly because it seems there's always something new."

She explained that Mike and Ruby had been married on New Year's Eve, and then in April Mike ran for mayor and won. "And now, only a few months later, we're talking about boardwalks and Christmas caroling at the covered bridge."

"Nic told me Santa's coming to River Street," Parker said, amused. "You've all been busy."

"It's an old story. A major employer shut down a plant and this town started to slide downhill. But we're turning that all around now. No more limping along. We're reinventing Bluestone River." She dramatically extended her hand in his direction. "And that explains why you're here."

Parker's jaw tightened for a second or two, but then relaxed. Hmm…she'd intended to amuse him a little. Oh well, so her act bombed. But why the tension?

"The board is busy luring volunteers." He smirked, adding, "And courting donors."

"Not such a bad thing for a not-for-profit to do." She looked away, annoyed by his snide tone.

When she glanced back at him, Parker's face was slightly red.

Served him right.

Parker stopped in place where the planking ended. "We'll decorate all this with white lights for the Christmas Eve event. The main building and the pier and our cabins will be lit up, too."

"It's making me look forward to Christmas," Emma admitted, turning to start back. The minute she heard it, Emma had taken to the sanctuary's new name: The Hidden Lake Bird Sanctuary and Nature Center. It sounded established, even permanent. It's what Mike's dad would have wanted when he gave the land to the conservancy.

"I can help out on Thanksgiving weekend." Emma didn't like the eagerness coming through in her voice, or the undeniable relief spreading through her body. It meant she admitted, at least to herself, that hanging out at the sanctuary gave her something to fill an otherwise long, even dreaded weekend. "Maybe I could be a greeter and entice people to join."

Parker shook his head and looked away. "Look, I owe you an apology for that remark about donors. My tone, I mean. I forgot for a minute that you're the one footing the bill for these renovations and other changes." His big gesture encompassed the woods and all the buildings. "I didn't mean to be sarcastic."

Oh, yes, he did. It was second nature to him. Probably every job he ever had depended on people like her. But as apologies went, she graded this one C minus. She held up her hand as if to stop him from going on. "Correction. I'm covering *some* of the upgrades here. And I *don't* micromanage. Consider me a silent partner."

Parker cleared his throat. "I only hope people around here have the good sense to know what a special place they've got."

"I think it's what got Mike elected mayor."

But will it point me in a new direction? She

pushed that question away for the moment and focused on Parker's rich, deep voice describing yesterday's cold downpour. Emma thought of her mom, who would have dispensed with words like *tenor, baritone* or *bass*. She'd have said he was born with a voice meant for radio and left it at that.

"The rain helped us identify the source of leaks in the office building roof," Parker said with a smile. "Admittedly, the water stains already on the ceiling and walls were pretty good clues."

She started to respond when a loud voice from behind interrupted. "Are you Parker Davis?"

"Yep, that's me." He put his hand across his forehead to shade his eyes from the shafts of afternoon sun coming through the trees. "Heater guys? I sure hope so."

"Yessir, that's us."

"I hope you're having those old oil heaters in the cabins replaced. It's way past time." Emma took a last look around. "I'll be on my way. Thanks for the walk and the updates."

Parker held up his arm in a silent message to the guy that he'd be right there. Polite. But unnecessary. With her free hand, Emma shooed Parker away. "Go on. Take care of business. I'm fine."

"They can wait a minute."

Since there was nothing tentative about his tone, she offered no argument. When they reached the gravel, she waved goodbye and started toward the lot, but turned around when Parker called out to her. "Will I see you on Friday at the reception? It's being billed as my formal welcome to Bluestone River."

"Absolutely," Emma said. "I wouldn't miss it."

He smiled broadly before turning his attention to the heating guy.

Nothing tentative in that smile, either.

NIC'S LONG BLOND hair blew around her head in the strong breeze coming across the lake. Even with her face partially covered, Parker could read her mood. With shoulders slumped and head lowered, she loped along the bare path to her cabin. In no hurry, or so it seemed.

Parker called her name to get her attention and waved his arm for her to come to the boardwalk. When she didn't respond the first time, he gave her the benefit of the doubt and called out again, louder this time. "Hey, Nic."

Finally, she looked up, still fighting a losing battle with her hair as it swished over her face.

Parker walked toward her. "The heater guys left a few minutes ago. You can warm up your place tonight."

That news changed her expression. "Yay! Finally." She looked past him at the carpenters, who were back now, unloading more planking off a dolly. They'd been around most every day, but from Nic's expression she might have been seeing them for the first time.

"They're the same two guys who were working yesterday," Parker said, amused by the way she was scrutinizing Will, who looked to be about eighteen or nineteen. Nic's age.

She responded with a halfhearted shrug. Man, much as he loved his daughter, she could wear on him sometimes. Wasn't a girl her age supposed to be lively, full of energy? Okay, that was a platitude, and sometimes she was those things and more. But lately, he never knew which Nic he'd be talking to. The teenager thrilled to be an adult going to college or the unhappy girl pining for simpler years gone by. Longing for the home they'd left, or wishing she was with her mother instead of him. When he challenged her, Nic defended her bad attitude by pointing out that he and her mother had forced her into this "new normal," as she called it. Hard to argue with that.

"So, how was your day?" *When* would he learn not to ask questions she could so easily dismiss with one-word answers?

"Fine." She changed the direction of her gaze from Will to him. "I have to study for my zoology test. And did I tell you I have an interview at the Sweet Comforts Bakery in the morning?"

"You mentioned that. Sounds like a good job to go after."

"See ya, Dad."

"Come to my cabin later. We'll figure out dinner."

"Okay, but as long as we have lots of veggies for a salad."

He clamped his lips together to suppress a snort of laughter. This from a girl who once considered the existence of carrots and kale a personal affront. "You got it, Nic. Green, yellow, orange. We've got them all. Even a purple something."

Did the corners of her mouth turn up?

Maybe, but then she remembered and flashed a withering look. "Leave the salad to me."

"Got it."

Nicole continued to her cabin but managed another surreptitious glance at Will, who was still stacking wood. As potential dates went, Nic could do worse, Parker decided. The kid sure worked hard enough. He and his dad had made great progress in the few days they'd been working at the sanctuary, inside as well as outside. On the rainy days the two concentrated on tearing out old rickety shelving in the office.

Most of the real work to fix up the two cabins, one for him and one for Nic, would wait until winter. The board had asked if he preferred to open up one large cabin for him and Nic, or would two small ones work better? Not a hard choice. Nic had taken to calling her one-room-and-an alcove cabin her studio—the only really good thing about their unexpected move to Bluestone River. She didn't care about the decay around her. Blue-turned-gray paint peeling off the cabin. Squeaky pipes. Limited hot water. Those were small prices to pay for having her own place.

Leaving Bill and Will to finish up their

tasks for the afternoon, Parker wandered down to the pier, also due for repairs in time for Thanksgiving. He looked across the lake to the marshes at one end, where a few dozen geese were gathering. Many more clustered in the field across from the woods. Parker expected most of the geese would move on, but a few would winter over. The sprawling Abbot family home sat back from the shore at the opposite end of the lake. At forty-five acres, Hidden Lake was big enough to be the centerpiece of the resort in the past, and now add to the appeal of the sanctuary.

Jackie, his ex-wife, would have called this land and the lake picture-postcard beautiful. The pretty brunette, Emma O'Connell, apparently agreed. He hadn't missed the look that passed over her face when she talked about her summer resort job and swimming off the pier.

Parker had to laugh at himself. As much as he'd tried, he couldn't stop looking at Emma, not from the first glimpse of her approaching him. Maybe it was the sassy way she'd twirled her cane that intrigued him. Straight dark hair set off large brown eyes that lit up in fun, but turned serious when something subtle shifted her mood. She was taller than average. Her body was curvy and strong—easy to picture her as that girl jock she brought up.

He bet Emma was a good dancer. He closed his eyes and there he was, holding her close and slow dancing on the pier. Now why had that occurred to him? He didn't know her. Not even a little bit. He gave the railing a little bump with his palm, as if that could knock her image out of his brain.

With no reason to let his mind go there, he wondered if the sadness rippling below the surface was about her losing her husband, a fact about her that had come in a casual conversation about how the sanctuary was funded. Or maybe she was doing fine and he was the one projecting sadness. He'd been walking around with a cloud over his head for a while now. Sometimes he forgot he hadn't always been grumpy and glum. Matter of fact, he felt pretty good walking on the boardwalk with Emma.

What made Emma tick was neither here nor there, he repeated to himself. Warm eyes and a smile to match aside, the woman was a donor. From his first interview with the three-person search committee, Parker got it. One person held his job in the palm of her hand.

She was a presence without actually being in the room, described as a wealthy widow who'd paid his predecessor's salary in order to keep the sanctuary open. And she would raise her contribution—substantially—in order to hire a professional, someone with the right experience and credentials. Someone just like him.

What wasn't like him was that he'd spared no stereotype in making assumptions about the donor in question. In his mind's eye, she was older than Emma, by maybe thirty, even forty years. His imaginary Emma was nothing like the real woman, who he guessed hadn't celebrated her fortieth birthday yet. He admitted being a little thrown that she relied on a cane. Likely, though, she was recovering from some kind of injury. He smiled to himself. She'd probably be dancing again soon.

Parker again tried to force his thoughts elsewhere. Emma's age and beauty were irrelevant. He knew that much. He'd accumulated a lot of painful experience working with organizations' boards and dutifully pleasing benefactors and courting new ones. He'd learned to hold funders at arm's length, at least as much as possible. His rules were simple: Be polite and competent, but don't confuse decorum with friendship. People with major bucks to hand out, no matter how worthwhile the cause, had a way of tightening reins on the organizations they propped up. This was true even in the smallest facilities, like the Hidden Lake Bird Sanctuary.

The geese in the marsh began honking as they took flight. He let the sound distract him from his own thoughts, which were making a beeline toward a dark, hurt place he couldn't afford to indulge. He stood in place and watched the birds soar across the sky on their late afternoon trip. In his last job, he didn't have a lake outside his front door. That particular rescue center for birds of prey sat a quarter mile back from a narrow creek off one of the estuaries along the North Carolina coast. At any given time, the center might house over one hundred birds in various stages of treatment.

Despite serious misgivings about saying yes to this new position as director of the sanctuary here on Hidden Lake, maybe breathing life into this run-down facility, it was exactly what he—and Nicole—needed to build a different life. That's what led him to sign a one-year contract to assure the stakeholders he'd launch their new vision for this wooded land and old buildings. In the fall, he'd plan his next steps. They could involve Nic, but maybe not. That depended on who she chose to live with. Right now Nic was with him. With some regularity, Jackie still dangled weak invitations to their daughter to come and stay with her at some vague point in the future.

Speaking of Jackie, he remembered the text that had come in and pulled out his phone. Nothing critical. Just a note about a loose end that once dealt with would sever any legal tie to each other. Parker stared at the screen. That was it? Jackie was his past. Her exact words were, "You're free, so go plan a great future for yourself."

Parker fought the impulse to call his ex-wife, maybe tell her to make up her mind. Did she want Nic with her or not? The vacillating wasn't helping their daughter adjust. Maybe, he'd drop a remark or two to remind her he'd never asked for his so-called freedom. That had been her idea.

He grasped the railing on the pier with both hands and sighed. He'd never planned to be on this pier overlooking this lake in a small Midwest town, either. But here he was. A chance at a bigger, better job had fallen through. Faced with no job at all, Parker reluctantly accepted what looked like a relatively easy stint here in Bluestone River. He had to watch his attitude, though. He'd already sized up the board and the donors as town booster types, which was okay as far as it went. But a legitimate bird sanctuary that rescued and treated its patient-birds needed dedicated advocates. So far, the board showed more interest in attracting locals and tourists to an ordinary nature center. Becoming a true bird sanctuary was a step in a five-year plan. Parker doubted it would happen at all.

Being blindsided over a job offer was one thing. A divorce was in a category of its own. The worst part was what it did to Nic. As an only child, and doted on at that, her spirit shattered in little pieces. Parker winced against the memory of Nic yelling at Jackie. Her mom betrayed them. She'd never forgive her, never. That had gone on for days, until the morning Jackie stood by her packed car and hugged Nic and asked her to come and live with her and Ben. One day. *Soon*. When she and Ben were settled. But the next time Nic saw her mom was almost six months later at her high school graduation.

Parker focused on consoling Nic. Something he apparently wasn't very good at.

Now, he stared overhead at geese flying in formation. He listened to their loud negotiation, as his daughter liked to call their attention-grabbing honking. With golden leaves dropping from the trees and the breeze ruffling the surface of the lake, he'd be a fool to complain about where he'd landed. What was a year out of his long career?

The upcoming reception wasn't his favorite type of occasion, but he'd managed to navigate his way around them before—almost every job he held required him to be the public face of an organization.

Strange how the prospect of seeing Emma again was almost enough to get his mind off Jackie.

While his good mood held, he left the pier and went to Nic's cabin and knocked on the screen door. "It's just me, Nic."

"Come on in," she said in a listless tone.

He stepped just inside the door, where the scent of spicy incense filled the air. It tickled his nose, and reminded him of coming into their house in North Carolina and being greeted with a mix of smells coming from the candles and incense Jackie and Nic had burned almost every day.

Nic sat at the table scrolling through her phone, earbuds in, laptop open in front of her, and textbooks spread on the table. The TV was tuned to a cooking show, but the sound was muted. He found Nic's multimedia world a little on the chaotic side, but he bit his bottom lip to keep his comments to himself. "Remember we have the reception on Friday. The board is rolling out a big welcome for us." Yikes. Where did a lame expression like that even come from?

"Why do *I* have to go?" Nic whined. "Can't you make up some excuse for why I can't be there? I'm in *college* now. It's not like you need to parade a perfect little family around."

Ouch. Nic couldn't know how much that hurt. The little things often did. When it came to those work-related duty nights, he'd counted on Jackie as a buffer. She could float around a room and be charming and chatty. He often wound up with his feet glued to the floor in one place holding a half a glass of wine he didn't touch. Some unsuspecting person would approach him and maybe ask a simple question about disappearing bird habitats or migratory patterns. Instead of giving two- or three-sentence answers, he usually fell back on a series of boring facts delivered in what Jackie called his doom-and-gloom voice.

"Hey, pal," Parker said, forcing a light tone, "I need you there to keep me from boring everyone to death."

She smirked. "Like that's even possible, Dad."

He smirked back. "All kidding aside, the folks on the board couldn't have been nicer to us. I'm trying to make it work here. I want you at the reception with me." He swallowed past the lump forming in his throat. "Like it or not, I'm really proud of you. Give your dull dad a break, okay?"

Nic flashed another look. Softer this time.

He stepped to the table and gave it a knuckle rap for emphasis. "C'mon Nic, I know Bluestone River isn't where we thought we'd be."

"An understatement," Nicole interjected. "Not exactly a major clinic for rescued birds, Dad."

"Maybe down the road, Nic, but not..." He let his voice trail off to stop himself from lecturing her. He stared at the window, his thoughts wandering deep into the past to better times.

"Dad? What's with you? You drifted far, far away. What were you going to say?" Nicole's forehead was wrinkled in a deep frown.

He waved her off and continued glancing around. "Uh, nothing. Just thinking about getting our places fixed up and ready for winter."

His astute daughter likely wasn't convinced by that little fib. Still, she sighed and said, "Okay, Dad, I'll go to your thing."

"Great, honey, thanks." He turned toward the door.

"Wait...not so fast. It's going to cost you."

Her impish grin immediately improved his mood. "Oh, really. What's the price? Clothes? Shoes?"

"Nope. It's *you*." Nicole jabbed her index finger at him. "You have to promise to wear a jacket and tie to the reception."

"Oh, no," he moaned, clutching his chest. "What a big price to pay. How will I manage it?" The jacket and tie were no problem, but he'd need to find a place to get a haircut.

"Really, Dad?" Nic shook her head, but at least she was laughing. "Your stand-up routine could use a little practice." She gave him one of her long-suffering looks. "Seriously, wear your gray tweed sport coat. It's like, up-to-date. I mean you did buy it in *this* century. It fits your nature-freak image, but still makes you look smart enough to be a professor."

"Okay, okay." He had to laugh. She'd been calling him a nature freak since she was about twelve years old.

"Seriously, you can't show up looking like a lumberjack." She gave him a once-over. "Like now."

He looked down as his jeans, almost tan from the sawdust clinging to the denim. "I think I can manage not to embarrass you for a couple of hours," he said, already halfway out the door. "See you later."

If Nic only knew how it lightened his load to hear her kid around, even at his expense. He could tolerate some teasing. Besides, he gave as good as he got, especially with Nic. Jackie claimed Nic's bond with him was even stronger than hers, mom or not. True, mother-daughter relationships could be rocky, and Jackie and Nic had their moments. In the end, though, Jackie better understood adolescent mountains and valleys—and quirks.

Or so Parker thought. Only in the last year had Jackie given him reason to question that.

"Dad, wait. I almost forgot. Mom said to say hello." She waved her phone. "She said to tell you she got your text."

"Oh, okay."

"What's that all about?" Nic asked in a wary tone.

"Nothing important. Another document to sign." Nicole's face darkened. She knew that meant it was the divorce.

"Oh." Nic shrugged. "Mom is okay...I guess."

Her expectant expression forced a response of some kind, so he said the first thing that came to mind. "Well, I hope she's doing well."

Nic looked down and got busy with her phone again. "Yeah, right, Dad."

Dead end. He closed the door behind him. Anger at Jackie rising up from his chest to his throat, he mumbled blaming words. It was her fault Nic was so moody—and torn. She lived in her new studio and claimed to like her classes, but on some days, Jackie's pull on Nic was like a magnet. When that happened, Nic could think about little else but her mom's life in Vermont.

Still, Parker had always believed Jackie was a great mom.

Right up to the moment she walked out the door.

CHAPTER TWO

EMMA LEANED AGAINST the back wall of the community room inside the town hall. She wanted to keep a low profile, and she'd likely succeed because the reception for Parker Davis drew a big, noisy crowd. All eyes would be on him. Including hers.

Stacey and Ty, co-chairs of the board, were making the rounds, stopping to introduce Parker and banter with the people who'd come to the reception. More than one hundred guests were there, by Emma's estimates, and people were still coming in. A better showing than anyone on the board expected.

Emma was certain some people had come to be part of the progress Mike had already made as mayor. Who could resist the new energy that had taken over in Bluestone River during the last six months? A welcoming event like this was a chance to put it on display.

Parker towered over both Stacey and Ty as

they steered him from one cluster of people to another. He still looked like he preferred the outdoors, even with the trimmed hair—maybe too trimmed. But she liked the professor-in-the-gray-jacket vibe. He looked almost as good as he did in dusty work jeans.

Maybe not quite as comfortable, though. Had anyone else in the room noticed him periodically tugging at his red tie to loosen its grip on his neck? Other body language spoke pretty loud, too, but not in a good way. Tall to begin with, Parker didn't lean in toward the person addressing him, and the social smile was just that and nothing more. He shook hands like his arm was a mechanical appendage. Maybe he preferred wildlife to people, but showing a little warmth wouldn't hurt. She'd had a glimpse of his softer side and wouldn't mind seeing it again.

Finally, Stacey and Ty led Parker back to the table with spiced cider and wine and trays of appetizers. A row of a dozen or so posters hung on the wall behind the podium set up for the business part of the reception. Stacey created the posters from four-season photographs of Hidden Lake and the woods. Emma had taken three of them. When Emma looked at all of them, she saw dollar signs.

They'd make a good item to sell in the sanctuary office.

"You keeping tabs on anyone special?"

Turning to the voice coming from the side, Emma let out an amused scoff at Ruby's conspiratorial tone. "Not really. Just taking stock of things."

"A likely story." Ruby's light brown eyes sparkled with fun. But that was nothing new. These days Ruby wore her happiness like a comfy pair of shoes. "From where I stand, Mr. Parker Davis is the combination of a hunky outdoorsy guy and not quite as smooth professional." She nodded toward him. "Hmm…he does wear that jacket and tie well, don't you think?"

"So he does," Emma said. "I'm glad you pointed it out. I wouldn't have noticed it all by myself." She had no choice but to volley her kidding back to Ruby. It was Emma's only defense against blushing. For all the good it would do her. Ruby could read her like a book. "Is Mike giving a welcome speech?"

Ruby shrugged. "Sure, but it wasn't anything he had to mull over too much. Stacey asked him to talk a little about the sanctuary as a driving force behind growing the tourist business here in town. That sort of thing."

"You're looking great, Rubes," Emma said looking down at Ruby's baby bump under her swingy purple dress. "You can talk about Parker wearing his jacket well, but I haven't ever seen anyone wear pregnancy with more flair than you."

"I've never felt better or..." She stopped in midsentence and touched Emma's elbow. "Oh, look. There's Parker's daughter, Nicole. She's standing by herself." She nodded to a far corner of the room. "Let's go say hello."

"I've not met her," Emma said, "so I'm glad you noticed her. Parker mentioned they'd met you and Mike when you delivered treats to their door."

Ruby nodded. "Right. And I hear Star hired her at Sweet Comforts a couple of days ago."

Emma immediately regretted not showing more interest in Nicole during her conversation with Parker earlier that week. She'd not wanted to appear too nosy, especially after hearing some talk about Parker being divorced.

"Hello, Nicole," Ruby called out as she led the way to the girl.

Nicole looked almost frightened at the sound of her name, but the muscles in her face immediately relaxed when she saw Ruby. Emma stepped forward and held out her hand. "I'm Emma O'Connell. I'm sorry I missed you when I stopped by the sanctuary the other day. I hope you're settling in okay."

Ruby laughed. "Right. Feeling at home in your *luxury* studio apartment."

Emma couldn't help but note the girl's timid handshake. But there was nothing shy about her hands. They were their own color wheel, each nail a different color from dark blue to sunny yellow. The girl rewarded Ruby's sarcasm with a quick snicker. "At least we have heat now."

"Wow, lucky you," Ruby teased. "So, according to all the busybodies in town, you're commuting to college and working in the bakery. I think I heard that from someone across the room a few minutes ago."

Emma playfully nudged Ruby's shoulder. "I'm sure Nicole loves hearing we're a bunch of gossips."

"Oh, I didn't need Ruby to tell me that," Nicole said, without a trace of embarrassment. "When I applied for the job at the bakery, the owner, you know, Star Lenski, filled me in on all the big holiday plans for the town. She told me about Ty and Stacey.

To tell you the truth I bet she hired me because of my dad and his new job. I can tell she thinks he's cute." She shrugged. "Lots of women do, even married ones like Star."

Emma's laughter sputtered out fast and loud. So, she wasn't the only one who admired the new guy in town. She covered her quick reaction by blurting a couple of questions to Nicole about school.

The girl spoke in a breezy way about her lineup of classes and credit hours. "It's a nice enough college, but I figure the credits will transfer when I move away and go to a different school." Nicole clamped her lips and stared at her flats.

Well, well, the girl knew immediately she'd let too much slip. Pretending she hadn't noticed, Emma said, "So far it looks like Stacey and Ty are keeping your dad pretty busy with the guests. Did you get some food or cider?"

Nicole avoided Emma's gaze. "Uh, not yet."

"You should go help yourself while it lasts." Ruby patted Emma's shoulder. "I'll catch up with you later, Em. Nice to see you again, Nicole."

"Ruby is my best friend," Emma said to keep the conversation going. "Only two people in the whole world get to call her Rubes, and I'm one of them."

Nicole laughed. "And her husband is the other. I heard him call her that the day we got here when she brought boxes of goodies. The pie was huge." She made a big circle with her arms in front of her. "I start my job at the takeout window on Monday morning. Like at *dawn*."

"That's terrific. Very popular newish hot spot in Bluestone River," Emma said with a laugh. "You've probably noticed we don't have too many."

Ignoring Emma's attempt at humor, Nicole said, "Only three, four shifts a week to start, but it's something." She gestured around the room. "You pay for all this sanctuary stuff, huh."

Nothing like a little frankness. "So, did someone tell you that?"

"No one in particular." She nervously tucked a tendril of her flyaway hair behind her ear. "But my dad said the place has the bucks…uh, funding…now and his salary was covered. Then, I don't know, your name came up."

Keeping her voice light, Emma said, "Volunteers and a lot of people make it all work.

I only help out. The sanctuary and the lake mean a lot to me." As she spoke, Emma studied Parker's fair-skinned daughter, whose hair was so much lighter than her dad's. Where his eyes were a deep, dark blue, hers were a distinctive shade of baby blue. "Uh, you mentioned going to a different school. Are you thinking about moving away?"

She scratched her cheek. "No, no, not now. I didn't mean…"

Keeping her voice low, Emma said, "Sorry, I shouldn't have asked." Then why had she? Surprise, maybe? Because she knew little about Parker, except what anyone could see on his résumé? Maybe it was a lot simpler than that. The girl intrigued her.

"It's okay," Nicole said earnestly. "My mom's in Vermont now and she said I could come up and stay with her, and like, switch to a college near her. Maybe…you know… when she's settled."

"I see." Not really, but Emma wished she'd kept her mouth shut.

"Lots of people showed up for this thing," Nicole said, her gaze darting around the room. "Oh, here comes my dad."

Emma turned her head and watched Parker cross the room toward them.

"So, you introduced yourself," he said, smiling at Emma. "I was hoping I'd get a chance to say hello, too." He fidgeted with the knot in his tie.

"You look good, Dad." Nicole pointed one purple-tipped finger at his neck. "And that tie is fine. You can stop checking it."

A laugh escaped from the back of Emma's throat just as Parker flashed a pointed look at his daughter.

"Nicole and I were just talking about her bakery job," Emma said to get off the subject of Parker's tie.

Parker nodded in acknowledgment, glancing at Nicole, who was now more interested in watching the food table, where Mike had joined Ruby.

"I wonder if they ever need a babysitter," Nicole mused. "I have a lot of experience. Their little boy is a cutie."

"Can't hurt to ask, Nic," Parker said.

"I think I will." Nicole said a quick goodbye to Emma and hurried away.

Parker gestured toward Ruby and Mike. "They seem like quite a pair."

Emma grinned. "They are. And they're over the moon about the baby. They live on cloud nine. Oh, and the stars lined up for them at last. Hmm...let me think. What other cliché can I come up with? How about 'they're made for each other'? That'll work."

She sensed Parker staring at her, so she looked directly into his eyes. "Let's just say they found each other after many years apart." Her voice suddenly husky, she added, "It's a long story, but it has a happy ending. That's all that matters."

"Well, to extend the cliché," Parker said, "I see the two of them as prominent movers and shakers in Bluestone River. Just like you."

Emma waved him off. "No, no, don't include me. I try to stay way behind the scenes." On purpose. End of discussion. Not that hiding always worked. She smiled up at him. "Nicole is lovely. The proud way you look at her speaks volumes without saying a word."

"That obvious, huh? I haven't said much about it to anyone, but this move was kind of an upheaval all around."

"And maybe kind of difficult?" The second the words were out she regretted them. Curiosity got the better of her. Again.

Parker's eyes flickered with concern. "Did she mention something specific?"

"No, no, not at all," she said, rolling her

eyes. "That was just a wild guess on my part. Or, I was thinking that starting college can be sort of a roller coaster." That wasn't precisely what she'd meant, but at least she'd backed herself out of her own nosiness. "You drew an impressive crowd. You'll likely see some of these same folks again at other events."

"They said it was a good turnout. I'll say a few words. I don't mind. I've got my routine down pat." Parker lifted one shoulder in a dismissive shrug. "These meet 'n greets go with the territory."

Not the response she expected. Emma shifted her weight, trying not to wince with the sharp pain shooting down her leg. Matching her dropping spirits. If he knew the territory so well, why wasn't he a little looser when he worked the room? Didn't he see the work that had gone in to welcoming him to town? Catered food. Wine donated from a new winery nearby. Printed programs. A reporter covering it for the daily in Clayton. Stacey and Ty's efforts had paid off. But it was just another meet 'n greet to him.

"I see an empty seat at one of the tables," Emma said, edging away from him. "I think I'll grab it before the speeches start."

"Uh, I see Stacey waving to me now."

She sensed him watching her walk away. Her first impression was right. Covert really wasn't his strong suit.

NICE GOING, PARKER mumbled to himself as he made his way around the tables to the podium where Stacey and Ty stood. He left no doubt where he stood. *He didn't mind? Goes with the territory?* Man, he'd let down his guard again. Even *he* thought he sounded like a jerk.

Parker took his place next to Stacey as Mike thanked the organizers and vendors. He quickly moved on to announcing some dates for the lineup of upcoming events. Busy place, Parker thought, as Mike listed the community Halloween party, the Thanksgiving sanctuary open house, Santa on River Street, caroling and Christmas Eve at the sanctuary.

"Watch for details about all events that are part of our Bluestone River Holiday Festival," Mike said. "But now, Stacey and Ty have asked me to introduce the Hidden Lake Bird Sanctuary's new director, Parker Davis. Since he's our neighbor, Ruby and Jason and I have had the pleasure of meeting him, and his daughter Nicole, who's now enrolled in Neville University." Stepping aside, Mike added, "Join me in welcoming Parker and Nicole to Bluestone River."

The applause showed more enthusiasm than he deserved. Glancing at his audience, he saw anticipation in the faces of people who'd taken time to come here and meet him and hear what he had to say. No one had welcomed him more eagerly than the Abbots and Emma.

Parker lifted the mic out of the stand on the podium, his way of reminding himself to move around instead of standing like a mannequin in one place. Jackie had warned him about his body language sometimes raising barriers and making him unapproachable. Sometimes his throwaway lines about donors did the same job. Now he was nervous and cringing at how arrogant he could sound at times. The truth was he should be thanking everyone in the room for giving him a job.

Looking at the friendly faces in the crowd, his heart pounded a little harder and his palms felt damp. But he saw Emma and Nic in the audience and something shifted inside him. He took a deep breath and started. "Thanks for taking the time to come here tonight. I hope you'll greet the changes at the sanctuary as warmly as you've greeted me. I don't want to be long-winded, so I'll give you a quick rundown of what we've got going on here." One by one, he ticked off the items on a list he'd jotted down and slipped into his jacket pocket, but his memory was working fine and his voice got warmer as he went along. The newsletter, coming soon. Social media, up and running. The new website, almost done. The boardwalk, under construction.

"So, I'll be around Thanksgiving weekend. Come in, have a look. Better yet, become a sanctuary member—the whole family can join and benefit from what we—you—are building. For sure, I hope to see all of you on Christmas Eve afternoon for the official relaunch of the new facility."

With his muscles relaxing as he got to the windup, Parker pointed to the wall of photos and the map of the future facility. "Tonight is about the future. I want your kids and grand-children to have the same chance to learn about the natural world as I did. I know you feel the same." Not caring if he sounded condescending or not, he added, "I took this job because Bluestone River made a decision to use this land well. I promise you won't regret it." He dipped his chin to signal the end and put the mic back in the stand before glancing at Stacey and stepping away.

Enthusiastic applause began, but one lone voice called out, "Not everyone likes everything goin' on, ya know."

"C'mon, Jim," Stacey said into the mic. "We know you had different ideas, going back more than a decade. But that time is over now. We're planning for the future."

Parker quietly observed the man standing nearby whose features were fixed in anger, his arms tightly crossed over his chest. But there was something else. Parker guessed this was a guy who suffered from feeling perpetually misunderstood. Even knowing only the sketchy history of debate over how to use the sanctuary land, Parker felt a little sorry for Jim. It was never easy to be a solo voice going against the crowd. He'd been in that position himself a few times and it meant being ready for ridicule—or worse.

"All I wanted was more time for debate," Jim shouted, red-faced as he approached the front of the room.

Voices in the crowd tried to shout him down. Although Parker didn't think the man looked especially threatening to Stacey, he moved in next to her and nodded to the mic she held and opened his hand. "Okay?" he whispered. "I can try to help."

She handed him the microphone. "Go ahead. But this is an old squabble and he doesn't budge."

Parker raised his free hand to quiet the crowd. "I may not be able to change your mind, Jim, but I invite you to stop by anytime. Let's talk about your concerns. I've been where you are. On the other side, maybe, but I know what it's like to take unpopular stances and be outvoted—in big numbers. You're frustrated. I get that."

Jim flapped his hand at Mike. "But you weren't here when *he* took over as mayor. He hadn't lived here for years. Then he waltzes into town and suddenly we're going to be some kinda Christmas village. Like that's going to bring jobs back? What about getting real businesses in town?" He turned as if to leave, but then stopped and said to Parker, "This foolishness goes back a long way."

"Why don't you take Parker up on his offer, Jim?" Emma spoke over the noisy reaction of the crowd. "Really. Visit the place. I was over there the other day. Did you know all the renovation work is being done by local businesses?"

Glaring at Emma through narrowed eyes, Jim opened his mouth as if to speak, but changed his mind. His already red cheeks were on fire. Finally, he said, "Well, I suppose you should know. *You* paid for all this."

Parker stiffened as he waited for Emma to shoot back a zinger. She didn't. Instead, she stayed silent while a few others in the room jeered at Jim. This had to end. Wanting to give him a way to save face and make his exit, Parker again extended his invitation. "I can't change your mind, but the invitation is open. Come by anytime. I'm at the center almost all the time. Come find me."

Parker gave the mic back to Stacey. A couple of seconds later, Mike tried to restart the festive atmosphere by urging everyone to help themselves to more food and wine. As the crowd began to move through the room, Parker watched Jim slip out the door without speaking to anyone.

With his speech behind him, a crisis sort of averted, Parker had loosened up. He made his way to the food table, looking for Nic. He spotted her pulling out a chair next to Emma. Based on the contemptuous way Jim had looked at Emma, even before his rude remark, Parker assumed there was no love lost between them from the start. Yet, Emma had jumped right into the controversy without breaking a sweat.

He got himself a glass of red wine and downed a couple of crackers topped with a shrimp concoction. When he turned around, Nic waved him to their table.

Nic grinned as he approached, looking happier than he'd seen her in...he couldn't remember when. "Nice goin', Dad."

"Thanks, Nic. And to what you said, Emma." Parker pulled out the chair on the other side of Nic. "I was obviously flying blind, but thought I had to say something. You all know the history."

Emma nodded. "I understand. Jim Kellerman never thought much of me or my husband, anyway. It's true. But I wasn't going to let that stop me from speaking. Besides, there's not much he can do now except show up at events like this and make a scene."

Parker wasn't sure he'd have described Jim's two minutes of disgust as making a scene. It seemed much worse.

Emma stared into space a minute, as if gathering her thoughts. "I thought your offer was great. The rest of us don't even try to deal with Jim anymore. That's what got to me."

Parker didn't know about great, but it lowered the temperature in the room. "I hope he takes me up on it." He had so much to learn about Emma, but she also knew only the top layer of him. But it seemed neither one of them was afraid to jump into a controversy.

"We haven't seen the last of Jim," Emma said, addressing both Parker and Nicole. "He's still clutching his grudge against Mike's dad for not selling the land—and the lake—to him. He's been on the town council for a long time. And now he has to deal with Mike almost every day."

"I'm used to going a few rounds over this sort of thing." Parker still felt for Jim without knowing exactly why.

Emma stood and pushed the chair back. Parker noticed the slight wince he was certain she was trying to hide. "I'm glad we had a chance to chat," she said, giving Nicole's shoulder a friendly pat. "And nice to see you again, Parker."

He got to his feet, ready to offer to walk her to her car, but Ty approached the table to take him to the interview with the newspaper reporter.

"We're lucky to get this kind of attention," Ty said as they crossed the room. "We may not be a factory town, and we don't have shopping malls. But maybe we'll become known as the nature town." Laughing, he added, "Or, who knows? Maybe our holiday festival will become the stuff of legends."

As he followed Ty, Parker took a quick look behind him and saw Emma taking labored steps toward the door. He reluctantly directed his attention back to Ty. Emma might be a donor, an important one, but she was obviously so much more. Parker didn't understand why, but he decided Emma O'Connell was brave.

CHAPTER THREE

THE WIND SLAMMED the rain against the patio doors with such force Emma could barely hear the updates from the weather service on the radio. For hours they'd repeated scary rainfall totals and flash flood warnings from the storm sweeping across the area.

Facing the patio doors she raised her arms over her head and joined her palms. Doing exactly as the physical therapist instructed, she drew in a deep breath and held it, counting slowly from one to five. Exhaling slowly she bent forward at her waist until she felt the first mild twinge. She kept going, letting her hands hang loose, bending, bending, bending a little more until the *eek* escaped her mouth. Her body had reached the familiar *eek* point.

She held her position, one second, two seconds, three…and trusted the quiet voice inside to signal when she reached her limit.

She finished her stretching routine, paying extra attention to her left hip and thigh that had stiffened up the last few days. Disappointing, but not unexpected. It happened sometimes. A year ago, Emma's back surgery had gone a long way in improving her mobility by relieving pressure on her leg and hip damaged in a fall over three years ago now. The neurosurgeon declared the surgery a great success. And it was. But she'd hoped the operation and rehab would eventually restore her full range of motion. She longed to walk and hike like she used to. That didn't happen, and she'd *almost* accepted the old injuries had healed about as much as they were going to. More surgery wouldn't help.

Stretching and strength training weren't optional for Emma. They made mobility—freedom—possible.

Ending her routine the same way she always did, Emma murmured her latest mantra, "I grow stronger every day."

Most of the time she believed it.

By the time she'd finished breakfast the sky had lightened a tiny bit, but the rain still fell in sheets and obliterated her view of the fields and woods from the patio doors. But for the moment she didn't hurt anywhere. Little victories.

The sound of her phone broke the silence

and surprised her, even more so when she saw Parker's name. It triggered a little buzz inside, too. Trying to be casual, she offered a chirpy, "Hey, good morning, Parker. Nice to hear from you."

"I hope I'm not calling too early."

"Not at all," she said with a laugh. "It's almost nine, hardly early. Looking outside, I imagine you won't be pounding planks on the boardwalk today."

"For sure. The Riveras are spending the day cutting wood in their shop," he said with a laugh. "I doubt I'll see Mike and his little boy out rowing around, either."

"I suppose not." What was with the small talk? They'd exhausted the weather in about ten seconds.

"There's a reason for my call, Emma. There's something here at the sanctuary I want to show you. I think it will…hmm, intrigue you. I'll leave it at that."

That took her mind off the weather, her hip, and everything else. "What is it?"

"Ha. I'm not going to give you even a hint over the phone," he teased. "I'd rather show it to you in person. Do you have time to stop by?"

Oh, yes. "When were you thinking?"

"Um, actually, I was thinking now…this morning."

Emma stared at the rain streaming down the glass doors. "Now? Haven't you heard about the flash flood warnings?"

An odd sound came through the phone. Was that a snicker? Was he making fun of her? Her shoulders stiffened. "Hey, are you laughing at me?"

"I'm laughing at myself." His voice carried an amused lilt. "Of course, you can't get in your car and cruise on over. I wasn't thinking. But I can come pick you up in my truck. It's made to handle weather like this. I remember you said you don't live far."

Emma chuckled. "Well, no, nothing is too far from anything else in Bluestone River."

"Right. So what do you say?" He paused. "I can leave now."

"Give me half an hour." She shifted into adventure mode. She gave him her address and directions.

"Okay, see you soon." He ended the call.

Silence. Emma stared at the phone, wondering what had just happened. The reception had been a week ago and she hadn't stopped by or heard from him. But he'd wandered into her thoughts. A lot.

She got ready in a hurry and was zipping up her raincoat on the porch when he pulled into the drive. He jumped out fast and went around to the passenger side to open the door. She grabbed the handhold overhead to help her step up and settle into the seat without looking too awkward.

"Thanks for going along with me on this," Parker said when he got back in and shifted into Drive. "I guess I was being kinda mysterious."

"Oh, just a little." Emma liked playing off his sheepish expression.

He looked at her with a mock frown. "I sure hope you'll agree this bumpy ride is worth it."

Parker navigated fearlessly through the ponds forming on the streets. A few downed branches blocked sections of the sidewalk on River Street and smaller ones skittered along the ground in the wind.

"The storm broke branches off out in the woods, like here on the streets in town," Parker said, "but I didn't spot any damage to the boardwalk. I'll give it a closer look later."

"This is so much fun," Emma said, laughing as Parker turned onto the road to the sanctuary and the wheels kicked up waves of water on both sides.

The smile he gave her was private, intimate. "Yeah, it is. But I suppose not everybody would think so."

"I used to be much more adventurous. That's why I'm so, so up for this." The minute the words were out of her mouth, she realized how silly she sounded. When had riding around town in the rain become something worth noting? Since she'd needed a walker to get around, a voice inside reminded her. But she was much better now—fewer limitations and ready for a change.

"I'll bet you have a yen for new things. And it's all just begun." He drove through the entrance arch and pulled close to the office building, angling the SUV so Emma's door faced the entrance. "Wait until I unlock the office door before you follow me."

When Parker waved for her to come she stepped to the ground, letting her good leg take the weight before reaching for her cane.

The office itself smelled oddly stale and looked in complete disarray. New shelving sat in piles waiting to be installed and every flat space was covered with boxes of tools and hardware or stacks of books and files.

"This way," Parker said, leading her past the long counter and into the alcove where a large dog kennel draped in a black cloth sat in the middle of a table. "Ready?"

Emma nodded and slipped out of her coat, but eyed the cage.

"Here she is," Parker whispered as he rolled back the cloth.

Emma gasped at what she saw—or who. A brown-and-tan owl stared at her through the wire. A one-eyed stare. The bird's other eye was shut and swollen. She stepped closer and peered into the owl's face. She'd counted herself lucky to see owls in her woods out back, but she'd never been close enough to have one to stare back at her.

She looked up at Parker. "What happened to her? Is she blind in that bad eye?"

"I don't know yet. It might take a while to find out. But to answer your first question, we suspect she was hit by a car." Parker sighed. "Truthfully, I've seen it too many times before. High winds and car headlights can confuse owls—they end up swooping in thinking they're going after prey."

"*We* suspect? You mean you and Nicole?"

Parker stared into the cage and nodded. "Nic found her. Nic was on her way to the bakery this morning when she spotted a sort of heap, as she described it, on the side of the road. She stopped to check her out thinking she was probably dead. Then Nic felt a heart-beat, so she swaddled the bird in a blanket to keep her from moving too much. Then she sort of wedged the owl on the floor of her SUV and came right back."

The owl inched away, as if trying to hide but didn't have the strength to launch a move that would land her in the corner in one mo-tion. "But you can help her now?" She heard the strain in her voice. "She seems so quiet for a bird not used to being in a cage."

"No guarantees, but I have a hunch she's got a concussion. Could be a bad one. But she's alive, and we can give her enough time to heal," Parker said softly. "I gave her wings a once-over, but I'll need to check them again." He pulled on a pair of thin leather gloves he'd taken out of his pocket. "I'll show you. Best to examine her as much as I can while she's still lethargic."

"Be honest with me, Parker. Could she die?" Emma took in a breath, preparing her-self for his answer.

Parker's eyes were soft when he nodded. "But losses are part of rescue work. It's not that different when dogs are found alone and hurt and someone drops them off at a dog shelter. No guarantees with any of this kind of work." Parker pointed to the gash. "I stopped the bleeding before I called you, but I see it's seeping. I'll clean it up again. You can help. But first I'm going to look for other injuries."

A hush fell over the room when Parker reached into the cage and gently took hold of the bird's feet with one hand, and with the other, he cradled her body to keep her wings immobile. When he lifted her out of the kennel, she offered almost no resistance. "When she starts feeling better, she won't sit still for all this handling."

"No, I suppose not." Emma let out a soft groan of frustration. "I'm so glad you brought me here to see her. It's a wonderful gift. But now I'll worry about this owl until she's back in the woods." She paused. "And I already know I'll miss her. How irrational is that?"

"Yep, that's the drill," Parker agreed with an understanding smile. "Not irrational at all." He paused before adding, "I realize I barely know you, but somehow I had a feeling you'd understand."

The rush of warmth in her body surprised

her and she couldn't find the right words to respond. Instead, she held his gaze and murmured, "Thank you for that."

"The center in North Carolina was so big—at times we had over one hundred birds—I didn't do as much hands-on work. We had a core of volunteers and a big staff. That was great, but it meant I spent too much time on paperwork." He tilted his head toward the bird to examine her closely.

"This isn't the kind of work that's typically represented at career fairs in school, is it?" Emma laughed. "It probably should be."

"That's true. Most of us more or less fall into this work."

She pointed to the tablet on the table next to him. A spiral notebook sat nearby. "Speaking of paperwork, do you document everything?"

"Sure. I'll keep track of the rescues here. We're not set up for this phase of the sanctuary yet, but it's good to keep records. I write down my observations and results of what we do for our patients." He grinned. "That's what they are when it comes right down to it."

"How do you know the owl is a female?" Emma asked.

"With barred owls it can be tricky, but the females are bigger than males. She probably has a mate out in those woods."

The owl struggled for a second or two to get out of Parker's grip. "*We* know we'll do our best to keep her alive, but she doesn't. Her instincts urge her to fight or flee, but she's too stunned to do either right now."

Still keeping one arm folded around the owl, Parker put her on the table in front of the door to the kennel. "I'm glad Nic had to veer around a deep puddle when she happened to see her. It's not the first time she's rescued a bird, I can tell you that. Nic's good at spotting birds and other wildlife."

"Where did the wire cage come from?" Emma asked.

"I came across some old equipment in the tool shed." Parker gently turned the owl on her side. "There were three small cages, basically dog kennels, and a bigger one. Five altogether, but only three were worth saving."

"I didn't know Millie was actually treating birds here."

"She mentioned helping a few that turned up and more or less taught herself some basic bird first aid." He glanced at Emma. "I'm doing this on my own time. The board didn't want to phase in rescue and treatment just yet."

"Priorities, or so I was told," Emma said. "But I don't see anyone objecting to rescuing a bird that's more or less handed to you."

"To do it on a bigger scale means staffing up, not to mention supplies."

Parker gently opened one wing and walked his fingers over it, pausing now and again to spend more time on a specific spot. "I'm looking for breaks in the wings, but I can also see if she has any injuries on her body underneath."

Emma leaned forward to get a better look at the bird's feet.

He said, "No injuries on her feet. Chances are she bounced off a fender, or maybe the windshield."

Emma's back muscles tightened just thinking about it. "Awful. I'll feel better if she moves around and tries to get away." Even as Parker examined her, the single good eye stayed open and still. Owl-like, Emma thought. "Looking at her huge open eye, it's no wonder owls got a reputation for being wise."

"That, and the way they do that 180 head turn. Or maybe it's their call. It always gets our attention. But they don't all sound the same. You've probably heard them in the woods around here."

"We'd hear them late at night when the resort was quiet." Memories of birdsong and the sights and smells of summer nights flooded Emma's mind. "We'd hear those first two *hoo hoos* and then one elongated *hoooo*." She laughed at her attempt to imitate the noisy call. "Those sounds carried through the woods when we were hanging out on the pier. It's like a snapshot in my mind. The lake shimmered in the moonlight, and sometimes the scent of sunblock would still cling to us after dark."

"Nice memories of a pretty special time and place."

Emma stared at the owl, still motionless in Parker's hands.

"Wanna know a secret?" Parker asked playfully as he adjusted the owl and opened the other wing.

"But of course."

"Owls are pretty smart," he whispered, "but the truth is, eagles are smarter."

Matching his hushed tone, Emma said, "Are you afraid she'll hear you insult her intelligence?"

"Hmm…something like that. Have you noticed how we've both been keeping our voices low? Not that we need to." Parker closed his eyes for a second or two when he again walked his fingertips over a bumpy spot on the owl's wing. "But ever since getting into this business, I've watched the way most people act around birds. No one shouts at them, any more than you'd shout at an injured cat or dog."

Parker asked Emma to get the gauze and a container of swabs off the counter, along with the bottle of disinfectant. "I don't detect other injuries, but I think she has a concussion. She's really not coming around—livening up. If she perks up soon, we'll know she was stunned. If it takes longer, that tells us the wound is more serious."

Emma brought the supplies to the table and saw Parker gently brush his fingers across the feathers on one side of the owl's eye. "That's the deepest part of the gash. She's still bleeding." Showing no hesitation, he pressed the gauze over the injured spot and then asked Emma to dip a swab in the disinfectant.

He drew the bird closer to his torso. "She won't like the sting." He held out his free hand for the swab, reminding Emma of a surgeon waiting for a scalpel. The owl's body jerked a little when Parker passed the swab over the gash, but not enough to stop Parker. "No infections allowed. Not in my clinic."

Emma glanced at him, admiring the confidence she read in his expression as he efficiently cleaned the wound and held the gauze in place. He didn't linger, though, but eased the owl back in the kennel.

"She can't live in this kennel for long. I'll put her in the larger wire mesh cage in the building. I'll get some plastic type mats and use it to wrap around a wooden perch." Parker chuckled and shook his head. "Keeping an injured bird around involves a lot of work."

"You mean getting the right food. By the way, what will you feed her now?"

"Chicken or fish," Parker said. "I'm not going to start ordering live mice, like we do in a big center."

Emma grimaced. "I hadn't thought about that."

Parker scoffed. "Most people don't. But the real work is keeping the cages lined and cleaned." He explained the daily routine, but with only one bird it wouldn't take much time. "Then, when she's well enough, we'll let her go."

Emma enjoyed the little shiver that went through her when Parker said "we." So maybe he wasn't necessarily referring to the two of them, but she was there only because he'd brought her into his world. She rested her weight on her forearms so she could relax and watch everything.

"Listen to that rain," Parker said, pointing up to the ceiling. The rain beat hard on the roof, but the alcove was warm and dry. "It's like someone is dumping nails on the roof."

She'd barely noticed the rain. Ever since she came inside and saw the owl, the space seemed charged with magic that left her lightheaded. Even her ears buzzed.

"Thanks so much for this, Parker," she whispered. "What a wonderful surprise." She shifted her gaze away from him and back to the owl, motionless like a statue now and resting on her side. "What made you think to call me?"

"I don't know exactly," Parker said, straightening his glasses. "It's not like it's a great day for a trip to the lake." He laughed. "But I forgot that when I called you. I haven't seen many wounded birds since we've been here, although we did splint the leg of a male cardinal a couple of days after we arrived." He grinned. "He's long gone now. Back to his mate and living the good life in the woods."

Emma smiled. "Living the good life, huh? But that's what a sanctuary is all about, right?"

"In order for people to care enough to protect the birds—or any other wildlife—they have to get to know them." Parker paused. "I haven't always valued that enough. I'm used to working in the kinds of places that aren't open to the public to come in and wander around. But taking this job shifted my thinking. If we can get kids—and adults—here, they can get a glimpse of the creatures who live all around them, they'll see that everything in nature works together."

"Is that why you're not big on things like receptions? You want to spend your time doing this?" Emma asked, curious about this man who could be both distant and warm.

"Uh-oh, you're on to me. My ex-wife used to coach me about loosening up. Nic warns me about acting like a stodgy professor."

She'd seen that side and had been a little critical herself. But there was much more to him. "You handled the situation with Jim

Kellerman like a pro. I was impressed. And I don't think I was alone."

"I appreciate that. I know I can be stiff and formal, but I've been the Jim in the room, fighting a losing battle over land or some kind of policy that's not popular in the moment."

Sensing Parker had more to say, Emma kept her questions to herself. But she wanted to know what he was all about.

"My ex-wife is in Vermont, by the way. She, uh, is with someone else."

"I see. I bet you're glad Nic is going to college nearby."

"I am. She's been with me since her mom left in January. That could change, but…" He swatted the air. "All that's up in the air. She's here now and enjoying having her own place—she calls her cabin her studio."

"A little perk. At the reception Ruby and I teased her about living in luxury. She has a good sense of humor."

"That she does." Parker moved into place next to her and rested his arms on the table, too. "I saw you leave the other night. I wanted to walk you out, but Ty set up an interview."

"I was hurting a little. My hip I mean." She pointed to the cane hooked on the table. "I had a fall a few years ago and broke a lot of bones. That's why I need the cane."

"Ah, I see."

Emma kept her eye on the owl, conscious of the two of them side by side in the space. If noise could fill a room, so could silence. Like now. Their breathing slowed and in a minute or two, they inhaled and exhaled in sync, while the owl lay silently in the cage.

Suddenly, the door pushed open, making the hinges squeak. Emma straightened up with a jolt. So much for magic in the air. It left in one big whoosh.

"Dad? You in here?"

Parker stuck his head around the alcove. "Back here, Nic. Uh, Emma's here, you know, to see the owl. She's doing okay. Come have a look."

Why did he sound exactly the way she felt? Unnerved. The surprised frown on Nicole's face was hard to miss, Emma thought, but the teenager quickly recovered a neutral expression and said hello.

"Must feel pretty good knowing you saved a life," Emma remarked.

"Like *really* good," Nicole said. "I could have missed seeing it…or her, I should say now. I was afraid I was going to be late for my shift, so I almost talked myself out of going back. I was telling myself that maybe it wasn't really a bird. But…" She shrugged.

"Given your dad's work, I imagine you have an eye for things the rest of us would miss," Emma suggested. "I've probably driven right past more than a few injured birds on the road."

Nicole pointed at her dad. "My dad the nature freak taught me back when I was a kid."

Amused, Emma looked at Parker, who was looking at his daughter and beaming with a special kind of pride.

"Well, your nature freak dad offered to pick me up at my house and bring me here to see the owl for myself. An offer I couldn't refuse."

Nicole opened her backpack and pulled out a bunch of paper bags and put them on the counter. "Jelly donuts, chocolate croissants and sugar cookies. Baked yesterday. The rain kept people away, so Star said she'd probably have to throw these out unless I took them."

"Lucky you. Their jelly donuts are my major vice," Emma said.

"Me, too." Nicole dug inside the bag.

Emma took the donut and napkin Nicole offered and listened to the father-daughter banter as she quickly polished it off. Parker asked about the condition of the roads, Nicole said they weren't too bad. Then she mentioned she had laundry to do, and Parker said something about throwing in a load later. And so it went, Emma thought. Ordinary life intruded into this otherwise extraordinary morning. Time for her to leave.

"I should get back to my house. Ruby is stopping by to go over some grants we're writing." That was mostly a little white lie. They'd dutifully go over the paperwork Ruby had already prepared. Emma would proof the proposals and offer a suggestion or two. Then they'd get a fire going in the fireplace and curl up and munch red licorice. Talk about everything and nothing.

"Don't leave on my account, Emma," Nicole said.

Emma cupped her ear. "The racket on the roof is quieting down. A good time to head home."

"Are you going to the Halloween party at the town hall?" Nicole asked.

"Sure, I always go," Emma said. "It's one of the few things the town kept up these last years when times got tough. I suppose your boss is supplying the food." It was silly for her to pretend as if she didn't know. Like every year, Emma's accountant had already transferred funds to cover the refreshments.

"I'll be there, too. Helping Star, but I'd go anyway. I want to see what it's like. And this year, I hear costumes for the adults are *required*. Something about new rules," she said, air quoting *new rules*.

"Ha! That's right. I'll let you in on a secret— they're Ruby's rules."

Nicole glanced at Parker. "We haven't talked about the party yet, Dad. You are planning on going. Right?"

Parker's eyebrows shot up and his expression revealed disbelief. "No. Why would I go? I don't need to be at a kids' party."

Nicole reared back in an exaggerated surrender. "Whoa, okay, Dad. I got the message. You don't have to be so rude about it."

Emma agreed. She was a little disappointed, too. He acted like a bad smell suddenly blew into the room. On the other hand, the party was supposed to be fun, not a chore to check off a to-do list. If he had to be dragged there, he shouldn't bother. She pulled on her raincoat, and Parker did the same. Then he grabbed his keys and waved goodbye to his daughter.

"Thanks for the donut, Nicole. See you soon." She restrained herself and didn't return Nicole's dramatic eye roll as she followed Parker out the door.

They got back to her house and she spotted Ruby already on the front porch.

"I'm sorry," Parker said. "I made you late."

"You did not," she insisted. "I made myself late, and I'm glad I did. I wouldn't have missed my morning with that owl for anything." *Or missed spending time with you.*

He started to open his door, but Emma touched his arm to stop him. "Stay where you are. I'll be fine."

And she was. She stuck her head inside to say a last thank-you and then closed the passenger door. Parker waved at Ruby before driving off.

Seeing Ruby's grin, Emma knew a grilling was in store and the questions would be all about Parker. But not today. Emma wasn't in the mood for even Ruby's fun teasing about the great-looking man that had landed in Bluestone River. She'd keep thoughts about Parker to herself for now. She preferred to savor that magical time with him—alone.

"Hi, Rubes. Sorry to keep you waiting."

"That's okay," Ruby said, grinning. "So, tell me, did you have an interesting morning?"

Emma thought for a minute before she smiled and said, "I can't wait to tell you about the owl at the center."

Maybe she wasn't up for talking about Parker. But the owl? She was another story.

CHAPTER FOUR

OPENING THE DOOR to Mike Abbot's law office sent the bell jingling. A bold, no-nonsense sound, but cheerful nonetheless. Kind of like Mike himself, Parker thought. A couple of seconds later, Mike's head appeared around the corner of his office door.

Parker hadn't called first, but now began to wish he had. But Mike looked pleasantly surprised. "Hey, Parker. I'm surprised to see you."

"I hope I'm not interrupting."

"Nah, not really. I was working on notes for a talk I'm doing later this week. Come on back."

As he sat in the client chair in Mike's office, his eyes were drawn to the vintage photos of the old resort. In one, he could see the two cabins he and Nic lived in a couple of hundred feet from the office building. Parker relaxed into the chair, his muscles losing the tension he hadn't been aware he was carrying until he could feel it easing.

Tense or relaxed, though, he'd had Emma on his mind more than made any sense at all. She came into his thoughts at odd times, like when he was working on the boardwalk alongside Will and Bill. He wondered how she was doing when he stood on the pier first thing in the morning with his ritual cup of coffee. She lingered again at the end of the day when he watched the sky streak with purples and pinks, or sometimes just pale gray as the light faded. She was always with him when he tended the owl. The bird was still passive, but she moved around a little more each day. She'd soon be ready for the perch Parker had installed in the larger cage.

Mike seemed unnaturally cheerful as he settled into his chair behind the desk.

"You're in a good mood," Parker said, aware of little stabs of envy in his gut. He knew he could be grumpy sometimes, but jealous of another man, a genuinely happy guy who'd apparently found the right woman? He'd never been that small and didn't want to make a habit of it now.

"I guess I am. My son is good. Ruby is having our baby." With a shrug he added,

"Tomorrow is Halloween. Always a fun time. At least in part, thanks to Emma. But you probably already knew that."

Using Emma's terminology, he wondered if Emma was throwing money at the party? Another of her projects? "Nicole mentioned the party. She works at Sweet Comforts, so she filled me in."

"Every now and then we manage to pull off an event without Emma's help," Mike said with a laugh, "but not often."

Parker stopped himself from blurting out questions about Emma that were none of his business. "Uh, I should explain why I stopped in. It's a legal issue, but nothing big. Divorce details."

Mike nodded. "Okay, let's see if I can help."

It took only a few minutes to lay out the one remaining item on the list of things he and Jackie did to separate their lives for good. A simple out-of-state property transfer.

"That's it?" Mike asked. "No liens, no taxes due, no disputes?"

"Nope. Like I said, it isn't a big thing. My divorce lawyer is in North Carolina. I don't talk to Jackie much, so I thought it was better to let the lawyers deal with it. She gets sole title to the cottage she inherited and I'm compensated for improvements I made." He passed the sheet of notes he'd written. "I wrote down the points we agreed to and the contact information for Jackie's lawyer."

"Consider it done." Mike scanned the agreement. "You're right. This looks like a straightforward transaction." He tilted his chair back. "But since you're here, Parker, don't take off. Tell me how things are going. Everything on track for the open house—and the Christmas ceremony?" Mike grinned. "My term for the relaunch."

From the faraway look in his eyes, Parker could tell this was a big deal to Mike. The sanctuary was nothing short of his parents' legacy. Parker stretched his long legs out in front of him and crossed his ankles. "I don't want to jinx it, but we're making good progress. We had a little tree damage back in the woods from the storm the other day. But the new boardwalk held up."

Mike squirmed in the chair. "What about our buddy Jim Kellerman? Has he stopped by?"

"He hadn't taken me up on my offer to talk. At least not yet."

"What happened the other night at the reception turned out okay," Mike said. "It's not so much that Jim has changed, but everyone in that room saw you make him an offer. The rest of us were groaning, wishing he'd go away." Looking sheepish about being so blunt, he added, "I admit I get tired of clashing with Jim all the time."

Parker took a second to gather his thoughts before telling Mike about identifying with Jim in an odd way. "In my senior year in college, I was part of a small group from the town and the school trying to keep some acres of woods from being cut down to make room for a giant mall. We lost that fight. It felt lousy." Parker shrugged. "Who knows, maybe we were wrong and the mall was worth it. I believe Jim is wrong now, but I have a little empathy for him."

Mike tapped his fingers on the arms of the chair. "I hear you, Parker, I do. But this is about so much more than Jim being a crabby old man about our holiday festival." Mike let out a cynical scoff. "I mean, who votes against Santa Claus coming to River Street?"

"Fill me in." Parker settled in his chair. "I'm never sure who to ask. I don't want to blunder in and offend people with sensitive questions."

"Jim's problem is with me. He didn't like my parents. Long before my dad deeded the land over to the conservancy, Jim was itching to get his hands on it to build—he's had a dozen different ideas about what to do with it. My dad didn't agree. When he left to come live near me in Ohio, he wanted the land to be like the sanctuary you worked in before you came here."

"And it will, Mike. The board wants to go slow and it'll take time. It's hard to please all the factions involved in change."

Mike nodded. "Tell me about it."

"I also get that Jim Kellerman hates to lose. Especially to you," Parker said. "I may not be privy to the history, but I know what a vibe is. And yours with Kellerman seems to go way beyond a piece of land." Parker hadn't meant to say all that, but he'd had a feeling that when it came to Emma and her friends Mike and Ruby, a whole lot was left unsaid.

Mike rested his cheek in his palm. "Bluestone River doesn't have a lot of secrets and scandals—"

Parker interrupted with a quick, "Oh?"

"The town's one big scandal involved my family—and Ruby's."

Parker grimaced. "Oops. I was being flip. Sorry."

Mike tightened his mouth. "The facts of what happened aren't that complicated. The aftermath was."

In the next few minutes, Parker understood why Mike was a happy guy—*today*. Going back twenty years, though, he could imagine how people in town reacted to finding out that his mom and Ruby's dad died together in a car accident, making their affair obvious.

"Our families fell apart. My dad never recovered. We all went our separate ways, and I came back so I could raise Jason here. He'd lost his mom in a fire and didn't speak for months. Ruby came back to help Emma through her back surgery a year or so ago."

At the mention of Emma, Parker's heart beat a little harder, a little faster. He didn't know why. "And now, here you are."

"With a whole new life. Together."

Parker grinned. "Now, that's what I call a happy ending." He paused. "Emma hasn't said a lot about her husband, but she did mention you were all friends back in the day."

"Neil and I were best friends," Mike said. "But I lost touch with them and didn't know Neil died until I was back in town."

Parker nodded, but would have liked Mike to confide more about Emma.

"My dad was a shell of his old self when my mom died and he never recovered. The only things he could keep the same were the woods and the lake. Jim acted like my dad was obligated to sell him the property. Jim didn't like losing that one."

"It all happened ages ago," Parker said, "and yet the aftermath lives on."

"So, now you know why Jim wasn't a fan when I ran for mayor," Mike said. "He associates me—and Ruby—with scandal."

"Guess he's not big on Christmas villages, either?" Parker said, laughing.

"Exactly. He's Scrooge," Mike said. "I mean, he asks what the payoff is for Santa to visit?" Mike raised both hands in the air. "Go figure."

Parker inched to the edge of the chair to get ready to leave.

"What about you?" Mike asked. "Are you happy here so far?"

He hesitated. "I am. My daughter likes Neville. And her job with Star Lenski."

"According to the board, we were lucky to lure a guy with your credentials out here."

That was true, Parker thought. He didn't

mind that Mike knew it. "And, uh, just between us you might as well know my wife—ex-wife—is in Vermont with someone else." "The whole thing blindsided me. And was hard for Nic."

Parker surprised himself by how ordinary it felt to say that. He must have turned a corner somewhere. He was usually embarrassed to say that, more out of foolish pride than anything else. "Unfortunately, our daughter bore the brunt of it. I think she's still hoping her mom will want her to move up there. But Nic is mad at her, too." Parker shook his head. "And at me. Just because."

"Your Nicole seems like a terrific kid." Mike frowned. "I shouldn't call a college girl a kid. She's a young woman."

"I know, but to be honest, I still think of her as my little girl." Parker got to his feet. "I try not to be harsh about Jackie. My daughter and her mom will have to work it out."

"Feel free to talk to me about anything. I'm your lawyer. Whatever is on your mind is safe with me." Mike smiled as he got up and walked Parker to the front door. "I'll let you know when I've talked to Jackie's lawyer. You'll need to sign the documents. So,

I guess I'll see you tomorrow at the Halloween party."

What was it with these people? Why would they think he'd show up there, like it was a part of his job? He waved off Mike. "Sounds like a good time for parents and kids. Nic will be there working with Star, but I'm in the midst of the renovations."

Mike's face showed surprise, and he looked like he was about to say something, but changed his mind.

As an afterthought, Parker added, "I sure enjoy watching you and your boy rowing around out on the lake."

"It's his favorite place." Mike's voice was pure joy. "It's kind of our thing. Pretty soon he'll be rowing me. Ruby comes with us sometimes. She tells me she wants to enjoy it before she gets too big. Imagine that?"

An image of a pregnant Jackie flashed uninvited through his mind. Round and healthy and happy to be having their baby. He nodded along with Mike and tried to ignore the lump in his throat.

Parker took fast strides to his truck, hoping to outrun the sadness threatening to overtake him. He could fool other people sometimes but not himself. He couldn't handle a Halloween bash in a roomful of giggly kids in costumes. Sometimes his memories were like little swords piercing his heart. Man, they wielded way too much power.

EMMA CAME TO a stop a few feet away from the table where Nicole was arranging cookies on platters. Her sparkly tiara doubled as a headband that tamed her long blond hair flowing loose down her back. No more multicolored nails. Today, all ten matched her light blue strapless dress with a full skirt, which in turn matched the color of her eyes. What flare, Emma thought. Nicole was a fairy-tale princess in a modern dress.

On her way into the town hall for the Halloween party Emma had spotted Star Lenski, also sporting a tiara and looking queenly in a flowing floor-length red gown. Queen or not, Star also was a business owner unloading more boxes from the back of her van.

Emma approached the table to say hello to Nicole, but the teenager's expression didn't match the party-like mood in the room. It looked more like the blue she wore. "Princess Nicole, I presume," Emma said tentatively. "And looking every inch like royalty."

Nicole offered a wan smile that quickly vanished. "It's my prom dress."

"And very beautiful on you." Another cheerful remark, Emma thought. No one could accuse her of not trying.

"Thanks. I'm glad to get this extra shift today," Nicole said, finally offering a real smile. "According to Star, this year's party will be bigger and better than ever." She studied Emma head-to-toe. "And look at you. A dancer. *Cool.*"

Emma glanced down at herself in a blush pink ballet dress. It draped over one shoulder, gathered at the waist and then fell loose just above her knees. She steadied herself with her cane and lifted her foot so Nicole could see her ballet flats with crisscrossed ribbons tied around her ankles. "I started with the shoes and built from there. This dress is from a costume I put together for a party years ago."

"Do you… I mean, did you take ballet?" Nicole asked, dropping her gaze for a second or two.

"For a couple of years as a little girl," Emma replied, dramatically clutching her hands over her heart. "Oh, I liked being a ballerina a lot, but then I fell in love with a horse named October. When my heart was stolen by softball, second base to be exact, I said goodbye to both October and ballet." Emma chuckled as she picked up the skirt of the dress and let the light chiffon swish into place. "But not to dancing, if you know what I mean. I was always the first out on the dance floor. Partner or no partner."

Nicole nodded knowingly. "Me, too. Wow, that costume suits you. Like Star said, being in that red dress just makes her feel good. Kind of like a queen. I bet you feel that way, too."

"I do. And I'm sure that Ruby will give us her seal of approval." She scanned the room, decorated with bouquets of orange and black balloons and skeletons and black cats mounted on the walls. Bales of hay and scarecrows sat on either side of the caramel apple booth.

"This is a noisy party already. And we haven't even had the parade. There's something going on in every corner," Emma said. "So many kids and parents are already milling around."

As the crowd grew, volunteers started organizing games. A few adults were filling orange-and-green paper bags with treats at the candy table. With everyone in costumes, the room was more colorful than Emma had seen it in years. Nicole had gone back to fixing up her platters of sugar cookies cut in pumpkin and maple leaf shapes and iced in a rainbow of colors.

"Uh, so tell me how's it going? Is school good?" Emma asked. "I hear the owl is on the mend—getting better every day."

Nicole started to answer, but when she raised her head tears had pooled in her eyes and threatened to spill down her cheeks. Looking as if she'd surprised herself, she turned her head and used her knuckles to dab at her eyes. "Oh, no, no. I didn't expect that to happen."

Emma extended an arm toward Nicole, but stopped short of touching her, unsure that the teenager would welcome that kind of comfort. "I could see you were upset about something. Can you talk about it?"

Nicole pressed her knuckles harder. "I'm being stupid...*stupid*." She glanced furtively around the room.

"No one is paying any attention to this corner, Nicole," Emma said, her voice reassuring. On the other hand, she cringed hearing Nicole call herself stupid. She fought back the urge to speak up about it, but a little inside voice cautioned, *let the girl talk.*

Speaking barely above a whisper, Nicole said, "Halloween was a big, huge deal with my mom and dad. Mom *made* our candy…really, she knew how to make chocolate drops with sprinkles. And she'd cook sugar and butter and make caramels."

Emma nodded along, wanting Nicole to know she was listening.

"The two of us used to go to thrift shops to find odds and ends to make funny costumes." She patted her arms and chest. "One year I went as a *garden*. We found artificial flowers and attached them to a green T-shirt and tights." Nicole's eyes were wet, but she laughed. "I looked like I was sprouting roses and daisies."

Emma held back a heavy sigh. No wonder Nicole was sad. Eighteen or not, she missed her mom.

"Then everything changed," Nicole said. "We won't ever have those times again." Then she shrugged. "I don't know why I'm thinking about it. I outgrew the little kids' parties a long time ago."

"But that doesn't mean this kind of holiday will be easy," Emma said. Was it worse because Parker dismissed the town party like it was beneath him?

"It was a really huge thing for my dad." Nicole shook her head as if resigned. "He and Mom took all the kids out trick-or-treating in a group. They helped out at the party at my school." She glanced around. "This kind of party."

"A family occasion, huh?"

"Oh yeah." Nicole dramatically opened her arms. "Way bigger than Christmas."

So much for the pretense of being too busy, Emma mused. It was all about memories he couldn't handle.

Nicole filled her lungs and huffed as she exhaled. "I'm okay now." She gave her head a little shake and smiled. "I'm not sure what came over me."

"I understand," Emma said. "Memories hit me like that sometimes. I can't order them to go away."

"That sounds like something my dad would say."

"He's really wise, huh?"

"Don't tell him that," Nicole joked. "He'll get a big head."

"It's a deal." Emma pulled out her phone. "Can I take a picture of the princess?"

"Only if I can take one of you," Nicole said with a big smile, her shaky moments behind her. She held up one finger. "Wait. Don't move. I want to go first." She retrieved her phone from the end of the table and then pointed it directly at Emma's shoes. "They deserve their very own shot."

Posing for Nicole, Emma rested her cane on the table and put one arm over her head and the other to the side in a ballet pose. She added some extra style with a tilt of her head.

Nicole let out a low laugh. "Oh, yeah, attitude. I like that."

It was Emma's turn to get her pictures. "I like seeing you at your first Bluestone River Halloween shindig. You're sparkling in your tiara and fabulous dress. Stand still, you. Here I come."

Nicole giggled, but Emma got her pictures— and a couple of selfies. Then Nicole's gaze shifted to the doorway, where Star was pulling a cart through the door. "Oops, I better go help."

Nicole raced across the room in time to help Star maneuver the wheels of the cart around the corner and toward the table. Then Mike appeared in the doorway in a tux with an exaggerated bow tie and a top hat. Emma watched as he made his rounds through the room saying hello to kids and parents, taking off his top hat and bowing to a bunch of little preschoolers playing a game. The room was transformed into a sea of quick hugs and greetings, and the buzz of "nice to see you again" greetings and hoots of laughter as parents herded kids down the atrium walkway where they lined up for the costume parade through the room.

The picture Nicole painted of past Halloweens stayed with Emma. She was used to parties like this one, full of laughter and silly fun. Alone for the moment, Emma stood near a wall and observed. Once upon a time, she'd been engaged and involved, particularly in the early years with Neil, when their marriage still stood a chance, or so she believed. When she came to town events with or without him, she knew most of the people who showed up. Not so anymore.

After almost three years eaten up by her fall and the aftermath, dealing with Neil's death, and her last-resort surgery a year ago, she was only now starting to redefine her life, and that included her place in town. Other than writing checks for things, she'd been outside what was happening in the wider community.

Why had she arrived so early? To wait around for the party to start, as if she had some job to do. But she didn't. It was all running along without her. The games, the food, the parade about to start.

Her spirits lifted a notch when Ruby's wave caught her eye. She was coming in with Jason, the seven-year-old dressed up to look like his golden retriever, Peach. Ruby and Mike had found a costume to match the orangey color of Peach's coat. This year Ruby was a ghost in a grayish-white caftan that almost hid her dark red hair. It didn't hide her pregnancy, though, not that she'd want it to. Emma watched Ruby offer her cheek for Mike to kiss. She took both of his hands and stepped back to admire him in his tux and hat.

Emma heard not a single thing they said, but she didn't need words to read their happy faces. After giving Jason a quick hug, Mike grabbed the mic and sounding like an old-fashioned carnival barker, directed traffic to start the parade. When circus music came over the loudspeaker, Emma moved to join a group of parents watching the children take a turn around the room one by one.

Mike's voice came through the speakers, crisp and cool as he began narrating the parade as if he was covering a high school football game. "And here comes Sally, a little brown-haired bunny. And a robot named... Nate... And there's Annie dressed as the real redhead Annie herself. Look at those big freckles!"

Parents called their kids' names as they came in so Mike could introduce them by name. Peter as a troll, and a little girl they called Cookie dressed like a sugar cookie iced in pink. Jason came in with the next-to-last group and Emma caught him on her phone when he was laughing and again when he curled up his hands at his chest, his pretend paws. When he was done with his moment in the spotlight he made a bee-line for Ruby who gave him a big hug and then scooted him off to the line forming at the treat table.

Watching Nicole fill cups with cider, talking and smiling like she knew everyone at the party, she felt even more irked that Parker had skipped it. Granted, Emma was probably the only person in the room who noticed Nicole glancing toward the door, subtly craning her neck to see around the clusters of adults circulating through the room. *She still hopes he'll change his mind and show up.* Her disappointment in Parker caught in her throat. As if it was any of her business.

Once the costume parade was over, Emma caught up with Ruby and Jason at the treat table. "Impressive," she said to Jason, flipping one of the dog's ears. "That costume does Peach proud."

"I want to be a dog every year," Jason said. He made three woof sounds in a row, getting the laugh he was going for.

"And you make ballet dancers proud, my friend," Ruby said, opening her arms for a hug.

"I came by to say hello—and goodbye—to the ghost and her dog," Emma said, smoothing her hand over Jason's head. "I got here early, so I'll be on my way. You have fun."

Ruby frowned. "You're leaving? Are you okay?"

Emma nodded. "Great. I got here for the main event—which is to see you and take a couple of pictures. I told Nicole I liked to tease you about your new costume rules. But it paid off. She and Star are glamorous in their dresses. We took lots of pictures." She glanced down. "Even my ballet flats got their own shot."

Ruby posed with Jason, but when someone called Ruby's name from the other side of the room, they said a quick goodbye.

Emma headed to the exit, waving as she walked. "See you soon, Nicole."

"You should stop by to see our patient," Nicole said. "My dad is always glad to see you."

"I will, thanks. Maybe tomorrow."

The cold air made her shiver as she walked to her car. Parker was a presence weighing on her mind. And if he was always happy to see her, he missed his chance to see her looking like a willowy ballerina. She chided herself for assuming he'd relent and come to the party, as if her recommendation would mean so much. Not even his daughter working there had been enough. Emma hadn't known that some special family traditions had kept him away. But did he know his daughter's memories of her family and the holiday could bring her to tears?

PARKER TURNED ON the hose and rinsed off the loosened rust and dirt he'd scrubbed off the metal mesh. Then he flipped the heavy cage to expose another side and ran the stiff brush back and forth over it.

"Hey, Dad, it's getting dark." At the sound of Nic's voice, he looked up to see her walking towards him where he was working outside on the cage.

"Oh, hi, Nic." The sky behind her had gone from a deep pink a few minutes ago to gray. He tossed the brush into the bucket nearby. "I'd hoped to get this one cage scrubbed today, but I'll have to finish up tomorrow."

"You should have waited to start until tomorrow. *You* missed a good party."

"Oh, right, Nic, you were working. But c'mon, what would I have done there? Stand around and admire the kids?" He closed his eyes, wanting to inhale both the words and the tone back in. He hadn't meant to sound so resentful.

"Yeah, Dad, that's exactly what adults do at kids' parties." She planted one hand on her hip and tilted her head. She'd gone from scolding parent to an exasperated thirteen-year-old. "Jason was dressed like Peach, for one thing."

"I bet that was cute."

"It was." She filled in the blanks about the

parade and Ruby as a ghost and Mike as a carnival barker. "But *Emma* was the best."

"Oh?" He jolted to full attention at the mention of her name. "What did she... I mean, was she in a costume?"

"If you ask nicely, Dad, I'll show you."

Okay, he could handle the teasing. This was the Nic he enjoyed so much. If she could read his mind she'd get a bead on his overwhelming need to know about Emma's costume.

"How nice? You want me to grovel because I chose scrubbing cages over the party."

She turned down the corners of her mouth as if considering a serious question. "Nah, I was sad about it at first. But then I saw Emma and her cool costume. Star and I got loads of attention in our dresses, so I won't make you suffer. I took a slew of pictures. I'll show you."

"Let's go to your cabin where it's warm." And he could have a better look in the light. Why did he care about Emma's costume?

"The party was like the ones we had in grade school," Nic said as they started walking. "I was telling Emma about you and Mom taking the neighborhood kids around."

Those memories had a habit of weaving

in and out of his days, chasing him, almost impossible to ignore.

"I told her it was our favorite family holiday."

He tried to smile as they went inside Nic's place and settled at the table. She was so right about the holiday.

"So, here's Jason," Emma said, handing him her phone. "And Star decked out in red. If you scroll back, you'll see Emma. She looks like a real dancer."

He dutifully commented on Jason and Star, eager to get to Emma. He glanced at the photo and swallowed hard. Her expression was full of fun and she'd posed like a ballet dancer. He hadn't forgotten the first day he saw her and imagined her on a dance floor.

"Go to the next one, Dad, and you'll see her shoes."

"Ah, I see. Those crisscross ribbons make them look like the real deal." He smiled. "You took great photos, Nic. She looks beautiful in both of them...and happy."

"She said she used to love to dance."

"Uh-huh, just as I thought."

"You did?" She frowned. "How could you tell?"

Because of his vision of holding her in his

arms and slow dancing around the pier. From the warmth spreading through his body, it was almost as if he was living it right then and there. He glanced at Nic, sensing her stare. "Takes one to know one," he quipped.

"I suppose." Nicole took the phone from his hand, stared at the photo, her forehead wrinkled in thought. "Mom's an okay dancer, but not as good as you. You sing better, too." She gave the phone back to him. "Keep looking."

It was true. Jackie was only a fair dancer, but he wasn't taking Nic's bait. He didn't want a conversation about himself and Jackie right now. He scrolled through the other pictures. "You really look like a couple of princesses, you and Star. Good costume idea. And you already had the dress."

He put the phone down and listened while she added details about this or that child's clever costume. She tucked her legs under her and rested her chin on her palm as they talked. For the moment she was the picture of a fresh young woman without a care in the world. She still wore her dress, but had changed into sneakers. When she brought up Star and the hundreds of cookies they'd handed out, she spoke with a happy lilt in her voice.

Finally, when Parker thought she was all talked out, she sighed. "Mom sent me a couple texts. I'll answer them before I go to bed. She said to say hello."

"Same back to her, Nic." How long would they keep up the ritual of saying hi through their daughter?

"She worries me sometimes," Nic said, nervously thrumming her fingers on the table. "She can't find a job."

"She'll be fine, Nic. She wouldn't want you worrying about her. Especially over a job." He got to his feet. "I'll leave you to your texts, honey."

Nic nodded and got up to give him a hug at the door, but she couldn't resist reminding him once more that he'd missed a good time.

He supposed that was true, but he couldn't make himself care too much. He missed seeing Emma. That's what he regretted.

CHAPTER FIVE

"I HOPED I might see you today." Parker walked toward Emma as she approached the boardwalk.

"You lured me here with that cryptic text, so now you owe me," she said. "When do you plan to let me in on the secret?"

Was it his imagination or did her voice seem a little on the cool side? "I hope I didn't overdo the buildup." He'd sent a text to ask her to stop by when she had a chance and hinted at a new development. Now he had to hope she'd find it worth it. Parker gestured toward the building behind him. "That's what I wanted to show you. I opened up that shed—it has some big windows and a long counter and bins. I'm moving our patient in there."

"Into the old garden shed? Good spot— nice and roomy. I spent a lot of time in the shed helping Mike's mom with her seedlings," Emma said with a sigh. "I used to help her plant flowers around the cabins. Year after year, she turned this old place into a showpiece."

There it was again. Nostalgia. Parker heard it every time someone talked about the old days. Whether it was swimming in the lake or scooping ice cream at the snack bar, it was always there. "You don't have to convince me. I've seen the photos. Mike has a couple in his office from way back," Parker said. "Come spring, we'll do some planting around the office."

She raised her eyebrows in expectation. "First things first. I want to see our owl."

He led the way inside the office. The owl was still, but in a bigger cage and on a perch.

"The swelling around her eye is down some, isn't it? She's looking better, Parker. From the way she's staring at me, I can pretend she recognizes me from the other day." She pointed to the smaller covered cage. "Is there someone in there?"

"Another surprise. A cardinal with a tiny fracture—not serious. She probably got tangled up in something."

"Where did you find her?"

"Out near one of the turnouts we're building in the woods. With any luck she'll be on her way next week."

"Is that why you're moving the cages? Because you've got two patients now?"

"That's part of it. But they don't do so well with a lot of people in and out." He tilted his head toward the birds. "There's a reason treatment areas in sanctuaries aren't open to the general public. Not like the huge bird refuge sites where species migrate and breed. Those sites are often like giant parks."

"I know you're going to remind me the owl and the cardinal aren't pets." Emma lifted her hand as if to stop him from covering that ground.

"Psychic, are you?"

"I admit to feeling, oh, I don't know what to call it, maybe a bond with this owl. For no good reason, other than feeling bad for her." She paused. "Maybe it was the storm. It was a bad one, fierce and dangerous. I hadn't thought about how vulnerable these birds are."

Parker was taken aback by the intensity in Emma's face. So much was going on inside her and she'd revealed so little. She could talk about Mike and Ruby and the resort in detail, but he knew nothing about how she spent her days. He knew nothing about her husband except his name. "Are you ready? I thought I'd move the birds now."

Emma's face brightened. "Let me get my camera out."

"A real camera," Parker teased.

"Absolutely." Emma shrugged off her backpack and dug inside for her camera. "Phones are fine, but I like the real thing, too, especially since I'm creating my masterpiece slideshow for the open house Thanksgiving weekend."

"You can wait here and I'll get the cart. I can move them both together."

The walk to the boardwalk gave him a chance to settle down—his thinking, anyway. His heart wasn't listening to logic. Earlier, seeing Emma walking toward him in jeans and sturdy hiking boots, her dark hair almost hidden under a cap, he was happier to see her than made sense. Now he looked over his shoulder and spotted her in front of the office moving the camera in front of her as if assessing each view. She walked tentatively with her cane hooked over her arm.

If taking photos would keep her at the sanctuary that day, then let the pointing and shooting begin.

"I need the cart for a few minutes," he called out to Will as he grabbed the handle. "I'll bring it right back."

"You need any help?" Will asked.

"Nah. We'll be fine." *We.* He liked that.

When he positioned the cart in front of the office, he went inside where Emma was taking photos of the owl.

"We don't want to use too many of those in the slideshow," he warned. "I need to focus on getting the community nature center part up and running. The boardwalk, displays, a membership drive."

"I'm sure the board wouldn't want you to ignore wounded birds that sort of drop in your lap," Emma insisted. "What would they expect you to do with the owl? Tell Nicole to leave her alone and let her die?"

He agreed, noting the irony of the situation. Professional help for an injured owl or any bird was far away. They'd have to go to the state university to find an avian vet. There wasn't even a zoo close to Bluestone River. "No, you're right. I need visitors to view this work as part of the sanctuary's future."

"Showing this bird in various stages of healing could be valuable." She gave him a long look. "I can't be the only person who has a special feeling about owls."

"And red-tailed hawks and eagles."

"I'll make a special section for it. We'll call it a vision for the future."

He grinned. "You make a good argument. And you are a donor, so I suppose I have to listen."

Emma flashed a mock look of disapproval. But she waved her camera in his face and gestured to the birds. "I'm spending time, not money. How I feel about these birds has nothing to do with being a donor."

"I'm sorry. I knew that." Old habits really were hard to break.

She held the door open while he rolled the cart with the cages out the door. When the two cages were side by side on the cart, Emma lifted her camera and grinned. "I'm not sure we'll want to use them, but I want them just for me."

"Gotcha," he said, returning her half-teasing grin. "Okay, my two avian buddies. Let's go see your new temporary home."

The owl was silent, but the cardinal exercised her vocal cords on the way to the shed. Other birds sitting in the trees called back.

"This must be traumatic," Emma said. "She's separated from her mate."

"I know," Parker said pulling the cart through the door. "It's a hard part of this work. Still, except for doing nothing and letting them die, this is the only other choice."

"I suppose."

"Think of it this way, Emma." He raised his head as he pointed toward the woods. "Birds have hazards all around them every day. They have natural prey coming for them. They get tangled in plastic bags or they bang into glass doors. We just don't see what goes on, unless we're paying attention and know what to look for. Even then we miss most of it."

They walked to the garden shed in silence and Emma again held the door while Parker settled the cages in front of the windows that let in light. He'd cranked them open partway.

"Is this the new clinic, then?" Emma asked.

"Just for now. I've got another idea. I need an area for a larger cage and practical things like better drains. I'll open an old cabin. We'll need the extra room later on anyway." Listening to himself, he sounded like a guy who intended to hang around for a while.

"We'll treat the ones I find or that others bring by. Some, like the owl, will need care for weeks, but some won't ever be ready to go back home." He stopped arranging the cages and grimaced. "I can't save them all. Some will die."

She nodded, but didn't say anything.

"Let's go down to the boardwalk. I want to show you the lookout we created at the marsh end. We can reach it from the beach."

"You know, I could get there on my own. I mean, I don't want to take up your day."

"Please do," Parker blurted. "Actually, I'm discovering how much I like showing the place off. Especially to you."

They walked slowly down the slope to the pebbly beach, going single file along the narrow strip of stones and sand. The trees thinned as the marsh grasses thickened. The whirring and pounding sounds of construction grew louder as they got closer to the lookout.

"I can see the boardwalk snaking along through the trees," Emma said, stopping to take a series of photos into the woods.

"Look at the sparrows hopscotching through the trees," Parker said, pointing to the low branches where the small birds looked like they were chasing each other. "Most of those sparrows won't go very far. Maybe down into Southern Illinois or maybe as far as Tennessee. They'll be back."

She lowered her camera and pointed to the patches of light and tried to catch the sense of movement. "What a sight. We used to see herons at the edge of the marsh. Maybe they'll come back."

He waited while she turned her back to the woods and shot some photos of the Abbot house across the lake. "Mike's house looks so different now with a new coat of paint and the green trim. It had turned a muddy beige color with age."

"I bet a lot of people will be drawn to that lookout point," Parker said, leading the way up a narrow path to the raised half-circle platform, where Bill and Will came into view. "It'll give visitors a good view of the geese— I've been told quite a few hang around all year round."

"I don't think any of us imagined a boardwalk that branches out and offers lookout points like this." Emma made her way closer to the Riveras working in tandem, one on the platform, one on the ground to secure the supports. Both men stopped and waved.

"Pay no attention to me," Emma hollered. "I'm doing the slideshow for the open house and I want you in it. You're a big part of the relaunch."

When Emma was done with her pictures, they retraced their steps and stopped at the pier.

"I know for sure I don't *need* even one more photo from this pier, but I can't resist."

"I've been bringing my coffee down here in the morning so I can have a look when it's barely light," Parker said. "Funny, Nic was surprised at how beautiful it is around here. I think she expected all corn and soybean fields. Lakes and rivers and woods like these weren't part of her image of Illinois. Needless to say, she's impressed."

"That's great." Emma smiled. "She looked gorgeous on Halloween in her blue dress. A real princess. Jason greeted her like an old pal."

"She showed me photos of all of you." His heart was thumping hard again, but this time with apprehension.

"We had fun with those. I think my ballerina costume impressed her a little."

"What an understatement," Parker said.

"She was blown away by you in your dancer dress."

"I'm glad I spent some time with Nic. She seemed a little sad at first, but perked up when she described her Halloweens as a kid." She cocked her head. "You raised a lovely daughter."

His face heated up. "Her mom, Jackie, gets most of the credit."

"I see I've embarrassed you," Emma teased. "Kind of you to give Jackie credit, but a good dad is worth a lot. She's a kick, that girl of yours. She was telling me about the year she dressed up like a garden in bloom."

Another one of Nic's trips down memory lane. Sometimes remembering those special Halloween adventures hurt. Like now. "Nic and Jackie went all out for Halloween. I don't know how she did it, but Jackie came up with all types of costumes. Nic was a cute little astronaut one year. It started with a silver snowsuit and took off from there." He laughed. "Oops, bad pun."

"Very bad," Emma said, somberly.

Emma meant well, but all she did was make him feel bad about not showing up at that party, like Nicole wanted. He just couldn't force himself to do it.

"You seemed so resistant to coming to the town party," Emma said, "like it was kind of a waste of your time—"

"I didn't mean it that way," he interrupted.

"Well, that's how it came off. Even to Nicole."

"You're crossing into territory you know nothing about, Emma."

She stared at the lake where half a dozen geese were gathering at the shore. She lifted her camera, but lowered it again. "I'm not trying to make you feel guilty, but Nicole was watching for you, like she thought you might change your mind."

"How do you know that?" he challenged.

"Because I was there. She told me all about Halloween being bigger than Christmas in your family."

Her voice rose with each word, in an intense, but not angry way.

"Look, Emma. Hear me out." He gripped the railing. "I wish I'd gone to the town hall party, but it's too late. When Nic came home, she was full of stories, but I saw her sadness. The truth is she probably missed Jackie. Halloween, all of it, was the best time of the year with her mom."

Emma tapped her mouth with her finger-tips. "This is *so* not my business, but I…"

"But you put it on the table. Truth is, it was my favorite holiday, too, probably because I caught Jackie's enthusiasm when we were first married." Seeing his knuckles turning white, he released his hands and leaned on his forearms. "I should have gone for Nic. I don't miss Jackie, but I miss all the hoopla around the holiday."

"Now that makes sense." Emma turned to face him. "My nosiness aside, I think your daughter is wonderful…smart and funny. She sure works hard."

"Yes, she does." Parker shook his head. "I'm adjusting to living in a place that triggers so many memories for me. You, Mike, Ruby and others talk about the old days and it strikes a chord in me. You're all so connected."

She tilted her head toward him. "I'm sure we've worn you out with our stories about this place and especially Hidden Lake."

"No, that's not it. I had a life and connections. I liked it. But it all blew up. Something as trivial as the big deal over Halloween made me aware of what I'd lost." He smiled sadly. "So, that's my confession. For a little while I missed what I had."

When it came to Nic, it was too difficult to explain that he didn't miss her mom, but couldn't help himself from mulling over some of his memories of their years raising Nic. Not to mention, on days like Halloween, he missed the little girl who called him Daddy. For years he joked it was his favorite word in any language.

Emma studied his face and gave him a fleeting smile. "I'm sorry for bringing it up, but I feel like I know you a little better now."

"I'm glad," he whispered in a voice more intimate than he'd intended. But he didn't regret it.

"I better go." She stuck her camera in her pack. "I can't wait to get these on the computer and find the gems."

"I can't wait to see them," he said.

"That reminds me. Why don't you come over for dinner on Friday? I'll have started working on the slideshow. But I have an ulterior motive, too. I need to ask a favor. Nothing big."

Parker smiled as they left the pier, happy to know that she trusted him this much. "Big or small, Emma, doesn't matter."

"Thanks." She added, "Asking that was easy. I look forward to seeing you Friday."

He felt the same, although he didn't seem to know the words to express how much.

"THE SMELL OF your pot roast is even stronger up here on the ladder," Parker said, sniffing the air.

"Part of my master plan," Emma said, "to keep you working hard for your reward of wine and dinner."

"So you're a schemer." Parker tapped the nail to secure the picture hook. Then he lifted the frame out of Emma's hands and slipped the wire over the hook. He stepped down off the ladder and stood back to check the spacing. "Looks good."

"Perfect," Emma said. "Two down, two to go."

"You are one talented woman."

She murmured a quick thank-you as Parker stared at the close-up shot of three monarch butterflies, so close together their wings appeared to form a single flower with yellow-and-black petals. It was one of her favorite photos. In the background, marigolds and blazing star were hazy, which made the butterflies pop out. The one first one they hung was a panoramic view of the whole butterfly garden. *"Many talents."*

"I have fun with photography. That's why I volunteered to do the slideshow." And it gave her a reason to be part of the open house.

"Stacey pointed out that three of the six posters hanging at the reception were yours. You're a pro," he said, moving the stepladder a few inches along the wall in her office. "Many people think they can do nature photography, but it isn't as easy as it looks. I'm sure you've discovered that."

She shrugged. "In a college photo class, as a matter of fact. I got better with practice. I've got albums going years back. Quite a few from my trips with Ruby. After my fall, I had to put the hobby aside."

"You must have missed it."

"By the time the butterfly garden was created, I was mobile again." She smiled. "Voila, the fruits of post rehab."

Parker measured the space for the bottom two photos, and then got back on the ladder and tapped in the hook. Emma handed him the photo, a shot of a single monarch sitting on the corner of a bench. "The bench is brought to you by the amazing Rivera father-son enterprise." Emma laughed. "They worked fast in the spring to get the flowers in. The garden attracted mostly monarchs."

"And it's on your land?"

"Makes it easy for me to walk over and see it."

"You like to mix things up, don't you?" Parker asked from his perch on the ladder. "I noticed on your living room shelves you have a photo of the butterfly garden next to one of Ruby on a walking trail in Italy. You've got Jason and Mike playing with Peach next to a shot of an old roadside vegetable stand. Extraordinary, really."

"I like the idea of having a blend of sleek and modern with warm and vintage," Emma said.

"You have the photographs of deer in curli-cue frames. Seeing deer in the mist at dawn never gets old, does it? Are they yours?" he asked, pointing his chin toward the pictures.

She nodded. "From last spring. Mixing things up is—for some reason—my way of working with photos. I've been accused of being overly organized, maybe even a little *rigid*. My photos and art are my rebellion against order." She laughed like she'd told a joke.

"You don't seem rigid to me. And your

house is warm and inviting. Not just from the scent of pot roast warmth, although that helps." Parker looked around again. "I look around and see the parts of your life you value. Friends, Bluestone River…"

She looked into his eyes, which were filled with curiosity. "Very perceptive of you, Mr. Nature Lover. But I suppose you see detail in places where the rest of us don't think to look."

He looked restless, almost fidgety.

"Is something wrong, Parker?"

"A game of tug-of-war is going on inside me. Should I or shouldn't I ask about your husband. You haven't said much about Neil. What was he like?"

"True, I don't talk about him much."

Parker nervously cleared his throat. "I'm sorry. I got nosy."

"After the probing I've done, I'm the expert. You don't get to take my title." She grinned.

"It's just that it must be hard to lose your husband at such a young age." He turned to put the fourth hook in the wall.

"He deserved more years, Parker," she said, giving him the last photo. "I'm not just saying that. I'll always feel sad—and even a little guilty—that he didn't get another chance. I don't really mind talking about him, but there's not much to say. About us, I mean."

Parker didn't look convinced. He hung the fourth photo, a picture of a hummingbird in flight over a bed of day lilies, and then got off the ladder. They stood side by side for a final check of even spacing and level corners.

"I'm glad you brought him up. I'm in the habit of not talking about him because he was so well known here. People thought a lot of him." She moved away from Parker, rested her hip on her desk. "The other day you talked about envying the connections so many of us around here have that go way back. It stuck in my mind. I get it. I'm grateful every day for Ruby and Mike."

He folded the ladder and stayed put as Emma lowered her gaze and rubbed her thumb across the palm of her other hand. "He was a good guy—for someone else. But Neil and I shouldn't have been married at all. We had a little harmless teenage romance and mistook it for grown-up love. And we refused to end it when we should have."

Parker started to say something, but closed his mouth.

"What? You were about to say something?"

Parker hesitated. "I admit I'm not the chattiest guy, but thought I should acknowledge what you said. But no words came to me. You took me by surprise."

"It's okay. It's hard to explain why I'm sad for Neil, but never went through what you'd call typical grieving. No one knows this except Ruby, and now Mike, but we'd agreed to see a lawyer about a quick divorce. And before we could even make the first appointment, he died."

When she lifted her eyes to meet his gaze, she saw kindness in his face.

"It's not complicated. Neil and I refused to take no for an answer." She mimicked a "go team" gesture. "We kept trying."

"Nothing wrong with that," he said sharply.

Without knowing why, she'd hit a nerve. "Maybe for some couples, but it was wrong for us." She bit her lower lip and tried to find a way to explain what happened. "We weren't trying to mend something workable. We were wrong for each other in the first place."

Parker widened his stance and crossed his arms. "I want to ask you something, but if

I'm being too personal, tell me to shut up. Okay?"

Emma answered in a dry tone. "Sure, now that I've said this much, it's not likely to get too personal."

"Did you and Neil ever try counseling?"

Emma sputtered her laughter.

"You surprised me again," Parker said.

"The question was so easy. Yes, we tried it. Many times. We were real troupers." She let her head drop as if worn out. "For a solid year we drove to Nelson Grove, a town more than halfway to the Mississippi River, to see a guy who was supposed to be a miracle worker."

"Seriously?"

"Uh-huh. In our case, though? Not so much. We weren't miracle material."

"I'm sorry...but you get credit for hanging in and trying to make it work."

She held up her hand. "No, don't. We spent half our time in counseling learning how to communicate better, and the other half wishing we had something to say. We kept up a good front for our families—and everyone else." She groaned. "It's sad, because he was a good man. And that's why I regret he died without getting a second chance. It's also why no one in his family and his friends know we'd agreed to split before he died. It was deceptive to keep that to myself, but it was kinder."

The room got very quiet. In a good way, Emma thought.

Finally, Parker said, "I asked Jackie—more than once—to try to fix what had gone wrong for us."

"And she refused?"

"Flat out. As it turned out, instead of working on us, she had an affair and one day she left."

An image of Nicole in her tiara and blue dress flashed in front of Emma. "And Nicole isn't over it yet, is she?"

Parker shook his head. "No. Even worse, she thinks her mom isn't doing so well. Nic expects her to pull into the sanctuary driveway one day. Unannounced. I think that's why Nic can seem like a happy college girl one minute and a moping teenager the next."

Emma's stomach dropped with a thud. "You're probably right." Maybe Parker was just as torn as his daughter. She started out of the room. "Come on into the kitchen. I promised you a glass of wine. We can talk there."

He followed her down the hall. "Oh, by

the way, my mom is coming to visit in December."

"Really? I guess we've never talked about your family. Is Nicole excited about seeing her grandma?"

"Oh, yeah. She'll probably tell you about it the next time she sees you. Mom's a high school counselor. She's going to a conference not far from here, so she'll add on two extra days to come to see us."

"Very cool." Emma got out glasses and held up a bottle of red wine.

He nodded. "Red is good. Nic pointed out that neither of us is set up for a houseguest, so we'll make a reservation for her in one of the hotels out by the highway."

Emma poured the wine and handed it to him. "I've got a better idea. I've got so much room. She could have Ruby's room. It has its own everything. It's a lovely room that's empty all the time now. I can show it to you."

He waved her off. "No, no. I take your word for it. But I don't want to put you out."

"You wouldn't be. You'd be doing me a favor. It would be fun for me."

He let out a hoot. "Come to think of it, my mom is gregarious and a lot of fun. I'm sure she'd find you very intriguing. Okay, I accept your offer."

"We have a deal." She held out her glass for a toast.

Smiling, he touched his glass to hers.

As Emma got their dinner on the table, she was lighter, freer. With the truth about her marriage out in the open, she had nothing to hide from Parker now.

CHAPTER SIX

PARKER TOOK THE hot pumpkin pie out of the oven and set it aside to cool. The scent alone made the day a little brighter. "Smell that, Nic? I've created a masterpiece. Again."

Nicole sat at the table, knees bent and heels resting on the edge of the chair. Her phone was on the table instead of in her hands. For once. "Bragging a little, Dad?"

"Go easy on me," he said with a laugh. "I don't have that many specialties. Pumpkin pie is one of them."

Nic took a deep breath. "It is such an awesome smell."

As he ran hot water in the sink to wash up the bowls and measuring cups he was struck by his upbeat mood. He was eager to kick off the holidays that were going to be so much better than last year's. Right before Thanksgiving, Jackie told him she was leaving, but wanted to wait to tell Nicole until after the holidays. One last holiday cycle as a family, she said.

Parker regretted going along with her on that. Later, when the truth came out, Nic had been furious with both of them and called them a couple of fakers. He didn't blame her.

This year was different, though. He'd made a mistake not going to the Halloween party. He wouldn't repeat that again. No more hiding out with old memories. Earlier, down at the pier, the sun rose in a clear sky and delivered the promise of another unseasonably warm day. The rest of Thanksgiving weekend was likely to be rainy and cold. Maybe not good for the open house, but he wasn't going to worry about that now.

Grabbing the dish towel to dry the bowl and utensils, he looked over at Nic staring at her phone. Back to normal.

"Mom just texted. She's not a happy camper, Dad."

How many times had Nic used that expression? When it came to Jackie, what did it even mean? That life wasn't one day of bliss after another? At one time he'd have taken secret pleasure in hearing that news. But those flashes of satisfaction had a short shelf life. He ended up feeling mean. By now, Jackie's problems only mattered if they spilled over to Nic. She looked up at him, obviously expecting a response.

He leaned against the counter and stretched his legs out in front of him, one foot crossed over the other. "Did she mention Thanksgiving plans?" He tried to keep his voice neutral.

"She and Ben are going to a potluck." Nic smiled slyly. "She says most of the food will be 'some combo of beans, zucchini and sprouts…even the pasta.'"

"Now that's your mom's sense of humor," Parker said with a chuckle. "She must be doing better than you think."

"I suppose." Nicole wiggled her shoulders, one up, one down in rapid succession.

"You're doing your shoulder dance. What's wrong?"

"In last night's text, she mentioned the job stuff again."

As in not finding one. Parker heard all about it. She even sent him a text complaining about the lack of teaching jobs in their town.

Nicole scrolled down. "Here she says the potluck is going to be huge. Oh, and it's cold and rainy."

"So, we're going to a *small* potluck," he

said, unable to resist adding, "on a warm, sunny, spectacular day."

Nic gave him a pursed lips give-me-a-break glance.

Give *me* a break. His ex-wife was not going to alter his mood. "What do you want from me, Nic? I can't help it if your mom is having a bad day." If, as Nic had implied on many occasions, her mom had some regrets, how would he know? She didn't confess them to him.

With a grimace nearly distorting her features, Nic stood and cleared their breakfast dishes from the table with a little extra disgruntled energy, as if the plates, sticky from pancake syrup, had done her wrong. "Okay. Sorry for caring." She put down the dishes and flounced past him to the window. She yanked the band off her ponytail and freed her hair and ran her hands through it.

This was getting old. "Nic, tell me what's really going on. Do you wish you'd driven up to see your mom for the weekend?" Had Jackie even invited her? "It's okay if that's what you're thinking. I'm not going to get hurt feelings over it."

She shook her head. "She didn't say anything at all about Thanksgiving until last night. Even if I wanted to be up there, I'm working this weekend. I've also got a bunch of stuff to do for school."

"For what it's worth, I'm not used to this kind of holiday, either. You know, having Thanksgiving dinner with four people we barely know."

"At least they invited us, Dad," Nic whispered, turning to face him. "Would you rather we were alone here? They're, you know, a real family." She chuckled. "Jason and that dog are hilarious. And Emma is fun. It's just so…so strange."

A real family like they used to be. He got that message, even if it bothered him. "Of course, I'm glad. That's my point. It's a different kind of day, but I'm looking forward to it." The words came easily because they were true.

Nicole's eyes flashed with anger. "At least we're not pretending. Like last year."

Parker lifted both hands. "You've got to let me off the hook. I made a mistake going along with your mom. I've said that, what, maybe a thousand times?"

Oh, there it was again. The long, pointed look. Nic was so good at those. But he wouldn't relive it all again. "I'm out of apologies, Nic."

Nic wasn't wrong about the facts. Jackie had told him a few days before Thanksgiving she planned to leave with her secret guy after the holidays. His ex-wife delivered this dose of reality in one speech. She was sorry. She fell in love. Ben was a great guy. She and Parker had had good years, but that's the past. Ten minutes later, he needed a divorce lawyer.

Still reeling from hearing about her affair for the first time, he'd been like a robot and foolishly gone along with her idea—demand—to get through the holidays before telling Nicole they were splitting up.

Nicole flopped on the couch. "I know, I know. I'm being difficult. But it's just…"

"Just what?"

"I guess I can't stop wondering if Mom's changed her mind. Or, like, maybe she wants to come back."

Parker pulled a chair out from the kitchen table and carried it closer to the couch so he could sit opposite her. "Honey, she's not coming back to *me*." He stifled all the platitudes about the good years they'd had and all that. He'd said all that when Jackie first left and they didn't make Nic feel better. Or him. "I know it doesn't seem like it now, Nic, but your mom never really left *you*."

"She's in Vermont, Dad."

Point scored. "You know what I mean."

"Yeah, I do. But it's weird I've only seen where she lives once—for two days while Ben was off on a camping trip with his buddies. I talked to him for like, half an hour."

He could see from her frown she was still perplexed. A man. An affair. A divorce. No obvious warning. He gave his daughter's knees an affectionate pat. "Meanwhile, kiddo, I like having you with me."

For the first time since Nic brought up her mom, she managed a smile. "I know, Dad. I don't want you thinking I don't like it here." Her tone turned sassy. "Not every girl has her very own studio apartment."

"*Heated* studio." Parker laughed smugly. "We better get ready if we're going to show up at Ruby and Mike's on time." He checked his watch and tapped its face. "Out front, fifteen minutes."

Nic hurried out, leaving him to brush away his negative feelings toward Jackie for complaining to Nic. Maybe even making their daughter think Jackie had regrets. Parker preferred the buzz of anticipation that stayed with him the last couple of days. Mike and Ruby were a lot of fun. And generous. He gladly accepted their invitation. Even better, Emma would be there. She was on his mind—a lot.

He quickly changed clothes and grabbed his jacket. After slipping the pie in a box, he joined Nic out front. She looked fresh and young in her skinny jeans and a heavy red sweater. She was like his old Nic when she said, "Lookin' good, Dad. I like your hair kinda longish again."

"I'm glad I pass inspection," he said. "But I think you're also telling me I need a haircut. Guess I'll have to schedule one with Georgia."

The bright afternoon sun warmed his shoulders as they walked along. Nic had been so right about last year's phony holiday in their house in the woods in North Carolina. But he was happy to focus on today.

When Nic led the way on a narrow section of shore the rows of metallic beads on the neckline of her sweater caught the sun and flickered. "If I forget to say it today, I'm proud to be your dad."

She rewarded him with a sweet smile. Then she tugged at the bottom edge of the sweater. "I went thrifting with a girl from my zoology class. This hardly cost me anything."

Thrifting? One of Nic's new hobbies? Nice and safe, Parker thought.

Nic thrust her arm in the air and put some energy behind a big wave. "We might have known we'd have a welcoming party. Peach is waiting to greet us."

"Yep, a dog and her boy," Parker quipped.

Jason ran to meet them, every part of him in motion and talking nonstop. "They sent me to welcome you. You're our guests."

"When I was your age, my mom and dad sent me to welcome guests, too," Nic said.

"Really?"

"Yep, but they just came to the door," Nic said. "We didn't have a special beach."

They hurried the rest of the way to meet Ruby and Mike in the front yard. Hmm… no Emma.

As if reading his mind, Mike said, "Emma's on her way. It's such great weather. I dragged the second boat out of the shed. We can row around the lake after we eat."

"We'll work off all that food, huh?" Ruby said, patting Jason's head.

Looking over Ruby's shoulder, Parker

saw Emma getting out of her car. "Here she comes now."

"She's bringing sweet potatoes," Mike said. "I'll go help her carry them."

"No, no, I'll go." Before Mike could argue, Parker jogged up to Emma. "I hear you have food. I'm the delivery man."

"Good." She pointed to the floor of the back seat. "Have at it."

Parker surprised himself by repeating what Mike said about taking a boat out on the lake later. He was glad Nicole couldn't hear him talking so fast.

Emma's face lit up as they started toward the house. "I'm game. I haven't been out on the lake in a long time."

"I suppose you saw the forecast isn't looking good for the weekend." He shrugged as they walked along. "But we've done all we can for the open house."

"So, how's the owl?"

"Livening up. She'll be on her way soon."

Emma's expression gave away her heart. "I know it's positive news, but I'll miss her."

He understood. "Everyone who works with these creatures has a pang or two when they fly off. That means we've been successful, but it's bittersweet sometimes."

"Hey, you two," Ruby called. "No time for chitchat. We've got work to do."

"Uh-oh. Listen up. Ruby's getting us organized," Emma said.

By the time Ruby divvied up the jobs, Parker gladly teamed up with Mike to set the table and open the wine. Ruby asked Nicole to help setting up the food in buffet style. Emma was put in charge of watching Jason and Peach in the front yard.

While Parker helped Mike, he tried not to be obvious about staring out the bay window at Emma. She was perched on the tire swing with her long legs extended in front of her while Jason pushed her and the dog sat and watched.

Mike glanced at him with a knowing expression. "She's like an aunt to Jason. Em and Ruby are like sisters, only without the rivalry."

"That's what Emma said."

Later, as they filled their plates with cranberries, dressing, sweet potatoes and Ruby's specialty, a corn casserole, Mike carved the turkey.

"You do that like a pro," Parker said. "You've mastered one of the manly arts."

Mike laughed. "I can carve a turkey and

row my family around the lake. I'm two for two."

"Before we eat, let's say something we're grateful for today," Ruby said. "Our families didn't always do that, but Mike and I want to make it our family tradition."

Parker glanced at Nicole, wondering if she was so quiet because it was Jackie's tradition, too. At times like this, it was as if her old childhood shyness had made a temporary comeback. He liked to joke about her being all grown up, but maybe not so much.

"I'll start," Emma said. "I'm grateful for the new center. And for all of you."

As they went around the table, Ruby talked about being grateful for Jason and the baby. Mike said thank you to his dad, who'd passed, for convincing him to hang on to the house and the lake.

"It's not exactly original," Parker said, "but I'm thankful for Nic and my new job."

"And I get to have my own studio," Nic said. "Who wouldn't be grateful for that?"

"What about you, Jason?" Mike asked. "What are you grateful for?"

Jason dug his spoon into the cranberries on his plate. "Today, it's cranberries. My favorite."

"You are so funny, Jason," Nic said, laughing.

"Thanks," Jason said. "Can we eat now?"

"Good question," Mike said. "I think it's time."

As they ate first helpings and passed the bowls for seconds, most of the talk was about how delicious everything was. At one point, Nic changed the subject and asked Mike if he liked being mayor. She soaked up the story of him announcing his candidacy over last year's Thanksgiving dinner.

Mike glanced at Jason and then at Ruby. "It was a big day all around."

"And now we're getting a baby, Nicole," Jason said, bouncing in the chair. "It's either a boy or a girl. We don't know which."

Parker chuckled along with everyone else, but Nic broke into a giggle. "How fun. You'll have a dog and a baby."

"Peach used to be Mom's dog," Jason explained, "but she belongs to the whole family now."

Ruby smiled softly at Jason. "With such a big heart, Peach has plenty of room for all of us."

Parker glanced at Nic, whose eyes were suspiciously shiny. Who could blame her?

His heart squeezed in his chest and for a couple of seconds he could barely breathe. Right now, this family had it all. No one was faking their feelings, or keeping up appearances, only to walk out the door forever.

Seeing Ruby and Mike brought him back to a time when they were getting ready for Nic and his pulse raced with excitement. He was impatient for her to be born so he could be a dad. Young as he was, it seemed he'd waited his whole life to say hello to Nic for the first time.

"I get to be an honorary aunt…again," Emma said, her gaze on Nic.

"Way cool." Nic smiled, but her tone fell flat.

As if sensing a subtle shift in the atmosphere, Emma pushed her chair back and stood. She looked expectantly at Parker. "Want some help cutting the pie?"

"Absolutely," he said, following her into the kitchen, where she got out plates and cups and saucers. "You know your way around, don't you?" he asked.

"I've spent a fair amount of time here over the last year. Ruby and I work together on lots of projects. She'll come to my house plenty, but I enjoy coming out here—and to the lake." Emma blushed and lowered her gaze. "But then, you know that."

"The birds and I are always happy to see you." It was true. He was lighter when he was with Emma. Sometimes she seemed to send him flitting all over the place like the chickadees and cardinals going from branch to branch, tree to tree. Right now, he was lighter than he'd been all day.

EVEN ROWING OUT onto the lake, the happy, playful sounds coming from Nicole and Jason on the shore carried across the water. It didn't take long for Emma to catch on to Parker. It was no accident he was keeping them a fair distance from Mike and Ruby in the other dinghy. Emma braced her palms on the seat and lifted her face to revel in the warmth of the sun.

"This is like a moment of perfection."

Parker smiled. "Not to mention having an oarsman at your service, ma'am."

"Ah yes, I'm getting a free ride." She leaned to the side and let her fingers drag in the water, cool, but not yet icy cold.

"The longer Nic and I are in town, the more she sees what having a real home is like." Parker pulled the oars into the boat and let it float aimlessly. "She grew up mostly in North Carolina, but her relatives were in Ohio, where I grew up. Jackie's were in Pennsylvania and Delaware."

"Makes my life in Bluestone River seem kind of dull. Born here, one house, one school." She grinned. "Only one college, too."

"But isn't your family kind of a big deal here?"

Emma shrugged. She hadn't thought about it in that way in a long time.

Frowning, Parker said, "Oops. Sensitive subject?"

"No, no. It's just that hardly anyone remembers the O'Connells anymore. My grandfather owned a farm machinery business way back when. He sold it at the right time, and being a smart investor, he called it dumb luck, he amassed the family money."

Parker's cheeks turned pink. "Actually, I wasn't talking about money. Everyone knows you."

"They know *of* me. Except for a huge, mansion kind of house, my parents were low-key. I'm the same." She waved to Ruby in the other boat. "I sold the house when my mom died and it's changed hands a couple of times since, so it's not the old O'Connell place anymore."

"You still live in a huge house," Parker teased.

Emma grinned and stared at the trees lining the lake as she gathered her thoughts. "I like my land, especially now that we have the butterfly garden on the edge of it."

"The woods here are pretty quiet now, but they'll be alive with birdsong in the spring and summer."

"I'm glad you're enjoying it here, Parker." She paused. "You're part of bringing Bluestone River to life. Even the diner is getting a new look."

"Jim Kellerman goes through my mind now and again. My invitation is still open," Parker said.

"He may be hopeless," Emma replied, a look of mild disdain passing over her face. "He even argued against reviving caroling at the bridge—an old tradition that fell by the wayside decades ago."

Parker chuckled. "Mike told me he didn't even want Santa Day. What harm could a little singing in the park do?"

"Good question." Emma bristled, knowing full well it wasn't fair. But maybe it was a little singing to him, but to her it was a statement, a sign. The volunteer organizers felt the same way. Bluestone River was taking something cherished in the past and polishing it up and bringing it out as a showpiece again.

Suddenly, Mike's laughter pierced the air and drew her attention to the other boat, facing toward the house again.

"I wonder what Ruby said to get Mike laughing," Emma mused. "This time. She makes him laugh all the time. I think that's half the reason he's so in love with her."

"Not a bad reason at all." Parker smiled and picked up the oars.

Emma was glad Parker rowed away from the shore rather than toward it. She was enjoying this too much to head back. She was curious about a remark Nicole had made earlier, but wasn't sure how to broach it. Emma wasn't even sure why it stuck in her mind or had any meaning at all.

"I'm curious," Emma started. "Nicole mentioned that it was snowing in Colorado and about going to another college. Is her mother moving there?"

Parker adjusted his sunglasses, one of his nervous habits, she'd noticed. He kept his focus on the water, not on her.

"No, that's where she expected to go to college. I'd accepted a job to start a new avian rescue center. Nicole planned to move with me. Actually, we were all going. Jackie hadn't left yet." Parker scoffed. "To be honest it was one of those offers that sounded too good to be true, and it turned out to be just that. The whole thing fell through last spring."

"I see." But she didn't. Or maybe she didn't like what she suspected was true. "So, we were your second choice?" *If that.*

Parker abruptly stopped rowing. "When you put it that way, then yes. That's how I landed here." He began rowing again. "Emma, surely that would make sense to you. You knew I wasn't a young guy looking for his first job."

"I just hadn't thought of it that way," Emma said, confused by a barrage of contradictory feelings. Parker was right. What had she expected? That someone with his experience would make their small center his last stop? She knew better.

"Look, I won't lie to you. I wanted that move to Colorado. I'd prepared my whole career for a job like that and had all the credentials for it. Anyone in my field would have jumped at the chance. But it was more or less a house of cards. I hadn't signed a new contract at the center in North Carolina. Nic was finishing senior year and we were going to leave after graduation. End of story."

Knowing the question was out of line, she stumbled into it anyway. "Then do you plan to leave when another opportunity comes up?"

Parker frowned. "Emma, these questions aren't relevant now. Have you seen even *one* sign that I'm not committed to the sanctuary? One hundred percent?"

"No, not really. But…" She searched for the words to make herself understood.

"So far, I've done everything asked of me." Parker's voice rose as he spoke. "And more. Much more."

"Yes, you have," Emma said. "I've enjoyed watching what you've done. Anyone can see all the time and energy that's gone into the sanctuary. I'm not criticizing."

"You've played a significant part, too, Emma." Parker nodded. "Look, let's settle this. I committed to the board for a year, with an optional automatic renewal if I want it. Beyond that, we'll see. But if you're wondering, I'm not actively looking for another job."

Emma ignored that grudging, frustrated tone that she'd also detected on other occasions. "Okay, my mistake. I never should have questioned you."

He studied her face. "Then why did you?"

A stark and frank question. An equally stark answer was on her tongue. "I really don't know." She stopped short of admitting she was drawn to him. That she selfishly didn't want him to leave. She settled for making a couple halfhearted remarks about the beauty of the land and its role in the town's renewal. It sounded like brochure copy, even to her. Finally, she more or less gave up explaining. "All that aside, you and Nicole seem to fit right in here."

In a gentler voice, Parker said, "And don't get me wrong. Even Nic noticed how nice you've all been." He raised his brows. "Not to mention an apartment all to herself."

"I'll bet." She glanced at the pinkish ripples of light on the water. The sun was fading now. "It's going to be dark soon."

"We should probably get back." He pointed with his chin to the shore. "Mike is dragging the other boat up on the beach."

"It's been fun out here rowing around," she said, trying to lighten up her tone. "Thanks."

"I'm glad we grabbed the chance."

The dull ache in her hip distracted her when they fell into an awkward silence. She shifted her position and bent her knee and tucked her left leg behind her right. Out of the corner of her eye, she saw Parker watching, a small wrinkle forming between his brows. It took an effort to keep her expression neutral.

When they reached the shore, Parker grounded the bow and jumped out. "Let me pull it up so you don't get wet."

Emma gripped the sides as she tried to figure out a way to gracefully lift herself up and off the boat. For the moment, though, she was stuck. Avoiding Parker's eyes, she saw Nicole watching while she pushed Jason in the tire swing. Emma had spent way too much time trying to dodge moments just like this one.

"Can I help you?" Parker's voice was casual.

She smiled up at him. "Um, thanks, but I can manage." She pushed off from her good leg, and almost got to both feet as she reached across the seat for her cane. Big mistake. The ache in her bad leg turned into a bolt of unexpected pain streaking down her thigh. She gasped and let herself drop to one knee to avoid falling over.

Parker's arm circled her waist and he steadied her. "That hurt, huh?"

"A little bit, but I'll be fine." As she started to straighten up, he held on with a looser grip but didn't move away from her. He kept his hand on her arm as she stepped out of the boat.

"You kind of had me worried there," he said, trying to keep his voice light.

She pulled her arm out of his grip. "Please, I can manage to take care of myself. I'm not helpless. I'm not one of your wounded birds." She gulped air and covered her mouth with her hand. An apology, an explanation, started to form, but Parker was faster.

"You? Helpless? Right." He turned away abruptly and took long strides toward Nicole.

Her expression troubled, Nicole caught her eye. She owed Parker an apology. But now he was talking to Mike and Nicole. Jason and the dog were running in circles around the three them.

Ruby hurried toward her, beaming, which meant her best friend hadn't seen her struggle to get out of the boat. Good. She would hide the ache in her leg long enough to say her goodbyes. Once she got home, she'd soak in a hot tub and the pain would go away.

"It was gorgeous out there, wasn't it?" Ruby asked. "Mike and I haven't been out much by ourselves. Jason is usually with us—and Peach."

"It was a gorgeous day." Emma put her arm around Ruby. "Thanks so much. Another special holiday with you."

Ruby pulled away. "Wait a minute. I'll get you some leftovers."

"No, don't bother now," Emma said. "I'll stop in tomorrow. I'm going to be at the sanctuary most of the day anyway." And she'd get Parker off by himself and apologize properly. Profusely.

Ruby eyed her suspiciously. "Are you hurting?"

She tightened her mouth and nodded. "A little. I probably didn't stretch enough this morning." A harmless little white lie.

"If you're sure," Ruby said, looking skeptical. "Well, I'll see you tomorrow one way or the other. If I'm not here, I'll be on the boardwalk."

Emma gave Ruby a quick one-armed hug and shouted goodbye to everyone. "See you tomorrow."

Jason ran toward her with Peach following. "You going to walk me to my car?"

"Uh-huh. Dad said we're going to be in the woods tomorrow. But our feet won't touch the ground."

Emma laughed and stroked Jason's brown curls. "That's right. You come visit me in the office. I have a slideshow. You can see pictures I took of lots of stuff. Would you like that?"

"Yep. Bye." With that he ran off to join the others.

Still angry with herself, Emma walked away as fast as she could.

When she got home, she peeled off her clothes and sat on the edge of the tub while it filled. Her cheeks were wet with the tears that had started the minute she closed her front door. Over what? Her thoughtless remark? Her tears certainly weren't about Parker. Well, maybe a little. No, this was all about her. She started her day with energy and anticipation, but now all that had drained away and this sense of defeat had taken over.

Poor me, she mocked. *I couldn't get myself out of the boat.*

Big deal. She'd stayed in one position too long and her hip and leg were like a frozen hinge that kept her from unfolding her body. If she'd laughed at herself and accepted Parker's help, it would have been a light moment between friends.

Emma thought she'd adjusted to her situation. Accepted that she had this one physical limitation. A minor one that had no real consequences in her regular life other than not being able to walk long distances. She needed a cane to ease the pressure off her lower back and hip. That was it.

And maybe occasionally, she had to grasp an outstretched hand to help her. She submerged into the water and let the heat do its magic.

PARKER WAS NOT about to apologize to Emma. He wouldn't back down and pretend he did something wrong. He left the treatment cabin and was on his way to the pier in the dark when his phone buzzed in his pocket. A call, not a text.

"Am I calling too late? Oh, why am I bothering to ask that. You'd deny it if it were true just so I wouldn't feel bad."

"Luckily, I don't have to deny anything. And it's not exactly the middle of the night."

"You know why I'm calling."

"I can speculate, Emma, but I'd rather not."

"I had no right snapping at you the way I did. I'm *truly* sorry. I hope you believe me."

"Of course, I believe you, Emma," he said, realizing his voice had softened nearly to a whisper.

"I was completely frustrated with myself, Parker. It had nothing to do with you."

He didn't believe that. He'd triggered something. And that's what he wouldn't apologize for.

"I know exactly how fortunate I am to be walking around at all. I don't wear self-pity well and I don't want to start now."

"Can I say something now?" Parker asked.

"Uh, okay."

"Well, I'm not going to lie and tell you I'm sorry for reaching out to steady you or help you get out of the boat. I'm just not. If Ruby tripped, or Jason got hurt, I'd jump in."

"I know, Parker. That's why I feel bad about what I said."

"It's not about intruding in your space, Emma. Maybe you would have righted yourself. Maybe not. But I wasn't going to wait around to see. But please, it's done now."

"And I can sleep," Emma said clearly

sounding relieved. "I didn't want to wait until tomorrow."

"Consider it done."

"Thanks. So, see you in the morning?"

"First thing."

She said a soft goodbye and ended the call. He went down to the pier, smiling to himself.

EMMA CRAWLED INTO BED, relieved by her conversation with Parker beyond what made sense. She'd blown this all out of proportion. Nearly asleep, she heard the signal alerting her to a text. She rolled over and grabbed the phone off the nightstand. She laughed out loud at the message: U r no wounded bird.

Sighing as she snuggled under the covers, phone in hand, she considered typing a reply, but couldn't come up with anything witty enough. Somehow, a simple "thanks" wouldn't do.

If more needed to be said to clear the air they could do it in person. Tomorrow.

CHAPTER SEVEN

STANDING ON THE pier, Parker looked through
the trees to watch the growing slice of red-
dish light eerily tint the horizon marked by
heavy, dark clouds. He turned to the sound
of footsteps behind him. It was barely dawn,
but Nicole had her travel mug in one hand
and her backpack hanging off one shoulder.
He remembered now she'd taken an extra
shift at the bakery this weekend. As she got
closer he could almost feel the heavy gloom
she brought with her that morning. Out of
duty, but not desire for an answer, he took a
chance and asked if she was okay.

She avoided his gaze and shook her head.
"Not really. It's Mom again."

"Oh? Did she tell you about her Thanksgiving?"

"She doesn't like some of Ben's old
friends."

Too bad. He couldn't dig deep and locate
sympathy.

"She hasn't made any women friends yet. She sounds kind of lonely."

Parker held back angry words and coughed like he'd swallowed wrong. Why was Jackie playing such games with Nicole? She'd never been that kind of person, not until she'd started sneaking around with Ben.

"Honey, I've told you a million times, your mom can take care of herself," he said. "Your mom absolutely knows how to make friends."

"But what if she and Ben break up or something?"

"She'll make another plan. She'll find a teaching job somewhere."

"What if she wanted to come here?"

"You aren't suggesting what I think you're suggesting, right?"

Nicole snickered and gave him a pointed look. "No Dad, I know you two aren't getting back together. But maybe she could live near here. Like over in Clayton. That's not far from my school."

It wouldn't matter to him one way or another. He also wasn't about to argue about some hypothetical breakup. "You know what I hope for? Whatever makes *you* happy."

Nicole nodded. She stared out at the water, dark and still under the thick clouds forming now. "I better go. But I'll be back to help you if you need it."

"No rush," he said. "Between you and me, I don't see this place overflowing with visitors. A cold front is coming through. It's probably going to be busier in the bakery than it will be here."

"Wow, aren't you the optimist? I hope you're wrong."

"Me, too, but I don't think so."

She started down the path, but turned back. "Is Emma mad at you about something?"

"No. We're fine."

"She seemed to rush off. Like she didn't hang around to say a proper goodbye."

"We had a little misunderstanding, that's all."

"Okay, I believe you." She grinned. "I think."

He waved her toward the vehicle. "Get outta here."

Parker went back to his cabin. Between thinking about Emma and worrying about this open house weekend being a bust, he'd barely slept and finally gave up and stood under a stream of hot water.

His hair was still damp when he went to pay a visit to the owl. Because of how protective Emma felt about the owl, it was hard to think that the time was coming soon when he'd need to let her go back to the woods. She'd likely stay in these woods through the winter, probably with her mate, along with a good number of cardinals and juncos. Crows might happen by as well.

"Okay, my friend, wake up and smell the coffee," Parker said, raising the dark fabric cover and eying the owl. The owl spread her wings and lifted her feet. The bird had a way of staring back.

"I promise not to treat you like my pet bird for much longer," he said. That's not to say Parker wouldn't think about his first patient in his new home. There were a couple of eagles that had long stays at the rescue center and the memories of watching them heal still lingered in his mind. Even Jackie and Nicole sometimes struggled to say goodbye to one of the creatures he'd saved.

Heading to the center, Parker debated calling Jackie. If he was going to make that call, he had to do it soon or postpone it another day. Once inside, he turned on the heater, and he set up chairs in the alcove for visitors to watch Emma's slideshow. By next year, one of the larger cabins would be converted to a classroom with benches, tables, a whiteboard and screen.

As he worked he rehearsed what he'd say to Jackie if he reached her. Finally, knowing he'd regret not trying to make the call, he went into the office and hit Jackie's number.

"Parker? Is that you? Do you know what time it is?"

"Yeah, I do. An hour later than it is here." Whoa, he sounded colder than he meant to.

"Is Nic okay? What is it?"

"Nic is fine. This isn't an emergency, Jackie. At least not on my end. It's you I'm concerned about. Nic is…" He searched for the right word.

"Nic is what? Is she unhappy out there?"

Anger started to build inside. "No, Jackie, she's not unhappy." He told Jackie about everything Nic liked about her life, from school and her job to Jason and Peach. "I don't want to blame you, but she's kind of gloomy about you. She thinks you're unhappy."

Silence.

"Uh, Jackie, I'm not saying it's your fault."

"Yes, you are." She spoke in her no-nonsense teacher's voice.

"Why don't you just explain yourself?

Why are you telling her you don't like Ben's friends or you don't have your own friends?"

"Oh, Parker, she's eighteen. Just because Nic says something that doesn't make it… entirely accurate."

"So it's only sort of true?"

"Let's just say I'm adjusting. New place. New…"

He silently filled in the blank implied in her pause. New man. She couldn't say it out loud.

"I'm looking for the right job. It's different."

"I get it, Jackie. All three of us are still adjusting. But somehow Nic has ended up feeling sorry for you. That's not right."

"Oh, that will pass," Jackie said, with an air of nonchalance. "She spent months feeling sorry for you."

He couldn't deny some truth in that. As much as he'd tried to avoid it, when Jackie first left, Nic dragged him into some gloomy pity parties. "That's all over now. I don't want Nic taking on round two by being overly concerned about you. And for what?"

"For nothing," she said, her voice softening. "It's none of your concern if I'm happy here or not."

"Absolutely. But make up your mind if you want Nic with you. Yes, no, or when."

Her heavy sigh came through the phone. "Oh, Parker."

"If you're unhappy, then in Nic's fantasy world, you'll pack up your stuff and find a place to live closer to Neville. You'll get a job and she can go back and forth between the two of us." He scoffed. "Until she's ready to break free and make her own plans. For all we know, move half a world away if that's where life takes her."

"My, my, so philosophical this early in the morning?"

"Realistic." Through the window he saw Emma's car nose into the lot. "I have to open up here. Think about what I said. And please, watch your words. Our daughter takes them to heart."

"I will, Parker, I will."

He ended the call. Knowing Jackie, she'd grumble about what he'd said, but in the end, she'd put Nicole first. He had that much faith her better judgment would make a comeback. Even when things had become strained between them, or even worse, indifferent, they united around Nicole.

Parker opened the office door and stepped

out into the chilly air and started toward Emma as she approached him walking faster than usual. "Good to see you," he called out.

Emma sent him a sheepish smile. "I'm on a mission."

"Oh? Well, I guess I am, too. I just hope people show up on this gray day."

Standing in front of him she turned to look at the lake and took in a long breath. "No, I'm serious. More than anything, I'm here to apologize. I was so out of line."

He waved her off. "No, we settled it. Don't give it another thought." He was being conciliatory, wasn't he?

"It wasn't nothing. The truth is I was in pain."

And in danger, Parker thought. He'd been keeping her from getting hurt. Speaking of, he had a case of hurt feelings. He liked her. Maybe too much.

"Okay, Mr. Boss Man. Tell me what you want me to do. What's up your sleeve?"

Cancel the open house and offer her one of her favorite jelly donuts with a cup of hot coffee? Spend time with the owl and show Emma how to check the gash behind the bird's ear? Put his arms around Emma and hold her for a good long time?

Parker cleared his throat. "Okay, why don't we finish setting up for our guests?"

EMMA POURED WATER into the urn and flipped the switch to start brewing the coffee. The weekend wasn't supposed to go this way. No one planned to offer coffee and brownies, not when the point was to get people out walking the boardwalk through the woods, hanging out at the pier, watching the slideshow in the office and going away with brochures and invitations to the official launch on Christmas Eve.

She stared out the picture window blurred by the rain whose steady beat was broken by gusts of wind. After expected poor attendance on Friday, cold rain on Saturday that kept all but a hardy few home, Emma decided they had to do something to make the visitors on a stormy Sunday think it was worth coming out. She came up with the idea of bringing her large coffee urn and paper cups. She enlisted Nicole to get brownies and butterscotch bars. If the people couldn't wander around and take in the beauty, they could chat with Parker. They could watch the slideshow and listen to Ty and Stacey explain future projects in the warmth of the office.

"Good idea, Parker," she overheard Stacey say as she opened a new package of paper cups.

"Emma thought of it."

"I knew there'd come a time I'd need to brew thirty-six cups of coffee in that pot that's been in my basement forever," Emma said, glancing at Parker, looking every bit the director in his forest green jacket, with Hidden Lake Bird Sanctuary & Nature Center stitched across the back.

"A lot more PR is going out for Christmas Eve," Ty said. "This was an experiment that didn't work so well."

Emma was glad to hear him admit this was not the best idea.

When the door opened and a man and two kids entered, Parker stepped forward to greet them. "As you can see the weather hasn't been kind to our open house, but please, come on in. Our slideshow is ready to go and we can all answer your questions."

"We thought we'd come to walk in the woods and see some birds," the man said, patting the heads of the little kids flanking him, "but I warned them not to count on it."

"If you come with me I'll show you a picture of an eagle sitting up in the tree." Parker pointed out the window at the giant oak in front of the parking lot. "He was sitting right up there. Come on over. Have a look."

The kids followed him to the alcove, where he started the slideshow. "It's about ten pictures in so we'll come to it. You can see the pictures of the geese and the ducks that like it here at Hidden Lake."

"Can we go see 'em?" the girl asked.

"When it stops raining, Caitlin," her dad said.

"When it's dry, you can walk out to the lookout. A lot of geese stopped here on their way to warmer places, but some hang out here all winter. You might see some cardinals and little birds like nuthatches, or bigger ones like crows."

Emma smiled when Parker cut his eyes to her. "You might even see an owl, although they like nighttime better."

As the photos changed, Parker explained what the kids were seeing and stopped on the one of the eagle.

"Wow, he's big," the boy said.

The dad stood behind the kids, amused by their curiosity. Emma tapped his arm and pointed to the urn, where he could serve himself.

"Will you be running classes for kids?"

"I believe so, at least, eventually." Emma pointed to Stacey and Ty. "They're the ones to ask about the current schedule for school trips and classes."

"My son finished a nature diorama, and now he wants to do more of that kind of thing. I wouldn't mind bringing him here."

Emma nodded. "The center's dioramas will be on display soon. Your son might want to see those. I'm only a volunteer, but I'll mention to the board that arts and crafts classes for kids might be a good idea."

She noticed Stacey and Ty listening to Parker's interaction with the kids. He was good at it. He'd moved them to the map showing the future plans for the sanctuary. Emma heard the energy in his voice when he told the kids about plans to rescue birds and take care of them.

"My two will think that's a pretty cool idea," the man said, introducing himself as Evan. "I've been following what's going on here. I'm impressed."

Good news for the sanctuary. "I hope you'll join us on Christmas Eve when we relaunch this as an expanded sanctuary and nature center."

The sound of the bell on the door gave Emma a lift. An older couple came and put their dripping umbrellas in the corner. Emma directed them to coffee. They helped themselves and took their cups closer to Parker and listened in. Suddenly, it seemed almost busy. And pleasant, Emma thought, with people clustered in the warm, dry office. With the fresh paint and brand new shelves, the counter rearranged, and the alcove set up for the slideshow, only traces of the old Hidden Lake Resort remained.

The trickle of visitors lasted through the afternoon. With Ty and Stacey there, and Nicole in and out, Emma was aware she wasn't especially needed, but she had no desire to leave. She had to laugh at herself. For someone who claimed to have no particular role in this venture, other than underwriting it, she sure hung around a lot. But she hoped to see the owl before she called it a day.

"That's a beautiful walking stick," an older man said, pointing his own rubber-tipped metal cane. "Do you sell them here? Or those posters on the wall."

"No to the canes, but I can give you a poster with a membership or sell you one. I imagine we'll eventually have a gift shop here. And I can show you where I bought the cane." Emma grabbed her phone and brought up the gallery on the screen. "Right over in Clayton."

Nicole, who had come in and chatted up the dad with the kids, came closer. "It would be fun to have him down on the pier doing his carving, wouldn't it? You know, a craft demonstration."

"The girl's a genius," Stacey said, making Nicole blush and everyone else laugh.

"You're all just getting started," the man said, nodding to Parker, who was talking with a young guy who'd just come in.

"Looks that way," Emma said, suddenly captured by the image of the wood carver on the pier. And a local science teacher— or Parker—doing nature projects with the kids. An art teacher doing crafts. And a gift shop? Wow.

"I'm glad it's coming to life. That's one reason why we came today," another woman said.

Emma moved aside as the visitors talked to each other and another person came in to fill out a membership form.

It was four o'clock when the last visitor had gone, but the wind and rain kept up. Nicole cleaned up the office and offered to load the urn and leftovers into Emma's car.

"Why don't we store that here? It's been gathering dust for years. It might come in handy here another time."

Nicole started to respond, but the conversation going on between Parker, Stacy, and Ty was impossible to ignore.

"It wasn't what we hoped," Ty said.

"A total of sixteen memberships over three days," Stacey added.

Parker threw up his hands in a gesture of helplessness. "We can't special order the weather." He gestured behind him at the alcove. "You saw me explaining the concept and talking about the future. You were mingling with the people who did show up. Whether they joined today isn't the critical issue. We've introduced them to the center. And I sure wouldn't count Friday in your evaluation. We already knew that was doomed to be a pretty slow day."

Emma winced at his harsh tone. Yes, Parker, this event was critical to the people using conservancy funds for what turned out to be a bust of a weekend. He could say he told them so, but what did that buy him? Apparently, Nicole wondered the same thing, because she stared at her dad wide-eyed, her eyebrows almost saying hello to her hairline.

"I still think it was an idea worth trying," Stacey insisted. "Keeps us in the news."

"I don't mean to be critical, but the TV cameras were here yesterday and the story wasn't the sanctuary, it was the weather ruining the weekend open house." Parker paused. "I'm not trying to do your job. But resources are limited and you want to make the most of them."

She gave him a D on the first point, a solid B on the second. They didn't need to be told their spot on the Clayton evening news was more or less wasted.

"On the upside, the people who stopped by this afternoon are potential volunteers," Parker said. "They came with ideas. Someone mentioned a gift shop, art classes and…"

"Like I said, craft demonstrations on the pier, Dad," Nicole interjected.

Parker smiled for the first time, and it was clear his change in expression was directed only at her. "Or, right here in the alcove this winter on a Saturday afternoon."

Stacey groaned. "Gift shops take so much time."

Parker's mouth twitched as if he might laugh.

"That's why we have volunteers," Ty said.

In a more diplomatic tone, Parker said, "You're starting from scratch and all this takes a lot of effort. I'd take away what you can from it and then let it go." He paused. "I know that's easy for me to say."

Emma found reasons to stay, but she didn't fool Parker. As soon as Stacey and Ty left, he said, "Hanging around for any particular reason?"

"As if you didn't know."

"Is this about the owl?" Nic asked.

"We're going to go visit. Wanna come with?"

"No, Mom texted. I think I'll call her back." She waved her phone at Parker and added, "Nothing serious." She left and broke into a run.

Emma slipped into her raincoat. Something always seemed to be going on with Nicole and her mother and even the mild tension could instantly change the atmosphere in the room. Like now.

"Let's go," Parker said, pulling up the hood of his jacket. He opened the door and Nic dashed out first and ran to her cabin in the steady rain.

"You can run ahead and save yourself," Emma said. "I'll only slow you down."

"Not a chance." Parker's face brightened. "Look in the corner. Someone left an umbrella. For us."

"It's official," Emma said. "The place is open and you have the first item for your lost and found box."

Parker laughed. "Never thought of that. Stacey and Ty will be pleased."

"I remember who the umbrella belongs to. Don't know her name, though. Maybe she'll be back."

"Probably not today." Parker closed the door behind them and opened the umbrella and covered them both, but mostly Emma. He put his arm around her shoulder to keep her balanced as she moved. She didn't argue.

When they got to the treatment building, the owl hooted.

"I'm pretty sure that's owl language for 'get me outta here'," Parker joked.

When he took the cover off, the owl was on the perch. Calm, but strong. One eye looked smaller than the other, but that likely wouldn't change because of the scar tissue.

She stayed still, as if observing them when they sat on a bench across from her large pen.

At the risk of opening a touchy conversation, she said, "You were so good with the visitors today. The little kids are your new best friends and their dad said he'd been following what we're doing."

"That part was fine. Having the snacks there kept people around and engaged. Great idea," Parker said. "My old days in nature centers kicked in and I dusted off my bantering skills."

"Your attitude and energy for the birds and the woods is infectious. It's one of your strengths." She nudged his shoulder. "Look what it's done to me. Turned me into a bird freak, as Nic would say."

"Another notch in my nature lover's belt," Parker said. "On a more serious note, I didn't mean to be hard on Stacey and Ty."

Stay out of it. "I guess all the attention is on Christmas Eve now."

Parker nodded. "And the Santa visit. I told Mike I'd help out. Then my mom arrives. Nic is looking forward to that. Then we have the fair at Neville." He frowned. "That should take her mind off Jackie."

"I imagine grandma visits are always fun for her."

"Next you'll start talking about the color of the owl's eyes," Parker teased. "Anything not to get entangled in the board business or what goes on between Nic and her mom."

"Haven't I intruded enough? I'm trying to be on my best behavior."

"Oh, no, don't do that," Parker said. "I like your curious side." He nodded at the owl. "Like how you are with her."

Emma gestured to the owl. "Well, she's part of my new life."

"Meaning?"

She scanned this makeshift clinic. "Being here, working with even this one bird. It's my something more, Parker."

His smile came slowly and wasn't entirely readable, but the look in his eyes told her he understood.

CHAPTER EIGHT

PARKER MOVED A couple of hawks' nests from the cardboard box and put them on a glass shelf inside a display case. He put an old label in front of it for identification until he could mount the remade descriptions of the variety of nests they'd display.

The cases were old, but cleaned up and fit the look of the wooden cabin. The Riveras had brought a crew to haul away the ancient gas stove and rusting refrigerator. They'd ripped out the kitchen cabinets that had warped with age. The building had fresh drywall, but the wooden floors had been refurbished. A table was pushed against the other wall, where a model of the sanctuary was underway.

The sound of his name was faint at first, but it was a man's voice that was louder with each repetition—and more frantic. Parker got down from the ladder and went outside. A man was standing outside the office peering through the window.

"I'm coming," Parker yelled, breaking into a jog. The guy looked vaguely familiar, but he'd never seen the woman standing by the car.

The man met him halfway and when he was close enough to shake his hand, the name Jim Kellerman zipped into Parker's mind. "Hey, nice to see you, Jim," he said, extending his hand.

"Not good right now. We found a crow out in the backyard," Jim said. "I remembered about you coming from a rescue place—"

"Where is it?" Parker interrupted. "In your car?"

"Yeah, my wife looked something up online and they said to wrap it in a blanket and put it in a box." Jim breathed heavily, his face flushed.

"Good, that's good," Parker said, walking toward the car. At the moment, he was more worried about Jim than he was about the bird. Ironic, Jim would be the one to bring in a crow. The only guy in town who'd openly opposed the sanctuary.

He introduced himself to Jim's wife, Ruth, who pointed to the back seat. "I emptied the biggest box we had in the basement. We didn't want to hurt him more. We saw some wings out by the woods—big wingspan, what we saw of it anyway. It said online to cover its head."

"You did the right thing. As long as the bird can breathe, you're okay." He looked at the box and judged he'd need the cart to transport the bird to the cabin. "I have a makeshift area in one of the old cabins. I'm keeping some supplies for situations just like this." Explaining he had to get the cart, he took off and left Jim with Ruth.

He moved quickly and a few minutes later, Ruth and Jim steadied the cart and Parker eased the carton onto the metal bottom. "I bought a couple of kennels the other day to replace some old ones here. One of them is big, a good size for this crow."

"I didn't think you were doing a lot of this down here," Jim said, glancing at Ruth, "what with the relaunch event on Christmas Eve. Other folks on the town council have been talking about it. I figured you'd know if the bird has any chance at all."

"We went out to the back to have a look and saw he was kind of bloodied up," Ruth said.

Jim nodded. "We figured maybe he'd just fly away."

"Sometimes that's what happens," Parker said. "They fall for some reason, get a little stunned, and then recover and take off."

When they got to the building, Parker slid the box off the cart and dragged it through the door.

"Uh, I appreciate you doing this," Jim said. "You and I didn't get off on the right foot, if you know what I mean. I'm not exactly a popular guy around here anymore."

Parker chuckled. "At the moment, you're pretty popular with this crow."

Ruth let out a hoot and gave her husband a friendly rib jab.

"It's just that there's some history about this land."

"Not my business," Parker said, hoisting a kennel from the floor to the table. Then he put on his rawhide gloves and explained that he would lift the bird, blanket and all onto the table to better examine the wounds. He stuck out his arm. "Stand way back close to the door. For all we know, the bird could come to life and these wings could knock us over."

The bird's body was warm and not especially heavy. Or resistant. "He's not putting up a fight," he said, glancing back at Jim and Ruth.

He went through his routine, held his arm firmly around the bird and pulled the blanket back to get a view of the crow's head. "Looks like he could have been another animal's prey. Feral cats will sometimes attack a crow. That would explain why you found him in your yard, where cats probably roam. It's not likely he was hit by a car and moved himself that far."

"Crows come around and perch on the back fence almost every day," Ruth said. "Sometimes quite a few of them and they stay for an hour or two."

"My grandmother believed crows were the storyteller birds," Jim said. "Always talking, always telling the latest news."

"Easy to see why people believe that," Parker said. "For one thing they can make such a racket. Sometimes a crow will perch nearby and stay for hours, like you invited him over for a visit."

"That happened to us last summer," Ruth said. "A crow spent all afternoon on our fence. I began to think he had a message for me."

"Now I told her that was a bunch of foolishness," Jim said. "But what do I know?"

Parker couldn't help but wonder how many

conversations in the couple's house ended that way. He saw torn feathers, some broken skin underneath. "We can fix those scratches and cuts. But we'll see about this wing. It could be just the feathers that are messed up, but I'll check it out."

"But you can help?" Jim asked.

"If his wing isn't too mangled, he has a good chance to survive. But if his wing is broken, he might not be able to fly again. I'll be straight with you. I've seen crows die when they can't fly," Parker said, thinking it was best to prepare Jim and Ruth for that possibility. "We had a couple of crows who couldn't fly, but they became permanent residents of the center." Parker reassured the couple that if the bird survived, they'd keep him at the sanctuary.

Over the next several minutes, Parker cleaned the skin under the feathers. "These are surface wounds, more or less. I'm not set up with an X-ray machine, but so far, I see only minor damage."

When Parker looked back at Jim, he saw the fatigue in his face. He'd been red-faced mad when Parker had met him at the reception. He didn't look much better now.

Ruth was staring at the large pen on the floor with the cloth draped over it.

"A barred owl is living in there, Ruth. She got hurt during a storm earlier this fall. From what I could tell, she had a concussion, but she's on the mend now."

"So, will she stay here?" Jim asked.

"No, that one probably came right out of these woods and will likely stay close by."

As if reading Parker's mind, Ruth patted Jim's shoulder and suggested they be on their way. "Parker says this might take a while."

Jim nodded. "I run outta steam quicker than I used to. My health isn't what it once was."

"I'm sorry to hear that," Parker said. "Don't let me keep you. I've got my work cut out for me, but you've done your part. I'll offer our friend a snack." He looked at the couple. "He'll be easy to feed. Crows are omnivores, a fancy way to say they'll eat anything."

Jim pointed to his wife and smirked. "Just so you know, this one has been after me to finally change my thinking about a few things."

Ruth's immediate burst of laughter led Parker to think she laughed easily and often. Grumpy husband or not.

"Looks like I'm outnumbered," Jim said with a huff. "Seems people want Santa parties and singing carols at the bridge."

Ruth rolled her eyes. "And I'm not going to miss the caroling and seeing people I've known for years. Since I retired I'm not as connected as I like to be. I told Jim I'll go by myself if I have to." She looked at Parker. "Big surprise. We've been arguing about this for years."

"For what it's worth, my daughter and I think this is a beautiful place," Parker said. "I walked the boardwalk yesterday and the woods were quiet, but full of cardinals hunting up some seeds. We took a ride down to see the covered bridge and the park. I'm glad she's feeling at home here in Bluestone River."

Ruth and Jim stepped outside and Parker walked them to the lot. Jim pulled out a business card and gave it to Parker. "I'd appreciate it if you let us know how he's doing. I don't want to bother you. You've got a lot to do around here."

"No problem. Call anytime," Parker told them. "I'll expect to see you down here on Christmas Eve."

Parker waited to take out his phone until

Jim and Ruth drove away. Emma had been on his mind anyway, but even more so when his newest patient showed up. Maybe she'd come right over. She didn't pick up the call but an hour later the door opened.

Emma pointed to the covered kennel. "In there?"

He lifted the cover, but it didn't have much effect on the bird. "I knew you'd want to see him. He's a crow who was likely attacked by another animal. Chances are, it was a cat."

"Where did he come from?" Emma asked.

"That's the interesting part," Parker said. "I bet you'll never guess. Jim Kellerman and his wife found him in their yard."

Emma's mouth fell open. "You're not kidding, are you?"

He shook his head slowly.

"You're a Jim Kellerman whisperer." Emma looked gleeful over her clever characterization.

Feeling smug, he said, "Guess so." In a more serious tone, Parker explained that Jim didn't look well. He'd lost some of his fight. "But I also made it clear that the crow could die. You know, Emma, we really can't save them all."

"But I bet you want the chance to try."

He ran his hand through his hair. "You're right. I do."

She took off her jacket and set it aside. "So, how can I help?"

Her eagerness took him aback, even when he might have known that's exactly what she'd say. "We can start with getting a better look at his wing. I'll walk you through the steps. You can see for yourself."

Her face lit up in response.

EMMA STOOD TO the side while Parker loaded the new kennels in the back of the truck. They'd already bought screening and hardware and remnants of what Parker called plastic grass to use for perches in the cages he was building.

"We got our supplies. Where to next?" Parker asked.

"Let's go to the gallery. It's down the block. With any luck Guy Hammond has replenished his supply of walking sticks and canes. His corner of the store was depleted the last time Ruby and I took a trip over here."

"You're the only person I've ever known who makes fashion statements with her canes."

"Consider me a trendsetter. Besides, I'm

probably just the *youngest* person you know who uses a cane," she said dryly.

Parker tilted his head side to side. "Not really. One of the best volunteers we had at the North Carolina center was a young woman who used a cane. She'd been born with a spinal condition. She was like you. She didn't let it stop her."

Emma wanted to take back her words. "Ignore me when I say things like that. They make me seem self-pitying, and I'm not." Not usually.

"You're the least self-pitying person I know," Parker said. "It was meant to be a compliment. You have a way about you, Emma. You just do. It's your own style."

"Then, thanks. I do like my bright painted ones, too. Jason likes the one that's painted like a candy cane."

"I'll bet he does."

"While we're in the gallery, we can browse around and see the kinds of things the board might want in a future gift shop," Emma said. "We can sell a few items online, like from a catalog."

"Way off in the future, I suspect. The board will have to build a crew of regular volunteers first."

Emma pointed to the women's boutique, an upscale bistro, an ice cream shop and the cedar-shingled gallery building dominating one side of the street. "The gallery opened ten years ago and all the rest followed. That's happening with Bluestone River and our outdoor spots, too. You're doing your part."

"I like the idea of the sanctuary featuring gift items made by local people. We've got lots of artists who could produce note cards and bookmarks."

"Like you."

"Possibly. I have more confidence in my work these days. I sold a couple of my own posters on Thanksgiving."

"Is the gift shop something you're thinking of taking on?" Parker asked as they approached the front door of the gallery.

Emma shook her head, irrationally bothered by the question. "No." Her blunt answer left no room for doubt.

"I see." Parker turned away to look at some framed pen and ink drawings on display in the window.

"No, you don't," she said. "Your question surprised me. That's all."

Parker met her gaze, clearly puzzled, as he opened the gallery door and they went inside.

"I'm not looking for things to fill my time," Emma explained. Had she expected him to know that? Somehow, yes, she had.

Parker followed Emma as she took a few steps deeper into the shop. "I didn't think you'd be filling time. But you take on a lot of things."

"No, Parker, I actually don't *do* much for the projects." She heard the testy tone in her voice and probably should have stopped talking. But she forged on. "It looks like I'm busy, but what I really do is *support* a lot of things. Like the sanctuary. I donate the money."

Parker stopped. "Yeah. I get it. But you're also genuinely interested in the relaunch. And you have lots of ideas."

"Maybe so. But I'll leave the gift shop to other people." Emma forced a smile. "Aren't you glad you asked?" She pointed ahead. "I see Guy Hammond's work."

Guy had a collection of new walking sticks and more traditional canes and dozens of intricately carved wooden boxes and picture frames. He also had exquisite carved birds. The eagles and hawks had strength, even majesty around them, but small birds and the geese and ducks drew her eye, too. "See?

I'll bet all his boxes include birds or flowers or both."

Emma picked up one of the oak walking sticks, taller than her usual cane. Thin and sleek, it had a flat top, but then gracefully curved in for a handle. It invited her to try it out. The wood of the curve was smooth under her hand. A perfect fit. Best of all, all the carvings were of hummingbirds and flowers. Her mood instantly lifted. "I found it. My new fashion statement."

"Can I see that?" Parker asked.

"Sure." She handed it to him and watched as he studied the detail, top to bottom.

"Made by a person who has paid attention to hummingbirds. The details on the beaks and wings are perfect."

"You would know," she said softly. "You can see why I think these might be good gift shop items, or they could be used for raffles and door prizes at fund-raising events. Even membership drives." Her mind jumped to an image of a glossy gift catalog sent to members, but she pulled back from that. Good idea, but not the right time.

Parker grasped the cane and exclaimed over the handhold. "Wow, Emma, this is perfect for you. I bet it would be good on flat surfaces."

"Exactly. Like the boardwalk." She smiled. "I'm glad you like it."

Emma turned in place, drawn by the beauty around her. Glass art and jewelry made from crystals and amethyst sparkled in the light. But her eye caught a quilt hanging on a rack, light blue and white, with a blue heron in the center surrounded by marsh grasses. Making her way to it, she said, "This is incredible." She rested her old and new canes against a shelf nearby and unfolded the quilt to get a better look. "We used to see herons in the marshes at the end of the lake. They looked just like this."

Her fingers began to tingle when a thought struck her. She used both hands to tug the entire quilt off the rack. "Oh, Parker, I'd really like to get this quilt for Nicole. It matches her eyes." She could picture the quilt in the teenager's cabin.

"That's kind," he blurted, "but...uh...really not necessary."

"*Necessary?* That wasn't part of my equation," Emma teased. But then her good feeling faded, along with the tingling, when she saw the flicker of anger in Parker's eyes.

Parker grabbed his wallet out of his back pocket. "It's perfect for her. I agree, and I'll certainly pay for my daughter's bedding."

"What?" She suddenly found herself without words.

"I mean, Emma, you don't need to…"

"To what? Give a lovely teenager a gift?"

"It's just that you already…you know. You've done enough."

"Ah, I get it." Maybe it started over his question about the gift shop, but now she'd slid from annoyance into anger. If Parker was angry, too, then so be it. She clutched the quilt to her chest. "Just because I'm one of those dreaded donors doesn't mean I can't give Nicole a gift, friend to friend."

"Like I said, you already do enough."

She turned to look directly at him. "How does it feel?"

Parker frowned.

"That chip on your shoulder. Don't you ever get tired of carrying it around?"

She looked away, wincing against regret for that extra bit of sarcasm. She grabbed the two canes and headed to the checkout. Despite trying to confidently navigate around the displays, the walking stick she awkwardly held under her arm threatened to topple a rack of earrings and her handbag slipped off her shoulder. Parker's long arm circled from the side and lifted the quilt out of her arms. "I'll take it to the counter."

Parker deposited the quilt and stood back while she paid for the items. As the saleswoman wrapped the walking stick, she offered details about the quilter's latest award. Her work had been hung in folk art shows all over the country. And she lived in a town only fifty miles south of Clayton. With the quilt tucked into the shopping bag, Parker stepped closer and eased it out of her hand.

By the time they got to the truck, Emma was jumping out of her skin. Apologize for her remark or be quiet? Maybe she'd said enough. But what was she sorry for? Not for calling him out over a gift. It didn't matter now. She had to do something. They'd talked about getting some lunch. She groaned inside. They had a good thirty-minute drive home.

They stood on the street, not looking at each other. Neither moved. Emma had no inclination to get into the truck just yet. Apparently, neither did Parker. The seconds passed. *This is ridiculous.* She pivoted on her heel to face him. He did the same. She blurted "I'm sorry" and so did he.

They stared at each other. And then they laughed.

SOMEHOW, AFTER INSULTING a woman he liked more than he cared to admit, they ended up sharing takeout sandwiches at her house. He started a small fire in the fireplace and after lunch they sat on the stone hearth to talk.

"I'll keep the quilt here at my house and bring it over when I know Nicole's home," Emma said. "I don't want to make it a Christmas gift. That could be embarrassing. I'd rather it be a 'just because' gift."

Parker nodded, unsure what to say. "I don't want to brag or anything, but she's doing well at school. She's made some friends, and likes her job."

"So, can we agree that sometimes a gift is just a gift?" she asked. "No hidden agendas."

His turn now. It would be easy to agree and write the whole incident off. Or not.

Emma frowned in the silence and gave him a look that sent a clear "what's with you" message.

"It's not that simple," Parker said.

Emma groaned. "I might have known you'd say that."

"But it's true," he said softly. "It's a beautiful gift. I'm touched that you noticed the blue matched her eyes. Nic will love it. I know she will."

"I agree." Cocking her head, she asked, "So what is it?"

"I heard the saleswoman tell you about the quilter. It's a mighty big gift for a teenager you barely know."

Emma squirmed a little on the hearth. "I was being spontaneous for a change. I'm not exactly known for my spur-of-the-moment decisions. That's why it felt good. I didn't think about the cost of it, frankly. It's beautiful. And think of it as a housewarming gift."

Parker was used to counting every dollar and making some tough choices. He and Jackie, a teacher, hadn't chosen fields that commanded big salaries. The offer in Colorado had come with a salary larger than anything he'd ever heard of for naturalists working in not-for-profits. For all that was worth. "It's hard for me to think of it any other way but as extravagant," he said.

"It *is* extravagant. But that doesn't make it wrong. Besides, your reaction didn't fit."

"So, we get to the chip on my shoulder."

"Uh-huh. I sensed it when your guard was down when you first met me. You didn't expect me to be your age, for one thing." She tapped her chest. "You were imagining the donor as a much older person. And maybe not someone as down to earth. You more or less came right out and said you knew how to *handle* donors. They're annoyances you've had to put up with to do the work."

Exactly, Parker thought. That was too close to the truth. That tension between the professionals and the funders was something he picked up at the very first nature center he worked in and the attitude was reinforced by every boss he had. He'd absorbed that tension like nutrients in food. Once in a while a demanding donor came along and reinforced the belief. "Do you sense that attitude from a lot of people?"

She shook her head. "Not really. Or maybe it's not as poorly hidden as yours. You seem to wear resentment like a comfy sweater."

"I could justify by saying I've had a few bad experiences," he said, "but that's too easy. You surprised me, though. That's true. But it isn't fair to you." He wasn't really apologizing, was he? He stood and grabbed the poker and stirred the embers around to revive the fire.

"When you asked if I might be interested in running the gift shop," Emma said, "I'm sure you could sense me bristling."

Even knowing what was coming, he had no impulse to flee. Emma meant too much to him already to settle for a flimsy truce. "Oh, yeah," he said. "I thought maybe you were tired of always being asked to do more."

"Nothing like that. The gift store is a good idea. A means to an end, a way to support the sanctuary and local craft artists. But I visit the center because of the birds."

"Yes. I had a feeling you would take to this work." So why had he even suggested that she organize a shop? It's like she'd changed hats and he hadn't noticed.

"When Neil and I got married, I did all that *doing* kind of volunteering. I helped sort books for the library sale and organized charity auctions for the food bank in town. I served on more committees than I care to count. I became my mom."

She stopped talking and stood and shifted her weight from one foot to the other. She's loosening her muscles, Parker thought. He'd seen her do that before. This time, though, her expression was serious, thoughtful, as if she was choosing her words carefully.

"I never had a career, not like Ruby. She found her purpose—her passion—in dealing with the aftermath of trauma. But when I saw that owl and watched you tend to the gash above her eye, it was as if I found what I'd been looking for."

She glanced up with tears in her eyes. He stood and took a few steps toward her. He smoothed his hand across her cheek, then leaned in and pressed his lips to her forehead. "Oh, Emma."

Wiping her eyes with the back of her hand, she said, "This must seem so ridiculous. But ever since my fall, I've put most of my energy in trying to get my old self back. But that old self had a missing piece. It sounds so trite, but I've longed to do something that matters."

"That doesn't sound ridiculous at all. That's what we all want." He took a deep breath. "But don't discount what you make possible."

"I don't. I enjoy seeing my money used well." She leaned in closer. "Full disclosure. I added extra cash to the fund for the renovation. You should know that, but I wish you'd forget about it."

"C'mon, I can't unlearn it, but you don't want me thinking of you in that donor role. No need, Emma. I really don't think of you that way." She was standing so close and when he tentatively put his arms around her, she returned the hug.

"This is much better than sniping at each other in the gallery," she said.

Parker smiled and pulled her closer.

CHAPTER NINE

THE NEXT SATURDAY morning, Parker positioned the cage outside, while Emma tried to hide her mixed feelings about sending the owl on her way. But if she was serious about this work it was something she had to get used to. Like Parker had said, once a bird was gone, there was nothing to do but get kennels and pens ready for the next visitor, assuming one would come along.

Emma had fallen into a rhythm with Parker. She felt expansive around him, sometimes even girlish. At home in the sanctuary, she was taking pictures with a seriousness she hadn't allowed herself before.

"This is an exciting day," Emma said, standing back and studying the owl. "She'll always be the first bird I tended, other than filling the bird feeder in the backyard when I was a kid."

Parker chuckled. "Big day for the owl, that's for sure."

"Oh, don't be a spoilsport," Emma said, scrunching her face in a disapproving expression. "That's a given. But this is the owl who changed my life." She'd been over and over it in her mind, finally realizing that she'd found her something more in a place she'd never thought to look. "This bird taught me so much...well, I should say *you* taught me a lot."

She liked Parker even more for simply nodding to acknowledge what she'd said rather than try to deny it was true. His gaze took a detour and he raised his arm in a greeting. "Here come our friends now. Hmm...minus Peach."

"I'm kind of glad about that," Emma said, turning to watch Ruby and Mike walking toward them behind Jason, who'd broken into a trot. "As quiet as the dog is, she's been known to chase the random bird or squirrel."

"She is a dog, after all," Parker said dryly. "It's in her blood and bones."

"Wow. That cage is hu...*mon*...gous." Jason slowed down as he approached the cage, his mouth hanging open in surprise.

Emma grinned. "You're right...hu...mun...gous." Jason played with words like they were toys. The more syllables the better, so he could draw them out and exaggerate their sounds.

Mike pointed at him. "Your eyes look humongous, buddy."

"Nic and I set up the cage we found here when we had a feeling she'd survive her accident but was hurt badly enough to need some help." Parker gestured at the bird. "We had a feeling she'd be our visitor for a few weeks before we could let her go."

"So, today's the day," Emma added. "She's ready to fly off to her real home."

"That's why I invited you, Jason," Parker said. "I thought you might like to see her up close. I've let a lot of birds go and there's nothing quite like watching them soar high above you."

"What's her name?" Jason asked.

"Well, Jason, here's the thing. This owl doesn't have a name."

"You could give her one, couldn't you?" Jason asked, his young forehead wrinkled up in thought.

Parker put both hands on his hips and took a deep breath. Emma had seen that shift in posture before, usually when the topic had special meaning to him. "I could. But it wouldn't be a good idea."

"Why?" Jason turned his head to look up to his dad.

Mike rested his hands on Jason's shoulders. "I'm sure Parker will explain."

Parker smiled at Jason. "If you give an animal of any kind, like a fish or a dog or a bird, then it becomes a pet."

"Like Miss Peach." He smiled. "That's Peach's whole name."

"Exactly. Your dog doesn't just live with you, she's a member of your family. You make sure she gets the right food and enough water. If she's sick you take her to the doctor. But the owl is different. It's not in her nature to hang out with a family. The owl wouldn't like bunking up with you."

"Peach sleeps on my bed," Jason said. "She takes up the whole bottom half."

Parker snorted. "I've had a dog or two like that myself. You're lucky she gives you any space at all."

Jason nodded. "Yep. That's how it is."

"You can play with Peach," Parker said. "She brings you sticks when she wants you to throw them. She understands the game. Some dogs are supposed to bark at strangers. Some dogs herd sheep."

Emma linked her arm with Ruby's. Her

friend looked amused by the conversation. Peach had been her dog first, but after she came back to Bluestone River, Peach's family expanded, just like Ruby's.

"But the owl has a whole different kind of life. It's not in her nature to be around humans. We want to help the birds when they're hurt or sick, but wild birds live in woods and the fields and they hunt for their own food. If the owl hadn't been hit by a car and Nicole hadn't found her, we'd never know anything about her."

For reasons Emma couldn't explain, a hush fell over them as the adults watched Jason stare at the owl. The owl stared back. Without understanding it, Emma had felt the power of that gaze. What gears were shifting in Jason's quick brain?

Parker cut his gaze to Emma and she gave him a single nod, understanding his silent question.

Parker picked up his long leather glove. "Here's what's going to happen next, Jason. I'm putting on the glove to protect my arm from her talons and beak. Then I'll reach in and take her out of the cage on my arm. You'll stand back a little and we'll see what happens next."

Mike held on to Jason's shoulders and backed him up. Emma became conscious of the cold morning air. It was a clear, crisp morning, with the lake sparkling under the sun. Any part she had to play with this particular bird was over, and Emma went to stand beside Ruby.

Without hesitating, Parker opened the cage and reached in, taking firm hold of the bird's feet to keep her in one place. Using one arm he folded her gently against his body. Emma couldn't keep her eyes off Parker carrying out the maneuver not only with skill, but with steady confidence. His confidence calmed her, but she didn't have the first clue how the owl experienced any of it.

"Is this the part where she gets nervous?" Mike asked.

"Not so much nervous as hyperalert," Parker responded. "This kind of maneuver is stressful and triggers a bird's internal warning system. Probably more so now that she's well—at least as far as we can tell."

Parker put the owl on the ground and let her go, stepping out of the way fast. "It might take her a minute." The owl lifted her wings and in a whoosh took off, flying, but not very high. She went to the corner of the wooden joint of the boardwalk railing twenty or thirty feet away.

Bringing Jason back into the conversation, Parker said, "She's getting her bearings now. See how she's lifting her wings?"

"Does she know where she is?" Jason asked.

"Well, that's a hard question. She's on alert now, but she doesn't think the way we do—putting words together and communicating. But her brain sends her signals to guide what she'll do. Like now."

"Where will she go?" Ruby asked. "Or how far."

Parker shrugged. "Hard to say. She could have a mate in these woods, or she'll find one in the spring."

"Are you gonna miss her?" Jason asked, his voice a little said.

Parker didn't answer right away. Emma watched his face, sensing he'd be cautious about how to explain himself. She suspected he would miss seeing the owl every day, at the same time he had the satisfaction of knowing the bird was strong enough to go away.

"I'll miss her in a certain way, Jason. But

I'm proud that she can look after herself from now on."

"Wow. You won't get lonely?"

Parker grinned. "There's a crow here still, but it will seem kind of strange not to have the owl around."

"But you have other people," Jason said, "and the owl will have other birds."

"Exactly. Mostly, I'm glad Nicole found her and we could help her get well."

Jason nodded. "That's pretty cool."

"It sure is," Emma said. "You can picture the owl and all the other birds living in the woods right around your house."

"Look, Jason," Parker said, "there she goes."

Emma shielded her eyes to watch the owl flying directly into the woods. She perched on a high branch in an oak tree left bare except for clumps of brown, drying leaves hanging from some of its branches. It acted like her camouflage.

"We can see her, because we knew to look, but she blends into the forest now," Parker said.

"She seems so small when she's that far away." Emma allowed herself a small sigh. "Okay, I'll admit it. I'm going to miss coming to see her every couple of days." She looked down at Jason. "It can be hard for me to remember her job is to be an owl and not to entertain me."

Mike laughed. "Right, Em. If you want entertainment, you'll have to count on Peach."

"She might stay close by for a time," Parker said. "We never know."

"Okay, buddy. It's almost lunchtime," Mike said, steering Jason away. "You need to let Peach out into the yard."

"Why don't you come back to the house and have lunch with us?" Ruby asked.

"Sounds good." Parker looked at the cage behind him. "The cage can wait."

Emma nodded. She'd expected Parker to beg off with some excuse. But he hadn't and now their day would keep going.

She watched Jason run ahead with Mike, while Ruby stayed with her to wait for Parker to lock the building.

"Are you going to walk, Em?" Ruby glanced at Parker who was coming alongside them.

"I'm thinking," Emma said with a sigh. Another decision point. Should she get her car or walk down the pebbly beach with Ruby. Almost every day it seemed a chance came her way to test her limits—or not. The walk appealed much more than a car ride. "I'm not giving up a chance for a walk with you."

"Good," Parker said.

Emma felt great that day anyway. Or even better, *strong*. She glanced to the tree where the owl sat. *Like you*.

"IT'S NICE TO be needed," Georgia said, as she removed the cape and brushed hair off Parker's collar. "You let yourself get a little shaggy, but I fixed you up."

With his glasses back in place, Parker could see he was a much improved version of himself. "No kidding," Parker joked. "I might have let it grow even longer if I hadn't needed to see Mike next door and Maggie later about the center's website. It's my River Street errand day."

"You don't know how great it is to hear someone talk about River Street as the place to run errands and, you know, do business," Georgia said with a pleased sigh. "We're seeing a positive turnaround on the street. The Santa Party this year will help, too, and the bath and body shop opening in the spring. Can a women's boutique be far behind?"

A couple of months ago, he wouldn't have cared much one way or another about these developments. But now he understood what was at stake. And he was part of it.

"I hope you'll come to the center's official relaunch on Christmas Eve." Parker followed Georgia to the front counter and paid for his haircut. "White lights on the boardwalk, snow on the ground—we hope it stays."

"We'll be there." Georgia gave him a look, simultaneously serious and lighthearted. "Like I was telling Mike, I'm glad you're here. You add a lot to our little town."

"Thanks," he said, embarrassed. And surprised. In the mirror behind the counter he saw his cheeks were pinker than usual. Supporters made a big deal of the work, but Georgia's words were personal.

"Don't wait so long next time." She tugged at the ends of her hair and sounded disapproving, but her smile gave her away.

"I'll try, but I can't promise," he teased. It was only a few steps to Mike's office, and he was still feeling good when he opened the door and the bell jingled. Mike was sitting in one of his reception room chairs thumbing through a catalog.

"Christmas shopping?"

Mike flipped the cover face out, where a sleeping baby was shown snug in a car seat. "Baby shopping. We get these catalogs almost every day now." Mike snorted. "Ruby has left nothing to chance. This new baby will outgrow the clothes before she or he can wear them. Come on back. I've got the papers ready."

Parker sat in the client chair and gave the papers a brief once-over before signing them. He pushed them back across the desk. "One day, Nic will own the cottage with her three cousins. Ten acres, woods and a lake. Sound familiar?"

Mike nodded, but seemed preoccupied. "Do you have a minute? There's something I'd like to show you."

"Sure. What's up?"

Mike hit a few keys on his laptop and turned it so Parker could see the screen. "Ruby and I converted some of the old footage from video that my mom and dad took twenty or so years ago."

Parker laughed at the images of Mike and a bunch of kids on a raft in the middle of the lake. "A few familiar faces stand out. What were you, fourteen or fifteen?" Parker kept smiling at the images of Ruby and Emma posing like bathing suit models. "Emma has a photo on a shelf in her house of her and Ruby in Italy. They don't look all that different than they did as kids."

"Years ago, they did a fair amount of traveling." Mike grinned. "Here we are as teenagers working. We're all in our Hidden Lake Resort T-shirts."

Parker stared at the screen and immediately picked Emma out of the group photo. She was taller and her long brown hair hung over one shoulder. A big guy stood next to her holding a mop over his head and pumping it in the air like a trophy. Pointing to the screen, he asked, "Would that be Neil?"

"Oh, yeah, that's Neil. He was the clown of our group." Mike bobbed his head from side to side. "Well, Neil and Ruby competed for that title. You can see he was a big guy. Neil grew faster and filled out and played football like an older kid."

"Emma said his family was like yours. They had deep roots here."

Mike nodded to the screen at Emma and Neil diving off the pier. "They're racing to the raft. Emma challenged everyone to a race. She knew full well she could beat us all."

The girl jock, Parker thought, amused. It

was one of the first things she said to him. The video captured the moment Emma braced her palms on the raft and easily lifted herself up. "She really was an athlete."

"I suppose. Ruby was always trying to keep up with her. But I think of her as more of a dancer. See?"

Emma and Ruby and a bunch of other girls all danced together. They had moves, as Nic would say. Even if he hadn't known Emma, she'd have stood out from the others. He'd imagined her as a graceful dancer, and he'd been right.

But there was more. Even in the giggly crowd, she was deep in her own world, arms raised, her head thrown back. She looked ecstatic as she circled around the other girls and created her own path.

Mike's voice broke the spell. "I'm not sure why my mom thought filming us eating hot dogs at the pier was worth preserving, but there it is." He gestured at the changing image. "But she gets the credit or blame for this footage of Ruby and me rowing away from the shore—off to be alone."

When the image switched to a woman in a heavy sweater and jeans and long blond hair,

Mike sighed. "That's my mom shooing away the person with the camera."

"Were you the cameraman?" Parker asked.

"I think that was Emma. Hey, look," Mike said, "your cabin, and Nicole's next door."

"Looking a little fresher than they do today. But we'll fix that."

He and Mike said little as the last few minutes of film played out. Parker scanned every shot for Emma. When she appeared, she was usually in motion. "Will you look at that?" He blurted the words as images of Emma turning cartwheels across the grass came into view.

"My mom dubbed her the cartwheel queen," Mike said. "I imagine my mom shot that when we were juniors or seniors. Mom would have claimed she liked all the kids the same. Ha! Hands down, Rubes and Em were her favorites."

Parker liked the sound of Rubes and Em. He wasn't in the select group that used those nicknames. *Yet.*

The silence got uncomfortable. Something was left unsaid.

"I was with Emma the other day and she told me about her fall."

"Whew." Mike let out a loud sigh. "I'm glad she said something."

Why would it matter to Mike? He must have looked puzzled because Mike spoke up again. "Then you know this is as good as she's likely to get. It's been an ordeal. The surgery helped, but not completely."

Parker nodded. "Seeing her doing those amazing cartwheels gives me a sense of what she lost." He lowered his gaze and studied the floor. "She was quite a dancer."

"Too bad Neil and Emma were a bad match."

"But Emma and Neil kept trying." Parker heard his voice rise with each word. "I mean she took her commitment seriously. When it comes to the subject of fighting for a marriage, I'm a little touchy. My ex-wife was in the walking away camp."

Mike tipped his chair back and laced his hands behind his head. "Seems you've come to know our Emma pretty well."

Mike couldn't hide the smile behind his words any more than Parker could stop the self-conscious chuckle. "I like her. A lot." Parker nervously adjusted his glasses. "Pretty obvious, huh?"

Mike's snicker answered that question.

Parker got to his feet. "I better get over to Maggie's and see about the website." He waved the envelope with his copy of the papers. "Thanks for handling this. And for showing me the video."

WHEN EMMA KNOCKED on Nicole's door, she didn't expect to hear a loud, "Come in."

She opened the door but waited to step inside. "Hi, Nicole. It's Emma."

Suddenly, Nicole came to the door in sweats and a long, loose sweater that reached her knees. A towel was wrapped around her hair and she had her phone in her hand.

"I see I came at a bad time," Emma said, nodding at the phone. "I can come back."

"No. Come in. I'm getting ready for work." She said a quick, "Emma's here. I'll call you back," to whoever was on the other end of the conversation.

"I'm didn't mean to interrupt."

"No problem. That was my mom. I'll call her back." Her eyes were drawn to the giant-size shopping bag.

Flustered at the mention of Jackie, Emma's hands trembled a bit when she held out the bag. "It's for you. Something I saw in a crafts gallery in Clayton. The same place I get my carved canes. When I saw it, I thought of you."

Nicole's eyes widened when she set the bag down on a kitchen chair and pulled out the quilt. "Wow, look at the color."

Emma caught the bottom corner and helped Nicole hold it up and see the heron in the center. "The color is why I thought of you. Like your prom dress and your nail polish, the quilt matches your eyes."

"I...I don't even know what to say," she stammered. "Except...except thank you. It's so much."

"Consider it a housewarming gift. My way of saying welcome to town."

"Can I give you a hug?" Nicole asked.

Emma pretended to frown and stared into the room. "Hmm. Let me think..." She held out her arms. "Sure you can give me a hug."

Nicole's shoulders felt light, but strong in her arms. "I smell cinnamon. Your shampoo?"

"A cinnamon candle. It's almost Christmas, ya know."

"I seem to remember that."

"This is going to look so good on my bed. Will you help me?"

"Sure. I'm glad you want to use it right away."

Emma held the quilt while Nic moved the screen that hid the bed, and the two of them arranged the quilt across the bed.

"See? Perfect. *Perfect*." Nicole smoothed her hand over the center where the heron stood in marsh grasses. "So real."

"So is the tiara sitting on that stuffed dog." Emma laughed. "Cute." She glanced at photos tacked on the wall. Some framed prints of flowers hung over the bed. "You've done a great job here."

"Thanks. Dad likes how I found the screen to turn this area into a little alcove bedroom."

Emma smiled. "Very homey. Well, I should go and let you get ready."

Nicole walked her to the door for a quick goodbye. She didn't see Parker's truck in the lot, so headed home, filled with a jumble of emotion. She was beginning to feel close to Nicole. Her moods could be like hills and valleys, but she knew how to have fun with life. At least it looked that way.

CHAPTER TEN

CHATTERING SPARROWS BROKE the stillness of the morning, with a little help from their neighbors, juncos and cardinals. These few minutes alone on the pier were all that stood between him and the day ahead and the people who came along with his job. It had been easier to hide out in the woods in North Carolina than here in Bluestone River.

He had to laugh at himself. It wasn't easy to say no to Mike, and then the neighborhood seven-year-old got into the act. When Nicole rearranged her Saturday so she'd be available for Santa Day, what could Parker do but agree to help wherever the organizers needed him? Besides, it was a good excuse to see Emma. His chiming phone startled him and when he looked at the screen, he smiled. Speaking of Emma...

Odd, only Emma hadn't tried to coax him to be part of this event. Parker knew himself pretty well, and if no one had roped him in to be there, he'd have skipped it and worked on displays for the nature center. But did he mind? Not really. It would give him another excuse to spend time with Emma.

Snowflakes the size of pennies and dimes swirled over the water, but sunbeams broke through the cloud cover and hinted at the promise of a bright day. This small lake, only forty-five acres, seemed to invite him into its orbit every day, and he was conscious of its quiet presence all the time.

The phone in his pocket buzzed. He checked the screen. It was Emma calling.

"Hey, you're up early," he said into the phone. Why was he grinning so?

"Want to meet me for breakfast at Sweet Comforts and head down to the Santa Claus Festival from there?" Emma asked in a cheerful voice.

Yes, yes, he wanted to say yes.

"I sure wish I could do that, but Nic sent me a text late last night. She's making her world-famous blueberry pancakes this morning. I'm expected to show up in about half an hour."

"Well, you can't disappoint your daughter. Especially when she makes you that kind of offer. I'm glad Nic likes her job and still has time for Santa on River Street."

"She sure likes you—and Star and Ruby. Sometimes I feel like I'm in over my head with Nic, though. She's a puzzle."

"Don't sell yourself short. You've got good instincts when it comes to Nic."

"Apparently, so do you. The quilt you gave her is one of the best gifts she ever got. Her words."

"I thought she would take to it." All business again, she said, "I'll see you on River Street. What job have you got?"

"That's TBA. Might man the donation table, could be handing out cookies or herding the kids. Whatever's needed."

"Like me. I'm just along for the ride. Well, see you then."

"Emma, wait. One more thing."

"Okay."

"Can I have a rain check on breakfast?"

"Of course. Whenever you're free."

"Good."

Parker showed up at Nic's cabin shortly after the phone call from Emma. If he'd been blindfolded, the aroma of bacon would have led him to the right door. He knocked and waited for her to tell him to come in before he opened the door.

"Smells like a café in here—in a really good way," he said.

"I hope you're hungry. I'm making a ton of pancakes."

"I know you'll stash the leftovers in the fridge to snack on." The idea of cold pancakes never appealed to him, but Nic and Jackie slathered them with butter and feasted on them.

He glanced around at the table with what looked like an old-fashioned tablecloth. It was blue with swirls of red and white flowers. It could have come from his grandmother's house. Each of their cabins had two folding bookshelves. Nic had one jammed with books and binders and odds and ends. Framed prints she'd hung over the table looked like illustrations of castles and towers and princesses from fairy tales.

"Looks nice in here, Nic. You've added some things, too."

Nic's face lit up. "I've been thrifting again with Cam, the girl from school. The tablecloth is from way back, you know, like the 1950s."

"A real antique," he agreed. "I like your art, too."

"Same store—I like the ones of Thumbelina and Rapunzel. I remember being really little and telling Mom I had hair just like Rapunzel." She didn't look at him, but kept her gaze on the prints. "When I was little you read fairy tales to me all the time. I remember."

Without warning his chest started to ache. Nic turned into a three-year-old sitting in his lap, her tiny fingers turning pages of the picture book. His voice caught in his throat when he said, "I remember, too." *We were happy then, Nic...you, your mom and me.*

Nic filled his plate with a stack of hot pancakes and crisp bacon and put it on the table. "And now I have the gorgeous quilt. Emma told me she thought of me when she saw it because of the birds."

"You saved the famous owl, honey, so you'll always be Emma's hero."

"She's really something, Dad. I suppose she'll be at the Santa party today."

"Yep, she'll be there. I just talked to her. She'll be a floater, like me. We'll go where we're needed."

"You already talked to her this morning?"

"I was down at the pier when she called. She wanted to know if I could meet her for breakfast at the café before the Santa thing."

Nicole pulled her head back, her eyes widening in disbelief. "And you said *no*?"

"Of course I said no. I'm having breakfast with you."

She looked at the ceiling and groaned. "I can't believe you did that, Dad. I could have made these pancakes tomorrow—or some other day."

"I took a rain check. I had plans with you."

"Fair enough. But I hope you realize how much Emma likes you."

"I like her, too," he said, aware he sounded stupid, like he didn't catch what Nic really meant.

"Good start," Nic said. "But do you like her like her?"

More every time I see her. "Where is this coming from, Nic?"

Nicole pointed to the chair. "Let's eat."

Grateful for the diversion, Parker sat down and avoided looking at Nic while he slathered on the butter and poured way too much syrup on the pancakes and took the first delicious bite. "Thanks for doing this. The pancakes are great, as usual."

"You know, Dad, I'm beginning to accept that Mom isn't going to change her mind—"

"Nic, stop." His voice was razor-sharp. He didn't care one way or the other if Jackie was having second thoughts. "We're divorced. Look, I realize I haven't talked much about what really happened, but—"

"Nope, *you* sure haven't. One day you two were like...you know...normal boring parents. You didn't even fight."

"We probably should have," Parker said, with a heavy sigh. "If you learn anything from what happened to your mom and me, maybe that's it. Don't go silent. Fight it out."

Resting her chin in her palm, Nicole stared off into the room, pensive and silent.

"But just because you didn't hear us fight, that doesn't mean I wasn't trying to work things out between us."

"Could have fooled me."

"Maybe, but none of it was ever about you. Parents are supposed to worry about their teenagers, like every minute. But kids aren't supposed to worry about Mom and Dad."

"I suppose. But maybe that's why I was so upset—well, shocked out of my mind is more like it—when she said she was leaving."

"I didn't know about Ben until around that

time. Time had run out on recapturing something we'd lost."

Nicole bit off the end of a piece of bacon. "You hover around me wondering if I'm okay, but what about you? I'm worried about you, Dad. I want *you* to be happy." She waved the piece of bacon in the direction of the window. "It's nice here. I like it. But it's no rescue center. You aren't spending all your time splinting broken legs or taking X-rays of wings. Is it enough for you?"

True enough. Her expression, the worry in her eyes, sent a message he didn't welcome. "You don't need to be concerned about me."

Nic swallowed hard. "You seem happy around Emma. I don't see any sign you're dating anyone else." She shrugged. "So that's why I asked if you like her."

Parker nodded. "You're the most observant person I know. You get that from your mom." He said the words to fill in some empty space, but in his mind he was fixated on Emma and his heart thumping in his chest.

"So, what about you, Nic," he said, steering the conversation in another direction. "Really."

"Hey, school and my job are good. This is a pretty friendly place. What's not to like?"

He'd have put more stock in her answers if she hadn't been pushing a piece of a pancake around the plate with her fork. She was holding something back. Maybe Nic herself didn't even know what it was.

BRIGHT SUN REFLECTED off plowed snow, forming borders on the sectioned-off end of River Street. Emma shaded her eyes to look down the street at the wreaths and banners mounted on the streetlights. The storefronts were decorated with multicolored lights.

Emma waved to Sam Wilson, aka Santa Claus. The padding and white beard couldn't fool her. He was another graduate of Bluestone River High School who'd not come back after college, at least until a year ago. Sam's wife, Lynn, was dressed in an ankle-length red dress with a white faux fur hood, a perfect Mrs. Claus. With kids and parents lining up, Sam looked about ready to begin.

Emma had to laugh out loud at Sam sitting on a gilded throne, probably borrowed from the prop room at the high school. The maintenance crew had built a plywood backdrop, and teenagers from the high school painted a sled being pulled across the sky by reindeer. Rudolph's red nose stood out against the dark blue paint.

She spotted Mike in his red down jacket and jeans meandering through the crowd with Jason at his side. He stopped to shake hands and chat with people who'd braved the bitter cold day to come out. Giving his considerable political skills a workout, Emma mused. Today mayor, tomorrow what? State senator, maybe? It could happen.

Still trying to find Ruby, Emma headed toward the event tent set up to hand out brochures and regional tourist guides and serve hot chocolate and cookies. With a heater near the tables, it was probably the warmest place on River Street.

"There she is." The familiar voice came from behind. When she turned around Nicole was hurrying toward her with Parker following. The three of them ducked inside the tent and out of the cold wind.

"I wonder where the organizers want us." Nicole bounced on the balls of her feet and rubbed the palms of her mittens together. "Looks like the goody table is covered. Lots of kids to pour the hot chocolate."

Emma added, "Our string of Christmas

festivals is providing the high school kids a chance to earn a slew of community service credits, I hear."

Parker scoffed. "More people already showed up here than we managed to lure to the sanctuary over a three-day weekend."

Nicole waved him off. "Don't be jealous. Dad. You were right in the first place. The open house was a dumb idea with no hope of working."

Emma let a hearty laugh escape. "Don't sugarcoat it, Nicole." She glanced at Parker. "Wouldn't the board love to hear that assessment?"

"They did," Parker said. "I was just a little more diplomatic."

"Let's not be Scrooges about it," Emma said dryly. She pointed around her. "For a Bluestone River native, it warms my heart to see a crowd like this on River Street."

"Will Rivera was telling me this is a big deal," Parker said. "His family used to take him to the mall in Clayton to do the Santa thing."

"Will, huh?" Emma said, giving Parker a quick glance.

Nicole tilted her head. "He's cute, but he has a girlfriend. He's off the market."

Emma groaned. "Off the market? I thought that expression died ages ago. Deep-sixed in the past."

"Seems it's made a comeback." Nicole lifted her hands. "Like Bluestone River."

Parker caught Emma's eye and they both laughed.

"It wasn't that funny," Nicole said, turning to look in all directions. "I'll go see what they want us to do."

"Mike said something about keeping an eye on the donation jar," Parker said.

"No fair," Emma shot back. "Ruby offered me that job."

Nicole rolled her eyes. "Are you two really going to fight over it? Let me go find someone in charge, so we can settle this." She pretended to go off in a huff.

Emma shook her head. "Your daughter is such a funny girl." When she looked into Parker's face, she saw pride, but something else, too. Nostalgia, maybe?

"I know. She throws me sometimes. She joked about us fighting over the donation jar. An hour ago she was pointing out that her mom and I never had loud arguments. That's why telling her we were splitting up came as such a shock."

"As shocking as her mother's affair?" Emma immediately grabbed Parker's arm. "I'm so sorry. Forget I said that."

Parker gave her a pointed look, but then his expression softened. "I guess you don't sugarcoat anything, either."

"Really, Parker. I apologize."

All she got was a quick nod before he used his height to advantage to get a good look around. "I see Nic found Mike. She'll come back with news."

"I'm surprised I haven't seen Ruby," Emma said, puzzled. "She was supposed to be here and we always find each other at things like this."

"Mike showed me some old video of all of you at the resort and the covered bridge. You two almost always turned up together."

Emma wasn't sure she liked Parker seeing her that young and fit.

As if they were standing alone rather than in the midst of a crowd, he leaned in and whispered, "You're a really good dancer."

Her cheeks suddenly caught fire. She patted them with her gloved hands as if she could hide them. "I wasn't expecting that. You and your daughter are experts at taking me by surprise."

"But it's true. You were in your own world in those videos." Parker smiled, as if remembering something. "One was down by the bridge. The other was on the grass at the resort." He paused. "And here I didn't know you not only were the best dancer, but the cartwheel queen, too. You really were a jock girl."

"No, no, I'm not going there." Oh, but doing those cartwheels was so much fun. She could almost feel the strength in her back and legs turning end over end. "So what about you? How are you on the dance floor?"

He pulled his mouth down in a silly expression. "I can find my way around."

"Aren't you smug?"

"You asked."

"I did." Her inner imp wanted to grab the flirtatious moment and make it last, but out of the corner of her eye, she saw Jason hurrying toward them with Nicole in tow. "Look who's here," Emma said. "Did you see Santa yet?"

Jason shook his head. "My mom has a stomachache."

"But his dad said it wasn't serious." Nicole stood behind Jason with her hands resting lightly on his shoulders. "Uh, I'm going to take Jason to Santa right now and look after him today. Mike is driving Ruby to Clayton to have her stomachache checked out. He wanted me to ask if it's okay if I watch him at your house."

Emma kept her voice casual. "It's fine. I'm always happy to have Jason around," Emma said, forcing a smile at the boy, whose attention was fixed on Rudolph's blinking nose. "I'll wait for you."

"Wait, Nic. Did Mike say who's in charge here at the festival?" Parker asked.

"A couple of town council people are taking over, so it's covered." Nicole looked down at Jason. "What do you say we see Santa?"

Jason ran ahead toward the line. Nicole took off after him.

"Could the baby be in trouble?" Parker whispered.

"I'm trying not to jump to that conclusion, but there's always that chance," Emma said, nervously rubbing her hand across her mouth. "But I'm a little concerned Jason might get scared if Ruby's gone for very long. I don't think Ruby's had so much as a cold since she first met Jason over a year ago. She's like a rock, you know, always there for him."

Parker's tone was thoughtful when he said,

"You wouldn't ever think she was his step-mom, and for only a year."

Emma had told Parker about Jason not speaking for months after his mother died in a fire. Peach and Ruby helped Mike and a therapist get Jason over the hump of trauma and grief. "He only started calling her Mom this summer. She'd assured him he could call her Mommy when he was ready, but he told her that's what he'd called his first Mommy, so she was Mom. That was that." She remembered Ruby's eyes going soft when she talked about it.

Parker's mouth dropped open. "Yikes. Such a grown-up way to think about it."

"Jason loves to play around with words, so it made sense to me." Her phone buzzed in her jacket pocket. Emma pulled it out and glanced at the screen. "Ruby...oh...they're leaving for the emergency room in Clayton." She looked at the screen and read, "Just in case." With the next line her shoulders slumped. "Oh, no..."

"What?" Parker asked.

"She wrote 'I am so scared.' Knowing Ruby, she's probably trying to put on a brave front. But we don't do that with each other." Emma sighed, remembering that she confided her fears to Ruby when she faced her surgery.

Parker put his arm around her shoulders and pulled her close. "You two are so lucky to have each other."

"We are."

"Okay, time to go." Nicole's voice surprised them and they quickly moved apart.

Jason hopped up and down. "Emma, Emma, guess what?"

"What, sweetie?" Emma said, avoiding Nicole's amused expression.

"Santa said maybe we could get a friend for Peach."

Now, that was pretty hard to believe. "Is that so?"

"A puppy?" Parker asked, incredulous.

Jason shook his head. "Dad said babies and puppies are a lot of work, especially if you get new ones at the same time. Santa said that maybe I could get goldfish for Peach. She could watch them swim."

Parker clapped a hand over his mouth to stifle his laugh.

"Now there's an idea for you. Very special." Emma couldn't resist adding, "Just think, Jason, you could have fish the same color as your dog."

Jason's eyes grew big in surprise, and so did Nic's. "I never thought of that," she said with a giggle.

"Speaking of Peach…" Parker cleared his throat. "Why don't I swing by their house and get her? I could bring her to your place to be with Jason."

"Good idea." And maybe he'd want to stay a while.

JASON LINED UP cars and trucks in neat rows in front of the TV in the office. That kept him occupied until lunchtime when they polished off a large pizza. Now Nic and Jason were making three miniature snow people in the back with Peach having fun getting in the way.

"The mama, papa and baby bear." Parker stood by the patio doors watching Nic help Jason create his snow family. Emma was at the table checking her phone again. Two texts so far, but nothing for an hour or so.

"No news?" Parker asked.

"Not since I checked ten minutes ago." She got up and joined him. "This is silly. I've got to stop staring at the screen. The doctor is just being careful. Mike said so himself."

Parker was aware that Mike and Ruby had

plenty of help. His presence wasn't essential, but he wanted to be there for Emma, Nic and Jason. He'd made himself useful picking up the dog and gathering a few toys in the kitchen. And he could take charge of bringing food in.

He was at home in Emma's house. They moved easily around each other at the sanctuary and here, too. Like a dance. It amused him to know Nic had been keeping an eye on him with Emma. Trying to not be obvious about it. Ha! He knew that maneuver from trying to study Emma without getting caught at it. He failed every time.

"They're almost done out there," he said. "The second head is in place. One more to go."

"Nicole is so patient. It must be getting cold," Emma said. "I'm going to start making soup for Mike to take home. And we'll need dinner, too."

"I'll go on home," he offered just to be polite. With any luck she'd squash that plan. "You don't need to feed me."

Emma rolled her eyes. "I meant dinner for all of us." Then she frowned, "But don't feel like you have to stay if you don't want to. I'm sure Mike will run Nicole home later."

Parker rolled his eyes and smiled. "I was offering to leave so you wouldn't think I was inviting myself."

"All right, let's get this straight. I want you to stay," Emma said. "Take it or leave it."

"I'm taking it."

"And anything you can do to keep my worrying mind off Ruby is appreciated. If I don't stay busy I'll stand here wringing my hands."

He squeezed her shoulders. "I know this is hard."

Parker found a quiet corner while Emma lined up sauté pans and mixing bowls, but then joined her at the counter to chop vegetables for soup. They could watch the antics going on outside. With the snow family complete, Nic and Jason were doing jumping jacks. Peach's paws were in constant motion, jumping and prancing in the space between them.

Parker chuckled. "She's showing Jason what I taught her about staying warm on the few icy cold days we had in North Carolina." Parker scraped the pile of celery into the pot Emma put between them. "Seems so long ago now, but we used to do jumping jacks in the yard and count out loud. Fifty was the goal."

Emma perched her hip on her stool. "They look so carefree. But I know that's not true for Nic. She has challenges. She's good with Jason."

"Jason's quite the little character, isn't he?"

Emma grinned. "Pretty clever of Santa to talk about a goldfish."

"Cute. Seemed to satisfy Jason, too. As for Nic, I think she's done letting her mother pull her one way or another. Maybe Jackie's less confused or something. I'm not sure."

Emma looked like she was about to say something, but the door opened and Jason came in still jumping and excited.

"Wow, that's quite a snow family you made." Parker's words were lost in the flurry of getting Jason out of his coat and boots before he paraded through the kitchen, dropping clumps of snow. Nic corralled Peach and rubbed her down with the towel Emma tossed to her. She passed a smaller one to Parker to use on Jason's hair.

"You got wet out there," Emma said, gathering up the dripping things. "It's taking three adults to dry off one child and a dog."

Emma went off to get some dry socks for Jason and Nic.

When Emma came back, Jason sat on the

kitchen floor to put on his dry socks and kicked his feet in the air and made the fabric flop around. "Too big," he said, laughing.

"They'll do," Nic said. "Uh-oh, here comes Peach."

The dog sniffed around Jason before flopping down next to him.

"You're a pushover for that dog." Nic playfully shook her head.

"Peach snores," Jason warned, but he got a big kick out of announcing it as he jumped up and pulled a chair closer to the counter. "Sometimes I wish I was a dog."

"Oh, yeah?" Parker said, getting back to work on Emma's soup. "Sometimes I wish I could be a bird."

"You could be like the owl and fly away into the woods and hide." Jason looked to the window.

"I could. Or I could be one of the little birds that flit around through the trees," Parker said, using his hand to do a pretty fair imitation of flitting about. "What about you? If you were a dog, would you swim in the lake? Chase sticks?"

Jason shook his head. "I'd let everybody pet me and in between I'd take naps."

"You'd get tired of that in a hurry," Nic said.

"No, I wouldn't."

With the same singsong lilt, Nic said, "Oh, yes you would."

It was like listening to music, Parker thought, almost embarrassed by the bittersweet emotions taking over. He stole a glance at Emma, who was looking down at her cutting board, but an amused smile had taken over her face. Her pretty face, with all her features set off by her big brown eyes.

"I know where the movies are," Jason said. "Wanna see?"

Nic squinted and pursed her lips in teasing disapproval. "I don't know. Did you ask Emma?"

"Can we watch movies, Emma?"

Emma grinned at Jason. "Of course."

The next couple of hours passed quickly. Emma made a triple batch of vegetable soup and the house was filled with the scents of garlic and oregano and the yeasty aroma of the rolls Emma heated. Parker was lifting the second of two pans of baked chicken out of the oven when Emma's phone rang.

She grabbed her phone. As Parker listened to her side of the conversation, her face got brighter and she glanced his way and gave him a quick thumbs-up.

Relief shot through Parker, the power of it surprising him.

"Nic and Jason are in the office watching movies," Emma said. "Shall I bring him to the phone. Oops, too late. Here he comes."

"Is that my mom?" Jason asked. He slid across the floor in his stocking feet.

"It's your dad." Emma handed him the phone. "Here you go."

"Is Mom coming home?" Jason frowned as a couple of seconds passed. "When are you coming to get me?" A couple more seconds went by. "Why?" His voice got smaller with the question. Jason looked at Emma. Then he said, "Okay." Silence. "I will. Can Peach stay, too?" A little smile appeared. "She'll behave. She always does, Dad."

Parker stifled a laugh and shook his head. Three pairs of eyes, four if he counted the dog's, were fixed on Jason and hanging on his every word.

Jason handed the phone to Nic. "He wants to talk to you, Nicole."

Her conversation was a series of one-word responses, but ending with, "Don't worry. It's all good." Then she handed the phone to Emma, who said goodbye and ended the call.

"So, Jason, I get to have you as my houseguest tonight. You can sleep in the big bed in one of my guest rooms or on the couch where you watch movies. Then your dad will pick you up in the morning. The best news is your mom is just fine."

"Sounds like fun," Parker said. "It's very grown up to be a houseguest."

"I want to sleep on the couch." He didn't look happy about it. "If my mom is okay, then why can't my dad bring her home?"

"Doctors like to keep an eye on things," Nic said, raising her hands in a helpless gesture. "Go figure. When I was about your age, I had a bad sore throat, so bad the doctor made me stay in the hospital overnight."

"I remember. We were scared at first, but Nic spent most of her time sleeping."

"I'm not tired," Jason said.

"Well, then, you can stay awake and play."

"I suppose we can go, Dad," Nic said.

"Don't be ridiculous." Emma crossed her arms over her chest. "No one gets out the front door before we have dinner." She glanced at the clock. "Like in the next fifteen minutes. Parker and I have been cooking all afternoon. I've got plenty for us and to send leftovers home with Mike."

"O…kay. Looks like I don't dare argue.

Not that I want to." Nic steered Jason out of the kitchen and down the hall.

"So, Ruby's okay?" Parker asked.

She nodded. "Seems so, but they're being extra-cautious. Mike wanted to stay with her. Jason will be fine here with me."

"Seems you're all set up for him. You can pull cars and books out of a hat. And his choice of movies and games."

"Ruby sometimes brings him and Peach along when we work on grants and things. I like to keep plenty of activities around to entertain Jason so he's happy while Ruby and I visit. When she has the baby, we'll figure out a new routine to do grants and spend time together. I'll want to help out."

"I'm sure you will."

As he got plates and bowls off the shelves in her cabinets, Parker felt oddly like he and Emma were hosting a party. Together.

"JASON'S DOWN FOR the count," Parker said, arranging a pile of pillows and blankets on the floor in front of the couch. "I know that at his age he's not likely to roll off, but if he does, it won't be a hard fall."

Emma closed the blinds and followed Parker and Peach out of the room.

"He fought so hard to stay awake," Emma said, going into the kitchen. "Can you stay a while? Maybe have a glass of wine."

"Sure. I'm in no hurry to leave. I'm sure Nic is having a good time with her friends."

Good answer.

While she opened a bottle of cabernet he took glasses out of the cabinet.

"I like how you move around in my house like you've spent a lot of time here," Emma said. She was conscious of the dimmed lights above the dining room table.

"You make it easy." Parker smiled. "Your home is like a person with long open arms."

Her heart beat harder in her chest. It took effort to steady her hand when she handed him the full glass. "That's sweet of you to say."

"The house matches—literally. Think about it, Emma. It has this large open space in the center, and then two long wings, like open arms."

"When you put it that way, no wonder I like it so much."

"And then there's the view. Come look outside." Parker pointed to the December half-moon casting its light on the snow.

"A perfect end to a day that had a few

scary moments." She sipped her wine and nodded to the outside. "My winter postcard. It can seem like the land really is asleep under that blanket of snow, just as sure as Jason is dreaming adventures on my couch."

She turned a chair to face the door that led to the backyard. "Let's sit here. I need to get off my leg, but I don't want to stop watching what's going on right outside my door. I'll douse the light so it's even clearer."

Parker pulled both chairs closer to the doors.

"It's been a remarkable day in many ways," Parker said. "I'll make that the last couple of weeks."

"Oh? Tell me more." Here in the dark with the moon lighting up the snow, everything was remarkable. They were dancing around something real, something good.

"Working with you, sharing Thanksgiving with new friends, releasing the owl, my mom's visit coming up. And then there was Jim bringing me the crow. Everything good going on comes back to you." Parker took her hand. "Even hanging pictures was a good time."

She could make a joke, tease a little, but she didn't want to. Instead, she said, "Yes, every moment is a good time."

Parker put his glass down and stood. He held out his other hand and Emma took it and rose to her feet. They wrapped their arms around each other as if their hearts were leading them to this next step. They held each other in the dark, quiet space. The kiss she knew was coming was everything she wanted, expected and so much more. She clung to him, bunching the fabric of his sweater in her fingers. They deepened the kiss and when they finally broke it, they both sighed happily together.

"So much is happening between us," Parker said.

"Kind of hard to describe." She looked into his eyes. "I can barely talk right now."

"Then we won't," he said, leaving a trail of soft kisses down her cheek to her neck before finding her lips.

Emma's heart was filled with new and wonderful feelings. She couldn't talk, and yet she felt she had so much to share.

CHAPTER ELEVEN

EMMA SCRUBBED THE plastic grass, as Parker called it, and spread it out to dry on the counter next to the sink. Then she filled the bucket with soapy water to make sure it was clean. "When you said I'd spend more than half my bird time cleaning up after them you were right." They both wore aprons and gloves. Emma had tucked her hair under a baseball cap.

"It never ends, especially now that I'm certain we won't be able to let the crow go free. But one bird or fifty, it seems the amount of work is always the same."

Parker's phone buzzed. "There she is. Mom will be here in a few minutes."

"Good. She'll get here before the snow starts," Emma said. "And I'm ready for her." Parker had finally stopped worrying about imposing on Emma. Instead, he'd taken a page from Nicole's book and asked her to send pictures of Emma's log house to

Grandma Sharon and text about the luxury suite. She'd even sent a photo of the butterfly garden on Emma's land.

"You're up for anything these days."

Her cheeks warmed from his intimate tone. "I suppose I am." Between the birds, the perceptible shift in the town's energy and Parker himself, Emma was content in a way she'd almost forgotten was possible.

"Nic can hardly wait for her to get here." Parker lined the pen with new paper and transferred the crow from the cage to the larger space. "Nic and my mom have had some unforgettable moments. Nic loved it when they put star stickers all over their faces and then went shopping like there was nothing different about them. Nic couldn't stop laughing for days."

"People who were close to really fun grandparents seem to have an extra something in their childhood," Emma said. "Mine lived nearby but were kind of formal and distant. They died fairly young, too."

Parker started to respond, but stopped abruptly and cocked his head toward the door. "I think I hear voices."

The door flew open. "She's here," Nicole

announced with enthusiasm. "Emma, this is my Grandma Sharon...uh, Sharon Davis."

Chuckling, Emma held up her gloved hands. "I'd shake your hand, but I've been handling the bird."

"No surprise to me." Sharon sniffed the air and wrinkled her nose. "I recognized the smell of a bird clinic from outside the building."

Parker grabbed a towel and wiped his hands, but Sharon shook her head. "I'm not waiting for my hug." She threw her arms around him.

"Oh, Mom," Parker said, as he returned the hug.

Emma stood back and watched the scene unfolding, including a three-way hug with Nicole.

"I haven't seen this guy for over a year," Sharon explained, turning to Emma. "I couldn't pass up a chance, especially when I was so close."

"Do you want to settle in your room at Emma's," Parker asked, "before we do anything else?"

Nic waved away that idea. "No, no, no. I want to show Grandma my studio first."

A couple of minutes of conversation settled

it. Parker stayed back to finish the cleanup and Nic played tour guide. Sharon flashed a bright smile at Parker and told Nicole to lead the way.

When they'd gone, Parker was all business, making notes on his tablet, documenting the crow's injuries, even noting the cleanup routine. "Our crow guest doesn't seem to be in pain, but since I have no hope he'll fly again, we might as well give him a name."

"I bet Jason would have some ideas," Emma said.

"Or maybe the perfect name will come to one of us."

"Ask your mom," Emma said, adding, "She seems excited to be here."

Parker nodded. "I'm glad I'll have a chance to talk to her. I didn't confide much about my divorce. I sort of shocked her when I called to tell her I was interviewing divorce lawyers. But Nic went up to see her last spring and filled her in."

Emma's questions came up as why, why, and why. But she sensed Parker was sharing more than he thought he should.

He frowned. "I don't know what it could be, but my gut tells me there's something else going on with my mom."

"Like what? I mean, could it be something serious?" So much for not prying.

"I don't know. She could retire anytime she wants to," Parker said, putting his tablet aside, "but she went to a conference for school counselors way out here. In Moline, on the Mississippi River."

"I see your considerable wheels turning," Emma said. "What are you thinking? I'm not good at mind reading."

"If you were, you'd see confusion. Let's just say she's been a little coy about her plans." He stepped back from the cage. "Like when she'll retire, or what she'll do when she does. But she's a planner and she likes to work. Maybe she wants to go to Florida or Arizona and teach part-time."

"She hardly looks like someone ready to retire." Parker resembled her in almost every way, except she was a small woman, not much over five feet tall. But her hair that fell to her shoulders was wavy and thick and dark blond like Parker's. They shared the same dark blue eyes and the wide smile. "I'm stating the obvious, but you look so much like her. It's almost funny. She has glasses that match her eyes, just like you."

"I hadn't noticed that, but you're right. I get

my height from my dad. And I hope I got his decent sense of humor."

She gave him a sidelong glance. "It came from somewhere."

Emma heard the voices again and Parker led the way out of the cabin.

"I told Nic she's a lucky teenager," Sharon said when she approached Parker. "I would have been thrilled to have such a great place all my own. Smells like lavender." She gestured around. "The woods, the lake, the buildings are reminiscent of the camp in Pennsylvania we used to rent when you were little. I'm not sure you'd remember the spot."

Emma saw a flicker of recognition cross Parker's face. He stared at the pier and the lake beyond.

"I didn't until just now," he said, "but the lake especially had a familiarity about it when I first saw it. Maybe I have traces of memories of that camp."

"Wow, Dad. That's like, sort of deep." Nic turned to her grandmother. "Dad was drawn to this land for real. He got a funny look on his face the day we moved in. And he knew it was sort of a dump."

Emma burst out laughing. So did Parker.

"It wasn't that bad," Parker insisted.

"Yeah, it was," Emma said. "You've both done wonders with those old cabins."

Sharon nodded. "I got the full rundown from Nic about how long these buildings were buttoned up tight and languishing."

"Rotting, Grandma, rotting. Languishing is way too polite."

"And there are a dozen more cabins we haven't even opened yet," Parker said. "Somehow, none of that mattered."

"No." Sharon took a step closer to Parker and patted his arm. "I can see that."

Emma hung back while they made their plans for the rest of the day, pleased to be included in this happy group.

"I KNOW I must sound like an old farmer," Emma said, "but I smell snow in the air." She threw her head back and inhaled deeply.

"Then we picked a good time for a walk," Sharon said. "Nic is the one who told me about your butterfly garden."

"No, no, it's not mine," Emma quickly interjected. "I don't have anything to do with managing it or promoting it. Other people are in charge of that. The acres are on the edge of the land my late husband and I bought to build the house."

"But the garden is built on *your* land."

"The acres were part of my land. A woman in town had the idea and asked for help and raised the money. She needed the acres. I happened to have them. It's the kind of land she needed because of the many miles of farms surrounding these acres. Some woods, too, but mostly fields. It was no big deal to donate them. I'm not going to miss three acres."

Emma played back the words and once again she'd minimized her contribution. Oh, yes, her default position. She hadn't fully broken that habit yet. But she could be proud of the butterfly garden. It had already made a difference in Bluestone River.

"I wish there was more to see," Emma said, "but the garden is sleeping for the winter now."

"Such a lovely town," Sharon said, opening her arms and inhaling deeply. "Parker said as much, but the minute I got out of my car, I knew this was his kind of place."

"Those of us involved with the sanctuary are glad he feels that way. We're not a full-fledged rescue center yet. I know he wants that."

Sharon offered an intimate smile. "He's mentioned you often, Emma. You're part of the reason he's so settled here. Like he's not simply passing through. I wasn't sure he would become attached to this town."

Of course not, Emma thought. "I understand why he'd have preferred a job in a big facility. As beautiful as it is, the center itself is on the dinky side, at least compared to what he's used to. Right now, it's a small community nature center."

Sharon gave her a skeptical look. "I was thinking more along the lines that *you* in particular have made him feel at home."

She blushed, avoiding Sharon's gaze.

Sharon thrust her hands into her pockets. "When I was with Nic in her place, she showed me the quilt you gave her. It's one of the most beautiful quilts I've ever seen."

"Which is why it caught my eye. The quilter herself is well known in this area. I couldn't resist it. It was a perfect match for her baby-blue eyes."

"It was generous. And I don't mean because of its value," Sharon said. "I mean you have a generous spirit."

Emma put her hand on her chest. "Oh, thanks. I'm probably blushing."

"Maybe a little." Sharon paused and then said, "I'm a bit concerned about Nic. She said something about her mother being at loose ends in Vermont. Well, more than that. Nic tells me Jackie's unhappy where she is. And then she mentioned she could change schools next semester. Has she said anything to you?"

This was probing, plain and simple. Emma feared that might happen. Being careful where she treaded, Emma said, "I haven't heard her say anything in a while. When I first met her she mentioned her credits from Neville could transfer to another school if she moved. But that's pretty typical. That's the extent of what she's said to me."

"Hmm… I see. Well, I bet that has more to do with Parker and her mom than it is about her and school."

"Well, I can't say. I don't know Jackie," Emma muttered, her way of begging off. Or trying to.

"I'll be honest with you, and I may be speaking out of turn, but I don't think Parker understands what Jackie is up to."

And she does? Emma questioned. "I'm in the dark," Emma said. "I know only the bare bones about what happened in the past."

Sharon stopped walking and shook her head. "I'm sorry. It's wrong of me to bring you into it. I know who I have to talk to for answers."

Emma smiled, acknowledging the apology. For being so far away, Parker's ex-wife could be a big presence.

"Here we are," Emma said, opening a picket fence that spanned the entrance.

"I'm surprised it's open," Sharon said.

"No reason to lock it up. It was planned to be bordered by trees and plants, and a fence set back. No fence can keep the rabbits out, but we can keep the deer from trampling through."

"Are you worried about intruders on your land?"

"Seriously?" Emma asked. "I had a stray cow turn up last summer. She got loose from the farm nearby. Some raccoons will come around hoping to find some food. But that's about it."

Everything in the garden had been cut back for the winter, but there was something special about seeing the benches and a couple of pools, dry now, but ready for next year.

"This is lovely. I'll have to come back to see it in the spring and summer."

"You should. This garden is thick with marigolds and blazing star. They've put in coneflowers and black-eyed Susans, and day lilies. Virtually everything a butterfly or hummingbird could ask for. Come to visit whenever you like. You'll always have a room in my house."

"I appreciate that." She let out a quick laugh. "You know, Emma, your reputation really does precede you. Nic thinks you're like no one else. She talks about how you run your own show, at least according to her."

"Now what show would that be?" Emma wondered, puzzled. But she supposed that to a teenager not having to scramble for a job was the best kind of freedom.

"She's aware of what you do for various town events, not to mention the sanctuary," Sharon said. "Besides, she sees you as a woman who follows her own star."

"Right now the birds are my star. Being at the sanctuary makes me happy, fulfilled. My photography is a guiding star, too." She stalled over the next line which would naturally follow, that being around Parker pleased her.

"All I can say is that Parker mentions you in all our conversations. Especially when the owl was here."

"Thanks to Nicole," Emma said. "But it

was very exciting for me. I'd never seen any-one examine a bird like that, and help the bird recover. I've always been behind the scenes with my Bluestone River projects. Parker saw how fast I took to it."

"Oh, he noticed all right."

Emma didn't miss Sharon's light tone. "Safe to say he's taught me everything I know."

Hoping she wasn't saying too much, Emma explained the lost years after her fall and rehab, and Neil's death. "I'd been looking for a new direction. The sanctuary is more than a cause for me. It's no longer something I fund to help the town. Turns out it's part of my life…my new life."

"Along with your photography? Parker tells me you do great work."

Emma jolted in surprise. He'd made com-plimentary remarks she thought were in pass-ing, but it never occurred to her he'd repeat them to someone else. "You'll see a sample in the house—in your room. Parker helped me hang some new ones of this garden." She raised both gloved hands to catch the large snowflakes drifting down. "Here it comes. We should start back to the house."

Sharon nodded. "But I'm sure Parker and

Nic have the good sense to get here for dinner before the roads get bad."

Emma smiled to herself, thinking of riding through town on the stormy morning with Parker. "Meanwhile, we can wait for them with a mug of warm spiced wine?"

Sharon's face brightened. "Great idea." She didn't seem in a hurry and continued looking around the garden. "Before the others get here, I wanted to say that I always adored Jackie. She's a great mom. A standout teacher. So, I'm not trying to criticize my son's ex-wife."

Then why bring her up?

"But I'm concerned about Nicole."

"I take it this isn't about college or her job," Emma said. No sense playing naïve.

Sharon sighed. "I'm afraid Jackie is beginning to realize she made a big mistake when she went off with Ben. Parker tells Nic not to worry about Jackie so much, but I think Jackie's getting ready to ask Parker if he wants to try again. Start over. There, I said it out loud."

Emma took in a quick breath. "Uh, I wouldn't know anything about that." But she would know about sweet kisses at her door.

"Well, Nic still has hurt feelings about not being invited to live with her in the first place," Sharon said. "As for Parker, he was blindsided. He... I don't know how..." She shook her head.

Emma stopped and focused on the woods where the snow was already starting to veil the trees in white. "I see with my own eyes that Parker likes having Nic with him here. Beyond that, I see a lovely college student finding her way."

"Finding her way to the resale shops with her friends," Sharon said, amused.

"She's a treasure hunter, all right." With the snow becoming heavier, Emma tried to pick up her pace, and Sharon fell into step with her. Finally, though, Emma had to slow down. "Sorry. This is as fast as I can go."

"Oops, sorry. Hey, what's a little snow?" Sharon stuck out her tongue to catch a couple of flakes." Exuberant, she extended her arms and made a full turn.

The two walked along in comfortable silence. When they reached the sliding door of the house, Sharon said, "I'm thrilled Parker took this job." She had a faint smile as she looked away. "For many reasons."

PARKER STOOD AT the kitchen sink, rinsing plates and glasses and handing them off to

Emma, who loaded them in the dishwasher. They'd finished their pasta dinner and coffee and thick slices of coconut cake from Sweet Comforts. Parker knew he should coax Nic away from the table where she sat with his mom. But his daughter showed no inclination to leave. Like him. Still, listening to the wind and looking at the huge snowfall starting to drift against the patio doors, he knew it was time to leave.

"Nic tells me she got you a speaking gig," his mom said.

"Tell her, Dad, you only got it because of me."

"It's true," he said. "Nic volunteered to be on a planning committee for a one-day fair. Next thing I knew the sanctuary had a booth and I have an afternoon talk."

"Lots of speakers and displays, Grandma," Nic said. "It's about all the jobs there are in the sciences. I bragged that my dad could talk about the sanctuary as part of wildlife management."

"I get to go, too," Emma chimed in, glancing at him and smiling. "I'm in charge of the booth and running the slideshow for the sanctuary. Everybody is getting involved. The co-chairs of the sanctuary board will stop in and help in the booth. Those careers are all well and good, but we're thinking about the tourists."

"I wish I could be there." Sharon looked out the window and sighed.

In the reflection in the glass door, Parker saw his mother's frown.

"But I have to get back to work."

Yes, something was definitely going on with her. He'd sensed it rippling beneath the surface since she'd arrived that afternoon. Whatever it was, he wouldn't find it out that evening.

Parker glanced at Emma. "Uh, I hate to break up this party, but Nic and I should go. It's not going to get any easier to drive out there."

"I was wondering when you were going to be a party pooper and say that," Nic said in a long-suffering voice. But she got up from the table and gave her grandma a hug.

"You're both welcome to stay," Emma said. "I'm serious. It's not like I don't have plenty of room."

Parker looked outside. It was tempting, but his truck would make it. "I think we'll be fine. If we get going now."

"I'll expect you back for breakfast," Emma

said. "I know Sharon will want the grand tour of the sanctuary tomorrow. Even in the snow."

They walked to the door for hugs all around. Parker kissed Emma's cheek. Whispering his thank-you, he breathed in the scent of her. Like the woods with spring flowers. Not for the first time, it left him light-headed.

He and Nic were quiet in the truck as they inched along the roads. He was mentally kicking himself for not leaving sooner.

"We probably should have taken Emma up on her offer," Nic said.

Parker carefully steered around a drift that spread into the middle of the road. His tires spun, but only until he pressed the gas pedal and accelerated his way out of trouble. "We're almost home. The plows will be out soon." Home? He hadn't spent much time there, but sometimes Emma's house seemed as much like home as his cabin.

"Safe and sound," he said a few minutes later. He put his arm around Nic's shoulders as they trudged to their cabins. "I'll get the driveway plowed first thing in the morning. Assuming the snow stops."

"I got a text while we were at Emma's. My classes are canceled tomorrow." She smiled sheepishly. "I'm glad. I get to spend more time with Grandma. I have a shift at the café, but not until late in the afternoon."

"It will all work out, I'm sure."

"How optimistic," Nic said.

"That's me." He kissed her forehead when they reached her door and they used their feet to push snow off the two stairs. "See you in the morning."

Too keyed up to sleep, Parker put his boots and jacket back on and using his flashlight to guide him, he kicked a path through the snow to check on the crow. The building was plenty warm for the bird in his pen. He turned on a low light, but lifted the cover only long enough to make sure he was okay. Earlier, he'd fed him nuts in the shells, and some chicken. "You're so easy to feed," he said aloud.

The lake was lost in the blur of snow, but he trudged down to the pier anyway. Not caring about how impractical it was, he wished Emma was with him to listen to the wind and see the snow. The lights in Mike and Ruby's windows were like haloed dots in the dark. It wasn't exactly a night for a walk. If he had Emma with him, he'd need to pick her up and carry her to the pier so she could appreciate this picture-perfect scene with him. Finally ready to get into bed, he trudged back to his cabin.

The next morning, his bare feet hit the icy floor, shocking him awake. He checked the heater. Cold as stone. The light in the kitchen? Out. He glanced out the frosty window. It was not only a white world, but a bone-chilling one. He checked the time on his phone and texted Emma.

CHAPTER TWELVE

LEAVING NICOLE AND Sharon huddled around the fireplace, Emma took her phone into her cold kitchen to pick up Ruby's call.

"Are you okay over there?" Ruby asked. "We don't lose power very often, but we've got a woodstove in the kitchen. You're welcome to join us. Mike's standing right here. He's happy to come get you."

"As a matter of fact, I've got three guests for breakfast," she said, reminding Ruby about Sharon's visit. "At the moment, Parker is scrambling eggs on the propane stove he had handy. Nicole and Sharon are playing a cutthroat game of Scrabble. And I'm just taking it all in."

Ruby's laugh came from deep in her throat. "And here we worried about poor Em in the power outage. Sounds like you're having a fine time."

"You're welcome to join us. Jason can pitch a tent in the living room and pretend he's on a camping trip. I'll be bringing out the hot dogs and marshmallows later."

"Ooh, sounds good. But as tempting as that is, I wouldn't crash your party."

"By the way, Sharon's terrific. The three of them seem right at home here."

"Like that surprises me? It's easy to feel that way in your house. You have a fun day. With any luck, the power will be on soon." In a stage whisper, Ruby added, "Details later."

"You bet, Rubes," Emma promised. "As it stands now, Sharon is supposed to start driving home tomorrow morning. Parker says the roads should be okay by then."

"Mike is staying in touch with the power company, so I'll keep you posted with my insider info."

Laughing, they ended the call at the same time Parker came inside from the patio with a pan of scrambled eggs. Nic entered the kitchen and Emma pulled out paper plates and the box of goodies from Sweet Comforts.

Nic bounced around the kitchen in her thick socks to see if she could help out. Emma was sure that for Nic the storm and the blackout were all part of the fun of Grandma Sharon's visit. Emma smiled to herself. She wouldn't disagree.

"Why don't you clear the coffee table, Nic? We'll sit around it on pillows."

"Definitely a paper plate day." Nicole took the pan from her dad and started spooning eggs onto the plates. "Lucky us, Dad," she said. "Emma's got jelly donuts."

"I'm glad you're having fun, honey," he said dryly. "I am, too, as long as it doesn't last too long."

"We've never lost power for more than four or five hours. Half a day tops," Emma said.

"I'll need to add an item to the budget I'm submitting to the board," Parker said when Nicole left. "We need a generator. There's an ancient one stuck in one of the storage buildings, but probably not safe anymore. I can also beef up the insulation in the cabins and work buildings."

"I always meant to put a woodstove in the office," Emma said. "I can sleep in there if I need to. I just never got around to it."

"So far, Mom and Nic are happy around your fireplace." He paused. "I'll install a woodstove for you this winter, Em."

Em…she liked the sound of it when he said it.

"Oops. I don't know why I suddenly called you that."

"That's okay. It's allowed. Trust me, I like it." How silly to feel her cheeks warming.

"Good," he said, keeping his voice low.

"As for the woodstove, you've got yourself a deal," Emma said. "Today is a gentle warning of storms to come."

Parker pointed to the blanket of unbroken snow from the patio to the woods. "It's so quiet out there now that the wind has stopped. But last night, I took a quick trip down to the pier. I was thinking how much you'd have enjoyed it."

"Oh, yeah." She so easily put herself in the picture. "I feel a lot like Nicole this morning. She's enjoying all this like we're having a little adventure. What could be better?"

He chuckled. "It's not just Nic. I'm enjoying it, too."

"Well, wait until you all see what we're having for lunch," Emma said, raising her eyebrows up and down to feign a mysterious expression. "I had some things in a little freezer in the basement just for this kind of occasion."

The morning passed quickly. While Parker plowed the driveway, Nic and Sharon dug out one of Emma's jigsaw puzzles.

"Ooh, the Chicago skyline. You picked a

hard one," Emma said, as she cleared the coffee table to make way for the puzzle.

"Okay, Grandma," Nic said. "We have our challenge, so get to work on those edges."

Sharon laughed. "That's what I used to say to you. Gotta start with the edges."

"You take this puzzle thing pretty seriously," Emma said after watching them pull out blue water and blue sky and toss pieces into piles, stopping only for what Nicole called sidebars to speculate whether a particular piece was the sky or the lake.

"Definitely part of a building," Emma said when Nic held up two pieces. "Trust me. Ruby and I put together this one last winter after she and Mike got married and he was running for mayor. We appointed ourselves co-chairs of his campaign and my house was the headquarters." Emma chuckled. "We worked pretty hard, too, but whenever she came over, we always spent a few minutes adding to this puzzle. We called it decompressing."

"You should meet that family next time you come to visit, Grandma," Nicole said. "They'll have their new baby by then. I've watched their little boy a couple of times."

"Parker told me about them," Sharon said, "and your Thanksgiving at their house."

"Speaking of Parker, he's been out plowing a long time." Emma said.

"I'm sure he wants it thoroughly cleared for you," Sharon said. "But I hope he comes in soon. I've got a lot on my mind and want to tell him about it—well, I want all of you to hear my idea."

"Nothing bad, I hope," Nicole said, straightening up as if she'd been put on alert.

"Nope, it's good stuff. I'll tell you when your dad comes back."

Nicole's eyes got big. "You've been keeping secrets?"

"Maybe just little ones."

"They better be," Nic warned as she got to her feet. "I should be helping Dad."

"You don't have to do anything," Emma said.

"Dad will want to make sure your stairs are safe." She stepped into her boots and hurried to get into her coat and pull her wool hat on.

"Whoosh," Sharon said with a sweeping gesture when the door closed. "And she's gone. She always did move like the wind."

"You know how to make a granddaughter curious," Emma kidded.

Sharon stared at the puzzle pieces she held in her palm. "Yesterday, during our walk you said something about having a new life, and I guess I'm ready for one, too."

"Well, I won't pry," Emma assured her. "But you've got Nic jumping out of her skin."

"I didn't mean to spark that much intrigue."

Emma took a couple of seconds to gather her thoughts before she spoke. "I hope this comes out the way I want it to, but the more I see of Nicole, the less she seems like other girls her age."

Sharon gave her a quizzical look.

"Parker tells me she can be moody, even a little morose. But from what I've seen she doesn't avoid being around Parker. She doesn't rebel or look for reasons to be mad at her dad. I mean, she loves having the studio, don't get me wrong." Emma shrugged. "Even Parker said she perked up a lot when she got her bakery job. Her boss, Star, is like a friend. She might tease her dad, but she doesn't treat him like the enemy."

"Nicole doesn't have much room for that, I guess." Sharon's grimace was fleeting, but

Emma didn't miss it. "When you're eighteen, it's easier to be huffy about getting away from home when you take it for granted. If you're not sure where home is, you're not so likely to act like you're planning a prison break."

Whoa. No mincing words. "You would know best about Nicole."

"If Nicole was one of the high school seniors I counseled," Sharon said, "I'd note that at the start of senior year, she was all set to move to the Rocky Mountains after graduation and start college there. But by the end of senior year, she was alone with her dad, who didn't have a job. Her mom was gone, presumably for good. She got late admission to Neville University."

Emma lifted her hands in a helpless gesture. "Of course. She isn't sure where home is, except that it's with her dad."

"That's why I'm concerned about how Jackie is doing. I'm afraid she's confusing Nic."

"Since I don't know the particulars, I'm only rooting for the best for Nicole. If it's any comfort to you, everyone around here likes her a lot. Talk about spirited."

"I used to say she brightened up everything around her."

"Like today," Emma said, touched in a way she couldn't explain.

"What's that I hear?" Sharon asked, amused. "A couple of people stomping snow off their boots."

"I'm ready to collect my fee," Parker joked when he came inside behind Nicole. "I heard something about fun food. And I've worked up an appetite."

"Kids' lunch, coming right up." Emma added another log to the fire before she went into the kitchen and gathered the thawed-out hot dogs and buns and mustard she'd hidden in the kitchen. She called for Nicole to carry in the food on a tray. She followed with the long forks and a tablecloth tucked under her arm.

"Now, when was the last time you cooked hot dogs over a fire and toasted marshmallows for dessert?" she asked, spreading the cloth in front of the hearth. She gestured for everyone to gather around.

"You weren't kidding about a stash of food in your freezer," Parker said, arranging pillows for his mom to sit. "I can't think of a better occasion for this lunch."

"The house is going to smell so good," Emma said, as she speared hot dogs on the forks and handed them out, while Nic took charge of warming the buns. "We have plenty, so eat all you want."

"These were meant for Jason?" Parker asked as he rotated the fork close to the flames.

"And for a situation like this," Emma said, positioning her fork. "Since I'll be watching Jason when Ruby has the baby and when she first comes home, I decided I better get ready."

"I can help watch Jason, too," Nicole said, "you know, in case you need to be at the sanctuary."

"He's a lucky little kid," Sharon said. "Everybody wants a chance to take care of him."

"And his dog, Grandma. You watch Jason, you get Peach as a bonus." Like her dad, Nicole put her fork practically in the flames. "This is taking way too long."

"I know," Sharon said twirling her fork. "It's so hard to wait."

Parker shook his head in a teasing way and made them both laugh. He examined his hot dog, which was almost on fire. Way too crispy for Emma's taste. He slid the hot dog off the fork and into the bun and took a bite. "Ah, food fresh off the fire. This is the best power outage ever." His voice was serious, but his face gave away his humor.

"For me, too, Dad. Much better than in North Carolina when everything flooded and we'd lose power." Nic made a face. "Sometimes for a couple of days."

"Flooding could get brutal in thunderstorms there," Parker said. "We had generators at the rescue center, but the battery lamp will be good enough when I go and check the crow."

"The lamps are okay for now," Emma said, "but not for long." Her vision now matched the kind of center Parker was ready to run. Thinking of the owl off in the woods and now the crow with cuts and missing feathers made her want that to happen much faster than the board planned. This outage was already lasting longer than any in Emma's memory.

When they'd all finished their first hot dog, they took their time roasting their second. Nicole took charge of clearing everything away and bringing fresh forks and the bag of marshmallows. Everything seemed to slow down as they moved on to dessert. Nicole threaded two marshmallows on the fork and toasted them until they were medium brown and passed them to Sharon. "Just the way you like them, Grandma."

Then Nicole fixed a fork for Parker and one for Emma. "Cook 'em to suit yourself. I like mine burnt black, you know, until it's nothing more than a soft lump of hot sugar and charcoal," Nic made two exactly that way and then licked the remains of the sticky marshmallows off her mouth.

Emma burst out laughing. "Now, that's the best description of a well-done toasted marshmallow I've ever heard."

Since Parker was struggling with a gooey blob himself he nodded his agreement.

"Hey, Grandma, we haven't forgotten about your news. Can we toast marshmallows and talk at the same time?"

"What news?" Parker asked.

"My news," Sharon replied.

"I had a feeling something was up with you. So?"

"I'm thinking about retiring from the school system. No surprise there. But I'm not ready to stop working altogether, not really. I'm taking a job with a college over in Moline. It's not far from here."

"Nice," Nic said, drawing out the word.

Sharon took Parker and Nicole through the real reason for her trip to the conference and the job interview that was part of it. "The university is right on the Mississippi River. I'd be teaching future high school counselors."

"You'd be closer to us, Grandma." She glanced at Parker. "Well, for as long as Dad is here."

"I have no plans to leave," Parker interjected. "I mean, yes, I have a one-year contract, but if they like me I could stay on."

Emma couldn't ignore her relief over how quickly he spoke up.

"They'll want him back, Grandma." Nic spoke slowly. "The people here like him…a lot."

"And that would never come as a surprise to me, now would it," Sharon said.

"Enough, enough, you two." Parker turned to his mom. "When did you come up with this idea?"

"I've been mulling it over for a while. I want something different. I like to work. I'm not interested in slowing down. I view this as my second career." Her face took on a dreamy look when she described the apartment she could rent with a view of the river. "A growing city, or so they tell me."

"You've made a decision, haven't you?" Parker said. "Did you already sign a lease?"

A knowing look passed between Parker and Sharon. Emma had to laugh to herself.

"Not yet. But if I take the job, I can move in June."

"So, you're going home to think about it. For what? Maybe five minutes?" Nic said. "Sounds to me like you've made up your mind."

Emma had purposely stayed quiet, but for some reason Sharon drew her in. "They're onto me. Want to add your two cents?"

Not a chance. "That's okay. I'll sit back and watch your decision pretty much unfold right in front of my fireplace on a cold day in December." Emma grinned. "And you'll always have a place to stay when you visit here."

"A place with hot dogs and marshmallows stashed in secret underground freezers," Nicole added, giggling.

Parker wagged a finger. "And it usually has heat."

As if his words were a practiced cue, recessed lighting came on over the fireplace at the same time the furnace cycled on.

"And soon will again," Parker said. "Well, I suppose I better check on the bird."

"I'd like a peek at your crow when you show me around the sanctuary," Sharon said. "I always liked crows."

"Me, too," Emma said.

"The bird is one of the stops on the tour, ma'am," Parker said, doffing an imaginary hat. "With any luck he'll add a remark or two about your move."

A little shiver of pleasure surprised Emma as she took in the uncomplicated love between them. It was almost too easy to march into the family picture, no fanfare needed. On the other hand, she was just as happy not to be part of their plans for the afternoon.

She started to unfold her legs so she could stand and maneuvered her body to get on both knees and go from there. Out of the corner of her eye, she caught Parker take a quick half step in her direction, but then hesitate. Of course, he'd think twice. Why risk a repeat of Thanksgiving? Smiling up at him, she held out her hand. He stepped forward and grasped it and in one quick motion lifted her to her feet. As she mouthed her thanks, she enjoyed his warm fingers giving her hand a quick squeeze.

"BE HONEST, PARKER? What do you think of my move?" His mom hung on to the railing and kicked snow off the edge of the plank.

"Are you kidding? It's the kind of change you've wanted since Dad died. You've not changed your life that much in the six or seven years since. Nic is your biggest fan and she's loving your plan."

Parker kicked the snow off his side of the plank as they strolled deeper into the woods. The day had passed quickly at Emma's house. Now the sunlight was fading. Parker felt better driving Nic to her job, even though the streets were okay. Nic wasn't used to driving in snow, not after growing up on the North Carolina coast.

"I'm her biggest fan in the way only a grandma can be. She's an adult now, but any move of mine, no matter where, isn't going to have much impact in her life."

"I don't know about that," Parker said.

"Oh, yes, you do," Sharon said as she brushed away snow from the top of the railing. "Emma said something interesting about Nicole. Pointing out that she's not an especially rebellious girl."

"It's true, she never really was."

"A lot of that is about you," Sharon said.

"That's my *professional* opinion. I see it every day. Girls who are good with their dads tend not to rebel so much. And that's you and Nic."

"So far, so good."

Sharon stopped walking and held up three fingers. "Since I've been here she hasn't stopped talking about the three incredible women she's met." She laughed. "She thinks Ruby is exciting and fun. She's in awe of her boss, Star, who's not all that much older. And don't get me started on how much she admires your boss, Emma."

"Emma is *not* my boss."

Sharon thrust out her hand so her palm almost touched his chest. "Sorry, sorry. I was joking. Why so touchy? *You* told me she's the donor who covers your salary."

"It's true I wouldn't have a job without her funding." He swiped more snow off the boardwalk, angry at his own defensiveness. "But this place would still be a bunch of boarded-up buildings if a lot of people hadn't wanted changes. The board is my boss." Softening his voice he added, "But you're right about Star and Ruby. And Emma, for sure."

"Who is very fond of your daughter."

"Look, Mom. I didn't mean to snap at you,

but I like Emma. As Nic would say, I like her like her." He laughed self-consciously. "She's around here a lot, learning about rescuing these creatures. We have a good time. If she was my boss for real, it could complicate things."

"I know. It's just…oh, never mind. Forget I said anything."

"What are you getting at, Mom?"

She flicked her hand dismissively. "Oh, nothing, not really."

"You're trying to bring up Jackie, aren't you?"

"I don't know what to think, Parker." She clapped her gloved hands and sent the accumulated snow flying. "Nic worries about her mom. Now she's torn. I think she's rooting for you and Emma to get together."

"Oh, come on, Mom. She teases. You know she kids around. But she's wrapped up in her own world. I don't think she gives it that much thought…"

"Ha! How much thought does it take to watch you and Emma together. Do you think you hide your feelings for her?"

"Only from myself, apparently."

"Now your face is turning beet red. See? I'm right."

"It's complicated," Parker said. "I didn't expect to be drawn to someone so soon after, you know, Jackie walked away. I've been pre-occupied with Nic…" he sighed in frustration "…and making a new start, even more for Nic than for me."

His mom stopped and looked into his face. "This is what I think. I bet if you said the word, Jackie would come back."

His stomach did a back flip. "First, I doubt that's true, Mom, but I'm not saying the word anyway."

"Just make sure Nic knows that—now," Sharon said. "Because it wasn't clear to me you were over Jackie. I thought you'd welcome the chance to try again."

"At one time, yes, I thought we could fix it. Work on it, you know, like you and Dad did. Was that so odd?" he asked impatiently. "I took our marriage seriously."

"So, there's no mystery why your daughter would not only worry about her mom, but read between the lines of her texts and phone conversations. Is she happy with Ben? Does she want to move down here, with or without him? Does she want to come back to you?"

"Those questions might be more in Nic's mind than in Jackie's," Parker said. "But it was a bad time. The marriage ending, the job falling through, and then feeling forced into taking this one."

Sharon stopped and gazed at the long stretch of boardwalk ahead and the pieces of it visible throughout the expanse of woods. "You've started rescuing birds."

"Yes. It's one reason I can see a future here."

"I'll enjoy being closer. You and Nic were onto me. I have made up my mind." She tucked her arm through his. "It's time for my new life."

He laughed. "Good. I'm beginning to enjoy my fresh start much more than I thought I would."

"I know that. I wonder if Emma does."

Good question. "She's like you, Mom, she doesn't miss much."

"I like her already."

CHAPTER THIRTEEN

THE CLUSTERS OF waving blue-and-green balloons attached to the walls ushered them into the gym turned into an exhibit hall.

"There it is, Dad." Nicole pointed to the sign on a beige background with forest-green lettering: Hidden Lake Bird Sanctuary & Nature Center. The banner matched all the others in the room. "*Awesome*, huh, Dad?"

Parker agreed. "Even better than I expected." The university's large gym had displays along each wall and two rows in the center. An impressive setup.

"My chemistry teacher said they started planning this fair over a year ago," Nic said. "The whole room gives me hope that I'll find exactly the right field where I can do some good."

"That's the spirit, Nic." Parker cut his eyes to Emma, who was looking at Nic with a touch of awe in her face. Hope. Wasn't that what his work had been about? He hoped to save birds, but he also hoped growing numbers of people would understand the natural world a little better. He'd be sure to add that idea to his presentation. He pulled the flat cart closer to the table to start unloading and setting up the booth.

"There must be dozens and dozens of careers that fall under the umbrella of science. And so many are represented here," Emma said. "Zoology over on this side of the room, and indoor agriculture has a display. And I'm seeing neuroscience and cancer research. Even the state parks have a couple of tables. So much to check out in one day."

"See? With all these choices, how am I supposed to pick one career? Right now, everything has its strong points." Nic lifted her shoulders in a happy shrug, obviously excited by her question and not even a little troubled. "I always thought I'd get involved with some area of wildlife preservation, kinda like you, Dad, but since I've been in school, other things keep calling my name."

"You've got time to decide, sweetie. That's what's so great about being in college. You can sample all the sciences before you settle on one."

"I agree," Emma said as she got to work setting up the computer for the slideshow they'd used on Thanksgiving. Everyone who saw it thought it was great. Emma had posters made from a few photos to give away with a family membership. Being optimistic, she'd brought a few along.

As Parker glanced around him, every booth had people like him, Emma and Nic working to get ready for the doors to open in half an hour. Wrong again, he said to himself. When Nic first mentioned the fair, he underestimated everything about it. Now he was grateful the group that managed the fair approved their application, late as it was. He— and the board—had Nic to thank for arguing for their late application.

"I'm glad you decided to bring the birds' nests, Dad." Nic held up a small, delicate robin's nest, and then a huge bald eagle's nest. She pulled out four more nests and set them aside. "I've got about ten minutes to help you set up, but then I've got to get to class."

It took only a few minutes to set up the heavy folding shelves and glass dioramas showing habitats and realistic wooden carvings of birds. The bird skeletons were arranged inside glass boxes to protect them.

"You should go now, Nic. We're fine here." He had the impulse to give her a quick hug, but held back. No sense embarrassing her. But as she was leaving, she ran into some kids she knew and pointed back to him. "That's my dad." Then she disappeared out the door.

"She's proud of you," Emma remarked. "You're proud of her. Everything's harmonious right now."

"Maybe so," he said, lifting a box of brochures off the cart. "She turned the tables on me. I'm supposed to be embarrassing her."

"Welcome, everyone," a voice boomed through the sound system. "The doors are officially open."

Students soon started trickling in as expected, but over the next couple of hours as he and Emma talked to more people passing by, they soon realized the fair was attracting a lot of folks who had no connection to the university. An older couple from Bluestone River approached the table. They seemed surprised to see the center involved in the event.

"Glad to see all that land and the buildings

getting some use," the man said. They became sanctuary members on the spot and spent quite a bit of time watching the slideshows with Emma. They remembered the days when Mike's grandfather ran the resort. When they left, they took a poster with them.

Leaving Emma to manage the table, Parker wandered around and introduced himself to other exhibitors. In a way he felt for Nic trying to make decisions about a career. Even if she narrowed her choices to a field in zoology or agriculture, that still covered a lot of ground. He picked up brochures at most booths, but his real mission was networking, making connections, seeing where cross-promotion might be possible. As he spoke to new people, he realized he talked about the sanctuary in ambitious, bold terms. How much had changed since he convinced himself to make the best of this job that he'd once considered a notch or two beneath him.

He stood across the room and felt a rush of pleasure watching Emma interacting with students who were looking at the slideshow. Her expression changed from serious to amused, and he saw her encouraging smile as she gave the students her complete attention.

Knowing he had more people to meet, he made himself move on.

EMMA DUCKED UNDER the table to grab brochures to replenish the stack she'd put between the two video screens. When she straightened up, she was looking into the face of Stacey Schwartz.

"Hey, good to see you," she said. "I knew you planned to stop by, but I wasn't sure when."

Stacey looked behind her and Emma followed her gaze to Ty and Parker standing together on the other side of the room.

"To tell you the truth, Emma, I didn't expect to see you."

What was with the flat tone? "I brought the slideshow I put together for Thanksgiving. We just met a couple from town who'd wandered in. They joined. The first new members today."

Stacey's pained expression hadn't changed since she'd said hello. "Are you okay, Stacey? Something wrong?"

"Sort of." Stacey thrummed her fingers on the pile of brochures. "Like I said, I wasn't aware you were helping out today."

"Well, now you know. I rode over with Parker and Nicole."

"But why, Emma? Did Parker really need your help? He knew we were coming."

Something didn't smell right. Stacey's pinched face and strained tone weren't like her at all. "Uh, what's this really about?" Emma folded her arms. She wanted to sit, but she needed to stand eye-to-eye. This Stacey standing in front of her was someone she didn't know.

"I hope I'm not speaking out of turn, but this is sort of sensitive." She looked to one side and then the other.

"Go on, please."

"Don't you think it's a little risky to get so close to Parker?"

Only to my heart, maybe. She cleared her throat. "Where is this coming from? He's divorced. You know perfectly well I'm free to see whoever I want to."

"C'mon, Emma," she groaned. "You know that's not what this is about."

"I do? What do you know that I don't?"

"You pay his salary."

Her head jerked back. "Are you kidding me? Are you afraid if Parker and I don't work out, I'll pull the money?" She stared at Stacey. "Well? Is that what you're afraid of?"

"It's been said that it could happen."

"Whoa. Who said?" Emma demanded.

"People talk, Emma." Stacey picked up a feather from the display bowl, but dropped it.

"About me? And Parker?" Emma braced her hands on the table. "Did I make funding the director's position contingent on anything?"

"No. But that's not the point." Now Stacey was focused on her shoes.

"Oh, so you have a better point?" Emma was desperate to stop herself from blowing up and saying something she'd regret. Besides, she expected a real answer.

Finally breaking the silence, Stacey rushed her words. "It's just that people see you together sometimes."

Emma rolled her eyes. "Better call the sheriff. Have me arrested."

Stacey sighed. "Please take this seriously. Someone mentioned seeing you having lunch over in Clayton."

"Another crime." She could almost taste the bile rising. "You know, this is the reason some people get sick and tired of small towns. Who has time to keep tabs on my lunch dates?"

"Emma, I don't like bringing this up, but I have to. I mean, I've been asked to."

Emma filled her lungs and slowly exhaled. "Do you seriously think I'm compromised in some way?"

"Do I think that? Not really," Stacey admitted.

"Do you object to anything Parker is doing at the sanctuary? Have you seen the work he's put in?" She pointed to the nests on the shelves, the dioramas showing birds and their habitats. The skeleton specimens. A glass jar of feathers sat on the table. "Everything came from him and what he's put together using old supplies. He's recycled everything. He's even using the ancient dishes he and Nicole have in their cabins. Good thing Nicole is big on vintage." Emma closed her mouth abruptly. She'd said enough. Nothing Parker had done needed defending.

Stacey had the look of a woman who was about to cry and was struggling not to.

Emma touched her arm. "Who asked you to talk to me?"

She raised an eyebrow. "To be clear, it's a person who isn't on the board. He brought up the issue of board members having relationships with employees, and how it's frowned on. The person writing the checks and the employee and all that."

"Ha! He needn't worry. I'm not on the board anymore. Remember? And the sanctuary has one employee." As an aside, she added, "But you may need to rethink that in the spring. Parker seems to be bringing more people around, even in the cold weather. And *to be clear*, my trust officer transfers the funds. You know perfectly well I don't write the checks. I stay out of that end of it. For this very reason. I don't want blurry lines. I make choices and the trust sends me reports."

Stacey rubbed her cheeks, her frustration clear. "Okay, okay. You've said your piece. I'm backing down. I didn't feel one hundred percent right about any of this. Not even ten percent. But I was pressured."

Emma didn't know who had talked to Stacey and didn't care. She busied her hands fanning out brochures on the table. "Let's be clear. I'm becoming more involved in the sanctuary, not less. I'm excited about what I've learned from Parker about birds and the work involved in saving them."

Stacey smiled. "I'm embarrassed. The thing is, I'm happy for you. If there's a choice, I'd find the money from someplace else rather than disrupt...whatever is going on with you and Parker. Oh, you know what I mean, Emma."

"Yeah, I sure do." Emma shrugged. "There's no need for that. Nothing is disrupted, and I don't intend to take a position on the board. Believe me." She looked over Stacey's shoulder and saw Parker and Ty coming to the table. "Here they are."

Stacey spun around and said hello. Parker said a terse hello to Stacey. Emma couldn't miss the phony smile Ty cast her way.

"I suppose we should be heading to lunch," Ty said, with what sounded like false enthusiasm. "We'll see you at the talk this afternoon."

Parker stood with his arms crossed over his chest as he watched the two leave. They were in an animated conversation and neither looked happy. From Parker's stance, Emma was certain Ty had sought him out for a talk. This situation was much worse for him, Emma conceded, since he did answer to the board.

"They're gone, Parker."

He leaned over and plunked his hands on the table and rested his weight on them. "From the look on your face, I gather Stacey questioned our *personal* relationship."

"Yes, but she backed down. She almost apologized for bringing it up."

"Lucky you. Ty wasn't that conciliatory," Parker said. "It took a second to understand he was serious. I thought he was sort of congratulating me on..." he pointed to Emma and then to himself *"...us."*

"Us. That's why Stacey backed off. She knows me. She thinks what's going on with *us* is kinda fun. On the other hand, I can't figure out who bothered to tell Ty and Stacey we had lunch together in Clayton. What is that?" Emma struggled to make sense of it. "At one time, I'd have accused Jim of being the troublemaker. Not anymore."

Parker tapped his fist in his palm. "My hunch is it's Ty himself. He was vague about some guy who had seen us around."

"Committing crimes, like being spotted together in a restaurant."

"Exactly," Parker exclaimed. "Ty made up that another person was involved and he lied to Stacey about it."

"So, you're saying no one complained," Emma clarified. "They're covering themselves." She pushed the point. "They really are afraid if things don't work out between us, I'll take my checkbook and go home."

Emma tried to shake the image of carrying her checkbook tucked under her arm like a ball. "And they'll be in trouble."

Parker growled in disgust. "It always comes down to that. Money."

"No, it doesn't." Emma would not give in to that worry. "I don't even think about it. I wish you wouldn't, either."

"You told me right from the start that you're hands-off when it comes to the decisions and operation of the center. Why don't they see that?"

"Seriously? If we're the talk of the town, let's enjoy it. We have fun. I like you and you like me. I don't care who knows it." She gave him a flirtatious smile. "Besides, you're a great kisser. I'm not about to give that up."

He smiled. "You're a pretty great kisser yourself, Emma O'Connell."

She gestured for him to come around the table. "Let's charm a few people into joining the sanctuary."

"I better leave the charm to you. I'll watch and learn."

"If you insist," she said, laughing. "We've still got a long day ahead. Might as well enjoy it."

She spotted Nic waving at them to get their

attention. "Speaking of charm, look who's here."

Parker turned around just as Nic approached with six or seven classmates, asking him about bird rescue and rehabilitation. Stacey and Ty no longer mattered.

CHAPTER FOURTEEN

"When you Bluestone River folks put your minds to it, you can draw big crowds," Parker said, pointing at the long line of cars and trucks flanking the farm road for as far as he could see.

"I might have known this many people would show up for the rebirth of Christmas caroling. If I'd anticipated these numbers, I'd have suggested we get here earlier." Standing next to his truck, Emma lifted her cane and then firmly planted the tip in the snow. "Nothing to do but forge on."

"Are you sure?" Parker's attempt to keep his voice neutral wasn't entirely successful. With the toe of his boot, he poked at the fresh snow in front of them, relieved it was only about three inches deep. They could walk in the tire tracks, which would be firmer for Emma underfoot.

Emma looked mildly concerned, but her voice was strong when she said, "Let's go."

Off in the distance Parker heard the opening lines of "Joy to the World." The music grew louder as more voices in the crowd joined in.

"Sounds like the high school kids are the opening act," Emma said. "They started right on time."

"Do you want to get there faster?" Parker asked.

"Sure, I do. Maybe you could arrange an airlift to the bridge."

"No need to be sarcastic," he said wryly, putting his arm around her. "Are you up for a little adventure?"

"Al...ways." By the time she was done drawing out the word, it might have been a sultry summer night.

"Good. Then you gotta trust me. Adventure about to launch...here goes." He bent his knees and scooped Emma into his arms. She grasped the puffy fabric of his jacket and slid her arms around his neck. "Hang on tight." She was light in his arms as he started down the road. His scheme might work after all.

Listening to her melodic laugh triggered the surge of adrenaline that made carrying her through the snow seem like a genius idea. One of his best ever.

Emma kept up her sultry tone. "Why, sir, you swept me right off my feet."

"I think you're close to a bad case of the giggles. But no humor allowed, m'lady. I won't be able to carry you and laugh at the same time."

"Got it," she whispered, glancing up at the sky and moving her head in time to the final bars of "Joy to the World."

"Do you know you're stepping to the beat of the song?"

She hummed along with the tune, not entirely on key, and sure enough his steps matched the rhythm. "I know it now that you've pointed it out," he said.

Emma sighed. "Wow, what a beautiful night."

"And it's just starting," he replied, keeping his voice low and full of promise.

The singing stopped, but it was only a few seconds before Emma began humming along with "Hark! The Herald Angels Sing." Another carol she claimed was her favorite.

"Ooh, the crowd is louder on this one," she said. "They must be warming up."

"There it is," he said, as the corner of the bridge came into view. He turned so Emma could get a glimpse of strings of lights spread across the opening arch and outlining the slanted roof. Other lights covered the side.

"The fairy lights are so pretty," she said as if in awe of the sight. "This is so, so special." Their contented silence was burst when she suddenly said, "I must be heavy. I could walk the rest of the way, you know."

He was still enjoying having her in his arms. That alone was enough for him to keep going. "I'll carry you to the edge of the crowd."

She let out a happy sigh. "I've never seen the park and the bridge this beautiful. Everything lit up and all these people. Even the usual summer weddings aren't this big."

Parker didn't know the names of most of the people he saw, but many faces looked familiar. He must have seen them around town or at the sanctuary. He also spotted people he thought of as friends now, like Georgia and Maggie and their families.

"Here we are," Parker said, gently lowering her to the ground, but holding her elbow until he was sure she was steady on her feet.

"Thanks. What a great idea." Emma slipped her hand through his arm and they walked up to where tables had been set up with town brochures and compiled song sheets of common Christmas carols. "Ah, they're singing another one of my Christmas favorites, 'Little Drummer Boy.'" She closed her eyes and began singing along.

"They're all your favorites," Parker teased. Looking around him, it struck him that he hadn't seen anything quite like the scene in front of him. Not just the decorated bridge, but also the lights circling the trees in the park and the spotlights surrounding a low stage set up at the back of the playground. One of the music teachers led the chorus of about twenty teenagers. There were some chairs in a row, mostly filled by older people.

"I may have needed a free ride, but I don't need a chair," Emma said, reassuring him. "I saw you looking at them lined over there."

"Oh, no, I wouldn't have suggested it." He drew back. "And have you get all huffy with me? Not a chance."

She squeezed his arm. "Aw, you know I wouldn't do that."

"Look," Parker said, pointing with his chin to Jim and Ruth sitting in chairs.

"After all that happened, I bet you're glad to see them. You're the one person in town who could bring out the good side of him." When the music in the background changed to a Christmas pop song, Emma said, "Oh, I love this one."

He grinned at her. "I think there's a rule that you can have only one favorite."

"Who would write such a rule?"

"What Child is This?" happened to be a Christmas carol Parker knew well. He used to sing it with Nic when it came up on an old CD of Christmas carols she played over and over when she was little. It brought on nostalgia as he sang, but here with Emma was where he wanted to be. Christmas Eve was only four days away. And a long quiet winter was ahead. He couldn't wait for Emma to open her Christmas present. He'd gone back to the gallery in Clayton and got her one of Guy Hammond's carved jewelry boxes, one with mostly hummingbirds.

"You have a nice voice," Emma said. "Not just like a radio announcer, but you can sing, too."

That was true, at least he could carry a tune. "I used to play guitar—sort of—and sing with a bunch of kids in high school. An old-style garage band. We were an odd assortment but we picked up gigs now and then. It was fun while it lasted—a couple of years."

"Okay, I'm officially impressed. I mean,

healing birds is great as far as it goes, but playing in a band?" In a voice full of enthusiasm, she added, "Now, that's cool."

"Hey, it got me dates," he joked. Specifically, it got him dates with Jackie, but he didn't need to say so.

When the music stopped, the music teacher, serving as emcee, went through a list of people to thank for making the event so successful. Before she stopped speaking, Emma nudged him and pointed to an area behind a couple of family groups in front of them. "Come on, we can get a better view over there." She pointed to a flatter spot on the edge of the crowd.

They moved the few yards, where it was easier to stand. And dimmer, Parker thought, with fewer people around them. The music teacher ended her talk and began leading little kids in the crowd in a kind of off-key "Jingle Bells," but no one cared. Conscious of Emma standing so close, Parker had a hard time paying attention.

"I always wished I'd had a halfway decent singing voice," Emma said.

"Who says you don't?"

She rolled her eyes. "No one has to."

She had him there. "Who cares? You have lots of other talents."

"Good evasion."

"No evasion." He leaned down and kissed her lightly on the lips. "You're smart and curious. And funny." He kissed her again. "Being beautiful doesn't hurt."

Emma let her head drop against his chest.

"Dance with me," he whispered in her ear. "You like to dance. You're good at it, too. You can't deny it. I happen to know a certain lawyer who has proof. On video."

She tilted her head back and held his gaze. "I don't know, Parker. I haven't... I've put that behind me now."

He put his arm around her waist. "I see the way you move. You're graceful, like the dancer you are. Besides, you walk everywhere, don't you? No reason you can't do it to music."

She didn't say no.

He picked up her hand hidden in thick, fleece-lined gloves. "There must be real fingers in here." His hands were just as protected. He gently drew her as close as their puffy down jackets would allow. "I've got you, Emma. I won't let you fall."

The crowd was singing the first bars of

"White Christmas." Parker smiled. "Hear that? They're playing your favorite song."

Emma put her arm around his shoulder, keeping the cane in her grasp behind his back. Parker took small steps at first, making a slow circle on the even ground and swaying to the slow rhythm. Parker softly sang the words, and with every step she relaxed a little more in his arms, trusting him, but mostly trusting herself.

He held on to her when the music stopped. "Let's see what comes next."

"Wait one second." Emma kept her right hand in his, but she stepped back and with her left hand, she tossed her cane into the snow. "I don't need it right now." She gave him a shy smile.

"Looks that way." He admitted to feeling a little smug, but this was one hunch he was glad he'd followed.

They stayed in the same flat spot and danced and swayed through the next two songs. The crowd got louder and the voices stronger, especially with "The Christmas Song," when everyone sang the familiar words about chestnuts and Jack Frost. He kept his arm around Emma when the music switched back to carols. He scanned the crowd and saw Mike and Ruby with Jason waving at them. When he and Emma waved back, Mike took a couple of steps in their direction, but Ruby touched his arm and stopped him. *Good. Thanks, Ruby.*

Later, Mike briefly took the mic only long enough to thank everyone for coming, and then the night closed with "Silent Night." The chorus sang in perfect harmony, and the crowd found its one voice to match it. He looked into Emma's eyes, glistening as the volume dropped lower and lower until the song came to an end. When the last bar closed, no one moved. Seconds passed in silence. Emma rested her head on his shoulder. Then, as if someone sent a signal, the din of conversation and laughter broke the hush that had settled over the gathering.

"Did you want to go say hello to Ruby and Mike?" he asked only because he thought he should.

"No, not now. I like being back here by ourselves."

He took in a deep breath and studied his surroundings. Next Christmas, the crowd would expand even more. Next winter. He'd included himself—with Emma—in that picture of a future night of caroling at the bridge.

He eyed the farm road, where a few dozen people were heading toward their cars. Within minutes, engines turned over and headlights came on and the atmosphere changed.

"Oh, I almost forgot to tell you. We have a new owl in our treatment cabin."

"Really? I hope it's not too badly hurt."

"Lots of cuts and gashes, but he'll be fine. He's a screech owl. They're on the small side," Parker explained. "A farmer brought him in. His kids saw the owl tangled up in broken fencing."

"I'm sorry I wasn't there when they brought the bird in."

"Oh, there will be plenty to do. I even had to bandage his feet," Parker said. "I told the farmer he should bring the kids before Christmas. He was a little afraid to let them come along when he delivered the bird."

"He was afraid it might die while you were taking a look?" Emma asked.

"More or less. Or even before he got to us. But those kids will feel so much better when they visit him on his perch." He smiled.

Emma snuggled up to Parker. "I'll see him tomorrow. I'm excited about it already."

"I thought you might be."

Emma nodded toward the line of people still leaving the bridge. "I don't mind being stragglers, but I'm ready to go when you are." She pivoted toward the edge of the woods where her cane had landed.

"I'll get it." He hurried to retrieve it and handed it to her. Then he held out his arms. "At your service."

She lifted her arms, and he picked her up. She leaned in and touched his cheek before tightening her arm around his back. When she kissed him, her lips were surprisingly warm and when she broke the kiss it was only for a second or two. Like him, she wanted another and another after that. Finally, she nuzzled against his shoulders and he started walking. "Keep hanging on tight," he whispered.

She lifted her head and lightly tapped his mouth with her index finger. "I have no intention of letting go."

"IT'S GETTING LATE," Emma said, taking a sip of wine, "but I don't care if you don't."

She'd expected Parker to take her up on her invitation to come in for a drink. Now they sat side by side on her couch and chatted about what a great evening they'd had. As if that was all there was to it.

"I've made some decisions," Parker said, shifting to face her. He smoothed the back of his fingers across her chin and through her hair. She closed her eyes, lost in his light touch, the sound of his breathing and the catch in her throat.

"Uh, do you want to hear them?"

She caught his hand in hers. "Okay, now I can concentrate."

"This pretty little town has grown on me, you know? It's grown on Nic, too."

"You mean Jackie's done hinting about great jobs for you in Vermont?" She'd had stomach flutters when he'd mentioned his ex-wife's texts complete with links to job postings.

"That's behind me now." Parker shook his head. "With any luck, she's finally finished with her antics that only confuse Nic." He blew out a breath of air in frustration. "Nic has been anxious lately, and I blame it on Jackie's mind games."

"I'm glad you settled it."

He caressed her cheek. "It means I can focus on other things."

Like her. She hoped she showed up in his thoughts as much as he visited hers.

She playfully tilted her head. "Tell me about these other things."

He lifted her hand and kissed her palm and pressed it against his cheek. "I wake up thinking about you. You're in my mind when I go down to the pier and watch the sky light up in the morning. Then I wait for you to show up at the sanctuary to see how our patients are doing. I like watching you with the birds—I know there haven't been many—"

"Yet." She smiled sheepishly. "Oops, sorry I interrupted."

"But you're right—I like your optimism." He laced his fingers with hers. "Mostly, I think about how I've fallen in love with you."

He raised his hand as if to ward off an objection, but he needn't have bothered. She had none.

"We haven't known each other that long, but…I like what I know."

She scooted closer to him. "Are you going to say something, Emma?" He paused.

She had so much she wanted to tell him. So many questions about him she wanted to ask. But not now. Emma let out a low chuckle as she ran her index finger over his lips. "Will a simple 'ditto' do?"

"I know it's early—probably too early—to say this, Emma, but I'm thinking this is for keeps."

"Funny how we think alike sometimes."

Parker's smile was sweet and she saw genuine affection in his eyes. "I'm getting used to it."

Emma relaxed into his arms and watched the fire, not wanting the night to end but knowing it had to.

As if reading his mind he released her and they stood. "See you tomorrow, early, I hope."

She stared into his eyes, such a deep blue in the dim light. The only sound was a log crackling in the fireplace. "You bet you will."

"So, for now," he whispered before lowering his head for a long kiss goodbye.

He was halfway out the door when she said, "Parker, thanks for convincing me I can dance again."

He stepped closer and kissed her cheek. "Be prepared for more of that."

She closed the door and leaned against it. He loved her and she loved him back. *For keeps*.

CHAPTER FIFTEEN

PARKER WAITED ON the pier until almost 8:00 a.m. before he made the call.

He was greeted with a happy hello. In his mind's eye, he could see Emma's bright smile. But he skipped the pleasantries. "Nicole's gone. She sent texts to let me know."

"She's gone to *Vermont*? To her mother's?"

"Right. She lied to me, Em." It wasn't the decision itself that hit like a punch, so much as the subterfuge. The sneaking around. The little fibs she had to tell to pull it off.

"I'll be right there."

Silence. She'd ended the call.

She hadn't given him the option to argue, which was his first impulse. Tell her not to drop everything. Who was he kidding? He slipped the phone back in his pocket and stared at the lake. The pier was like a magnet pulling him there to make the call to Emma on a morning so cold he exhaled a dense cloud of white air.

When he'd come home last night his head was spinning with happiness. He might as well have been a sixteen-year-old asking a girl to go steady. He'd laughed at himself over plodding through the snow, kissing her and not caring who saw them. And they'd danced.

Now this.

He clutched the railing and leaned forward, trying to stretch away the tension in his back. One more time he went over the last conversation he had with Nic. Where were the clues, the signs he missed? Now it was like a hard punch that came without warning. He was so deep in his thoughts, he startled when he heard Emma's voice calling his name.

He started toward her and wrapped her in his arms.

"This is the opposite of what you thought was going on, isn't it?" Emma asked when she stepped back from the hug but hung on to his hands.

He nodded. "I thought Jackie had settled things with Nic, made her understand no reconciliation was in the works." He shook his head sadly. "Nic teased me in her funny sort of way, when I told her I was serious about you."

"So she left when we were out together." The sound Emma made was low, guttural.

"Exactly. When I got home her car wasn't there, but I didn't think anything of it. It's not like she has a curfew."

"And she was supposedly out with friends?"

"That's what she said, but…"

"She waited to leave until she knew you'd be gone long enough for her to slip away."

"Right." He took the phone out of his pocket and brought her text on the screen and tilted it so Emma could see it. "Here it is: need 2 be with mom now. ben may be gone… not sure mom says you refuse 2 look at jobs in vt…still wants to try with u again N."

He scrolled down. "Then, after I called, she wrote another: sorry dad…luv u lots… don't worry."

"When did the first text come in?" Emma asked,

"In the middle of the night. I'd dozed off but woke up to go check for her car. When I didn't see it I looked at my phone. She timed it all. She knows I usually sleep like a rock. She figured it would be morning before I'd know she hadn't come home."

"She concocted quite a scheme, I'd say.

Not something you'd have expected from Nicole."

He ran his hand through his hair, reliving the anxious moment when he knew her car wasn't there.

Frowning, Emma stared at the screen. "Let's walk to the building while we chew this over."

"Sure. Sorry. You're getting cold. My fingers are already numb."

"What's next?" Emma asked. "You wait for her to let you know when she gets there?"

"I left a voice mail telling her to get off the road and check into a hotel. I didn't want her driving straight through—it's like a fifteen-hour drive." He waved the phone. "So far, nothing. I told her to text me when she stops." He raised his hands in a helpless gesture. "Like she'd listen to me now."

"I agree that's a long drive. At that age, Ruby and I used to do roads trips during our spring breaks. But we switched off driving. I didn't drive more than half the day alone in the car."

"She's eighteen, Em. Almost nineteen." He laughed cynically and stopped walking. "She's invincible. Earlier, I wished she had a dog with her in the car. Even a marshmallow like Peach would make me feel better about my girl on the road at night. It's so hard not to be Daddy, you know. Daddy could order her home. Dad doesn't have that sway."

Parker stopped and pointed at a stand of birches protected from the wind by surrounding oaks, so snow built up on their branches. "Man, it was like two days ago Nic told me your photos of those birches would make great greeting cards for the sanctuary to sell."

"A project for next year." She leaned against him. "You don't want to think about that now. You want to figure out what to do."

"Not much I can do except wait for her call." Parker patted his pocket that held his phone. "I hate feeling helpless."

"Did you look inside her cabin?" Emma blurted. "What did she take with her?"

"I… I'm not sure. I opened the door, called her name. I got scared when she didn't answer, so I wasn't thinking about that. Her texts sounded so final." He studied Emma's expression. "What is it? What are you thinking?"

"Let's go into her place," Emma said. "It's not snooping, especially if she packed everything up."

"I hope she didn't," he said. "She and a

couple new friends are always thrifting these days. I thought she was having fun fixing up her cabin."

"She was. That's not your imagination."

When they got to the cabin, he glanced at Emma, who'd hung back a few feet. He turned the knob. As he predicted, the cabin wasn't locked. Neither of them locked their cabins very often. He pushed the door open and switched on the closest lamp. Puzzled, he said, "Her computer is gone, but the pictures are still on the wall."

Emma went deeper into the room just as he checked behind the screen blocking Nicole's bed from view. "She took the quilt you gave her. And her pillow."

"But only some of her clothes." Emma stared into the half-empty closet. "It's kind of mixed."

He brushed his hand over the shelf of textbooks and notebooks. "She left those. She had her last final a couple of days ago." He sighed. "I thought she liked her classes at Neville."

"She did, Parker, she did," Emma insisted. "Don't second-guess yourself. We all saw it."

Parker nodded. "She was a big fan of yours. I thought…"

Emma turned away so she wasn't looking at him. "Maybe you moving on with me wasn't as easy for her as we thought...or hoped."

"Now she thinks Ben left her mom—"

"Maybe, maybe not," Emma interrupted. "Let's wait and see what's really going on. Seems Nicole doesn't know one way or the other."

"Unless..."

"What?"

"Unless she's not being honest with me." He scoffed. "Or maybe it's Jackie who's manipulating her. My ex wasn't always such a master game player, either." Parker needed to get out of his daughter's space. It only confused him, made him doubt himself and his decisions. He rubbed his hand across his forehead. "Let's check on our newest patient. And say hello to the crow, too."

When they went inside the cabin, he flipped the electric heater on low. He uncovered the owl, who spread one wing. "Chipper today, aren't you?" he said.

He and Emma sat side by side on the bench letting the owl get used to the light streaming through the window. The clear sky in Bluestone River gave him little comfort, though.

He got out his phone. "I'm checking the weather again for storms out east," he said. "It's not a great time of year for a long drive."

Emma covered his hand with hers. "Nicole has good sense. She knows to get off the road in the snow."

Annoyed, he freed his hand and waited for the screen to show the weather in the northeast.

"Uh, I'm sorry. I didn't mean to make light of your concern."

"Driving in snow is new for her." He knew he was being unfair. His words. His tone. They were off, but he couldn't help it. "She's only had experience driving in North Carolina. On the coast, where snow is a novelty."

"You're right. My mistake."

"I'm worried about her driving through mountains in the snow…if it snows." His nerves were raw. Overwhelmed by his mixed up emotions, he couldn't figure out the simple weather forecast displayed on his screen. Besides, he couldn't pinpoint where she was, anyway.

He got up from the bench and braced his boot on the edge of the low platform where the bird pen sat. With his back to Emma, he said, "She and Jackie have had their mother-daughter drama, but I thought…" he searched for the words "…oh, I'm not sure what I thought."

"Speaking of Jackie, have you texted her?"

Parker shook his head. "I will soon, though. I really wanted to talk with Nic first."

"It may be small comfort, but no matter what she's up to right now, anyone can see how much Nic loves her dad. And I know how much you want her to be here with you."

"You're right. It's small comfort." His whole body was jumpy. He turned to Emma. "I thought you got it. It's not about wanting her to be with me. She's not a little kid. She's an adult. Soon to be completely on her own."

"Parker, I didn't mean—"

Agitated with the situation and with Emma, Parker didn't have the energy to hear her out. "I'm upset because of what Jackie's been doing with Nic. And with me."

Emma had no response. But why would she? He more or less shut her down. And he couldn't help himself.

"I'm obviously confusing the situation," Emma said. "I'm not helping to make this any easier on you. And I get it. You're not sure what to do now."

"Like I told you there's nothing for me to do."

"Maybe Jackie isn't playing games, Parker. You told me you had wanted to fix your marriage. Now your ex-wife is finding jobs for you, hinting her boyfriend is gone." She shrugged. "Somehow, she enticed Nic up there. *Four days before Christmas.* Maybe this is her way of finally trying."

"Maybe. If I took a job in Vermont, Nic would come, too. She knows our daughter wouldn't feel as torn if we were in the same place."

Emma stood, but kept her distance. She looked beyond him to the owl on the perch. "So, you can't say Jackie's wrong about that."

Something was way off, knocking his thoughts all over the place. "What is this, Em? It sounds like you're taking her side. Are you inviting me to go back to my ex-wife?"

"Are you kidding? I've been falling in love with you since the day I twirled my cane and pointed it at you a few feet from where we're standing." She closed her eyes and rubbed the back of her neck. "But something has you thrown. I've never seen you like this before."

"Like I said, Nic doesn't make a habit of lying. And slinking away in the night isn't her style. Or so I thought."

"Something happened that looks a whole

lot like a jumble of misunderstandings. Add some manipulation to the mix and all you get are more questions. Maybe Jackie will keep on doing this." She shook her head. "You and I can't move on with this hanging over you." She nodded to the owl and the crow. "You have so much you want to do here, but…"

"But?" He peered into her face. Not move ahead? He thought they had a problem to solve. Apparently, she thought differently. "Go on. But what?"

"Confront Jackie about her games." She grimaced. "At least get her to be straight with you about what she wants. Be clear about what you want."

"I told you," he said, confused, "I need to talk with Nic before I hash things out with Jackie."

Emma took in a breath. "Why don't you follow Nic? Go up to Vermont yourself and have it out."

He dismissed that idea with a sharp look. "C'mon. Why would I do that?"

"You claim things are settled between you and Jackie."

"They *are*."

"Right. You've signed all the papers. But what about the emotional fallout?" She moved toward the door. "I mean…until you confront your ex-wife I think Nic will keep on worrying about her mother and fall victim to every complaint. Even Nic will wonder what you and Jackie really want."

He was stunned. "Drive off. Just like that."

"Better now than later." She pointed to the crow and the owl. "You taught me well. I can feed them. Will and Bill will help me clean the cages. The board and Mike, any of us, can stand in for you on Christmas Eve. It's a family emergency, Parker. No exaggeration." She sighed. "As far as I'm concerned, it's an emergency for us."

His stomach was churning in a kind of disbelief. "But I love you so much, Emma."

She stared at him and the seconds ticked by before she answered. "I know. And I love you. But I want you to be sure—one hundred percent—you want to be here with me. No matter what." She put her hand on the doorknob. "I'm going to leave. Let me know your plans. Please."

Then she was gone…*gone.*

RUBY WAS EASY to spot in a back booth. In spite of her low mood, Emma was amused to see her friend thumbing through magazines and sipping a giant chocolate milkshake like she didn't have a care in the world.

"There you are," Ruby said, looking up as Emma approached. Then she signaled to the waitress and pointed to the old-fashioned shake glass.

"I already ordered one for you. And you won't argue."

"Don't worry, I don't have the energy."

"I just got a text from Mike. He and Jason are in Clayton doing some mysterious Christmas shopping," Ruby said, raising her eyebrows and smiling. "What could that be about, huh? Anyway, I've got plenty of time."

Emma glanced around at the diner, mostly empty in the late afternoon. "When you picked up the call, I heard loud whirring in the background. I had no idea it would turn out to be the shake mixer. This is the last place I imagined you'd be."

Their teenage hangout had always been a little shabby and only got worse as the years passed. But some things never changed, including the demand for milkshakes and malts. Spruced up now, the River Street Diner was bringing in people nostalgic for traditional diner food.

"You can't believe the cravings I get for these," Ruby said, pointing to the glass. "Always chocolate," she added with a grin. "I have Mike bring one home almost every day. Might as well enjoy 'em now." Ruby cocked her head. "Enough about that. You're upset. Start at the beginning."

Emma waited for the waitress to deliver the milkshake and walk away. "You know how Parker and I became friends. And last night you saw us dancing at the bridge." Emma filled in the blanks about all that happened between swaying to the music warm and safe in Parker's arms and calling Ruby twenty minutes ago. She explained Nicole taking off and the confusion in Parker's deep blue eyes. His agitation, his constant motion. Her voice quivered with the words, "Only now, it's sinking in. *I* sent Parker away. But…"

"Aw, Em, no knocking yourself over that. You had to be sure. From what you told me, Jackie is good at games." Ruby flashed a knowing look. "We've seen it for ourselves. Nicole can be pretty talkative. She probably dropped a little detail here and there about her dad and his friend. Thanksgiving dinner at our house, tending the birds, the fair at Neville."

"And we can't forget that her grandmother stayed in my guest room," Emma added. "Oh, and the quilt I gave her."

Ruby nodded. "Yep, there's that. Let's be honest. Maybe Jackie seriously regrets letting Parker get away. Now, it's probably worse because he met you. He's really gone now."

Emma scoffed. "Yeah, finally, something Jackie and I have in common. Letting go of Parker."

Ruby grabbed Emma's hand. "Sweetie, you've completely bedazzled the guy. I see it. Mike sees it. And we're not alone. Lots of people get it. I don't believe for a hot minute Parker will change his mind about his ex-wife—or you—because his daughter has mixed-up feelings about her parents' divorce."

Emma wasn't so sure. "In any case, Nicole is confused."

"She's still a teenager, Em, so of course she's confused. But at the same time, she's almost an adult. Parker isn't trying to keep his family together for the sake of their young child."

"It's true, that ship sailed years ago, Rubes. But according to Parker, he wanted to go to counseling to work on their marriage. Jackie wouldn't go. Then she met this other guy and wanted out." Emma sighed. "He'd have put everything into it, if she'd made the effort. What can I say? I fell in love with a loyal type of guy. He takes commitments seriously."

Ruby nodded. "Good."

"I was honest with him about Neil and me and how we refused to give up. Big mistake." Emma knew Ruby wouldn't argue with that assessment. She'd lived it with her.

Ruby pointed to the shake. "Drink up, Em. My guess is you haven't eaten all day."

She dutifully took a few sips. On any other day the rich chocolate would have been irresistible. Even the aroma of burgers and onions sizzling on the grill couldn't entice her to order her usual go-to comfort food. She glanced out the window. The day was drifting toward twilight. If he'd listened to her, Parker could be on his way north.

"I got Parker one of Guy Hammond's birds for Christmas—the most beautiful goose. Its wings are spread in lift-off position."

"You'll get a chance to give it to him," Ruby said. "You will. This isn't over. Not by a long shot.

"Even if Nicole stays in Vermont," Ruby said, "I don't believe she'll shut her dad out of her life."

Emma took some comfort in that. "She gets such a big kick out of teasing him. He'll always be her nature freak dad. It's so much fun to watch."

"Seems the two of them are like puzzle pieces that discovered where they fit." Ruby's expression was full of thought. "And it's here in Bluestone River."

"They need Bluestone River and we need them." Emma's shoulders sagged as she exhaled a heavy sigh. "My days have been so full the hours usually fly by, but not today. I soaked in the tub, I sorted a box of photographs, I channel surfed until I came to a movie I've seen half a dozen times. My phone was never out of reach." She'd waited all afternoon for a call or a text from him, followed by a whole train of thought about Parker needing space.

Ruby jabbed her finger at her. "You'll call me when you hear from him. Promise?"

"You know I will." Emma managed a smile as she slid out of the booth.

She gave Ruby a big hug. Then, in no particular hurry, Emma turned off River Street and drove the long way home on the streets behind downtown.

PARKER WAITED ALMOST an hour in his truck, fighting against his growing impatience. Not so much with Emma, but with himself. What he had to say wouldn't work in a text. Or a call. She needed to see him standing in front of her when he told her what he'd decided. But it was dark now and calling her might be his only choice.

Restless, he got out of his truck and paced in front of her house. He took off his gloves and blew on his hands to warm them, painfully aware of how ridiculous he was being. Finally, he pulled out his phone and called Mike, happy to hear his cheery, "Hey, Parker."

"Uh, I know this is a long shot, but do you happen to know where Emma is?"

"On her way home from the diner, I think," Mike said. "Hang on a second."

Parker heard the back and forth of muffled voices in the background.

"Ruby met Em at the diner late this afternoon," Mike said. "Ruby tells me Emma left first, but Em didn't say anything about making another stop."

"So, you don't think she went away for the weekend or anything."

Muffled voices again.

"No, no. She wouldn't leave town without telling Ruby," Mike said firmly. "My hunch is she'll be there soon."

"Good. I need to talk to her. Right away."

"Uh, well, like I said, she shouldn't be long."

Parker saw headlights sweep across the road to the drive. "I think she just turned in. Thanks, man."

He stood and met her as she left her car and walked toward him. She nodded at his truck. "Are you leaving? Have you heard from Nicole? Is she okay."

"Nic is fine. I talked with her right before I drove over here. She's warm and safe in Jackie's house. She beat the storm."

Emma swiped her hand across her forehead. "Whew…you must be so relieved."

"You bet I am." He glanced at the door behind him. "Uh, will you invite me in?"

That seemed to startle her and she started toward the stairs. "Sure. How long have you been waiting?"

"Not too long." He heard his flat tone. But it matched his mood. Every part of him resisted what he was about to do.

"Why didn't you call me?"

He smiled sadly and peered into her face. "I needed to see you. A phone call wouldn't have been good enough, Em."

She nodded, and fumbled through her key ring as if flustered. "I'm surprised to see you."

"Did you think I'd leave for Vermont without letting you know?"

"No, not really. But I was watching my phone. I wasn't sure…" She didn't finish the thought, but turned to open her door. They stepped inside the entryway. She shrugged out of her coat and kicked off her boots.

He stayed on the mat as is. If he got comfortable in her house, he might not do what he knew he must. He was close enough to her to breathe in the sweet scent of her hair, but he didn't take her in his arms. That wouldn't be fair to Emma. He had no choice but to keep his distance.

"So, tell me," she said. "What's going on?"

"A lot's happened, but I'll give you the bottom line. I'm going to Vermont."

"Now?" she blurted.

"But I wanted…needed…to see you first. It seems your instincts were right. I realized I can't settle things with Nic over the phone." He stared beyond Emma into her house. The fireplace, the view from the patio doors, the way the place seemed to invite people in. He shook off those thoughts in order to keep going. "I also need to find out what's happening with Jackie. I won't feel right until I see her."

Emma crossed her arms. "What about Ben?"

"I don't know. Nic seems to think he's gone, but I'm not sure Jackie is giving her the real story."

"And the launch?" Emma searched his face for answers. "Oh, and the two birds?"

Nodding, he said, "It's a bad time for this, but like you said, I've done the work. The center is ready. I've let Ty and Stacey know what's happened. They have the launch covered. And, Em, I know you can take care of the birds until I get back or…"

Emma's features pinched in hurt and confusion. "Or, what?"

He couldn't say. He hadn't thought that far ahead or figured out anything except getting to Vermont. "I'm not sure. I don't want to hurt anyone, especially you, Em."

"All right," she said in a cool tone. "But let's not pretend I'm an expert about those birds. I know the basics. I'll do my best."

Parker looked away, not wanting to meet her eye. "If I'm going to go, I probably should be on my way."

"I hope you get some answers," Emma said. "And watch the weather."

"I will." He gave her a quick hug and then turned away to let himself out.

CHAPTER SIXTEEN

"YOU TWO ARE good for my heart," Emma said to the owl and the crow as she pushed the workroom door closed behind her. The bitter wind was blowing fiercely. At the moment, her one consolation was being certain that no matter what happened with Parker—even if he walked away from her—she wouldn't abandon what had become a passion.

Should she be proud or angry that he felt free to leave on a moment's notice because he knew she could care for these two patients? It seemed she was a little of both. She'd thought about Parker through a sleepless night and a restless day, but she showed up this evening, as he trusted her to.

The owl looked about the same as he did when she'd examined him the day before, battered and bruised but alert and apparently on the mend. She couldn't say as much for the crow. First, he hadn't touched any of the food she'd left for him a day ago. Not a good sign. He usually gobbled it up. Even more troubling, and unusual, he didn't react to her presence. He always lifted his good wing and made his friendly cawing sound. According to Parker, crows have an unusually good memory for faces, well, good in the bird world, anyway.

"What's this?" she said aloud. "Are you becoming a picky eater? We already feed you like a king."

He didn't turn his head in response to her voice. He was off his perch and sitting on the mat. The cage was a real mess, too, which meant she had a huge cleaning job ahead.

She dumped out the old food, but before refilling the stainless steel tub, she opened Parker's log. Leafing through his detailed notes about the last few days, she saw nothing out of the ordinary. "Never mind, I'm still going to figure out what's up with you." She stared at the crow, but got no response.

As she went through the log, she settled on two symptoms, lethargy and loss of appetite. Emma took a couple of deep breaths to ease the tension building in her body. Even her hands trembled slightly as she scanned the information and weighed the probabilities that the crow either had a simple infection or the more serious salmonella, likely fatal. She wasn't ready to accept that. In either case, there was little to do but watch and wait.

She lifted the crow out of his pen and set him on the mat of the holding cage. No resistance, no sound. "I wish you could talk to me," she said. "It's not my fault Parker is gone." And without any commitment to coming back.

Well, when she'd first suggested it he'd rejected the idea of going after Nicole. It didn't make sense, he'd said. Now she wished they'd talked about it more. If he'd stuck around a little longer they might have come up with a solution. And not one that meant he'd head out exactly when snow was predicted for large swaths of the Midwest and New England. If she weren't so worried about him, she'd say it served him right.

Her hip ached and her body craved sleep, but frustration produced enough fuel to get through the cage cleaning routine. After switching out the mats she put the crow back in his pen. Then she eased herself down on the bench and rested her back against the wall. Normally, she'd leave and come back in the morning. Christmas Eve morning, she thought. Nothing about the launch or the holiday would be as she envisioned it. Nothing. She leaned forward and covered her face with her hands and rubbed her eyes. And now she had a sick bird to care for.

"What am I supposed to do?" she asked, as if the birds could answer her.

Luckily, the answer to her question wasn't that complicated. And she already knew the answer.

WITH THE WINDSHIELD wipers barely keeping up with the falling snow and a salt truck close behind him, Parker pulled off the highway and into a gas station plaza filled with semis likely waiting for the roads to be cleared. This is exactly what he'd feared when Nic made the drive. She beat the snow and was safely at Jackie's house, but here he was catching the tail end of another storm.

Before leaving the truck, he checked his phone. Nothing from Nic, nothing from Emma. What could he expect? He'd always remember the pained look on Em's face when he gave her such vague answers when she asked when he'd be back and what would happen next.

He went inside the store and picked up hot coffee and a sandwich that he took back to his truck. He resisted checking his phone again. Watching the snow come down, Parker was struck by the notion that the vehicle was pointed in a direction he didn't really want to go.

He ate quickly and swallowed the last of his coffee and let his head drop back against the headrest. He closed his eyes. When he opened them again, it took him a second to realize he'd dozed off. The wind howling outside the truck had startled him awake.

Thankfully, it had stopped snowing. Fewer semis were in the rows of parking spaces and more were leaving now. He could be on his way, too, if he wanted to. What he wanted wasn't the point. This was about Nic. He scoffed. If it was about her, it was time to let her know he was on his way.

He tapped her number and was prepared to leave a voice message, but then he heard her cheery, "Hi, Dad?"

"Hey, sweetie, I wanted to let you know I'm on my way. It's been slow going what with the storms."

"On your way here? Vermont?"

"Yes. I'm at a rest stop in Pennsylvania. I should be there—"

"Why, Dad?" she interrupted.

"Why? Why do you think? I'm worried about you. You left without telling me."

"Because you would have tried to talk me out of it," she said, her voice louder now. "I needed to come and see Mom. You know, see what's going on. I told you that."

"I get it. I just don't want to see you disappointed, or worse, Nic." He paused, knowing how irrational this all sounded even to his own ears. "I thought I should be there for you. Put my mind at rest."

"What about Emma?"

"She's looking after the birds we have."

She let out a low groan. "I wasn't talking about the birds, Dad. I mean you and Emma. I know you're in love with her."

That gave him a jolt. He hadn't expected Nic to come up with that. He didn't know what to say in response.

"Right, Dad?"

"Yes, Nic, but that's not as important as you. I need to know you're okay."

"Oh, Dad, of course I'm okay. I love you. I like Bluestone River. And Neville, and my job."

"So, if that's true why did you sneak away?" The thing that hit the hardest.

"I love Mom, too," she said in a low voice.

"We haven't talked about heavy stuff yet, but I hadn't seen her since June."

"Oh, sweetie, I've never said you didn't have a great mom who loves you," he said defensively.

"Please, Dad, I'm not ten years old. I have to work this out with Mom on my own." She paused. "But I always thought you and I were good."

"We are, Nic, we are." A whole new way of looking at this situation was taking form.

"Even if I stay with Mom for now, it's not like I'll never see you."

"I'm sitting in the middle of nowhere, Nic, and I've dodged snow and slick roads since I left home." He shook his head. "Only now, this minute, am I seeing the truth of what you're saying."

"You know, Dad, I don't want to see you get hurt or disappointed, either. You have the big launch you've been working on since we moved into those cabins. And you have Emma."

His daughter was making so much sense he was already calculating how quickly he could get back. Since the minute he'd pulled out of Emma's driveway, he'd forced himself to think about Nic, and how she and Jackie were doing. And, as usual, worrying about her getting caught up in Jackie's problems. All along, he should have known Nic was capable of handling it herself.

"Okay. You're right, Nic. I've got to go back and hope Emma will understand."

When he heard Nic's girlish giggle come through the phone, his heart soared.

"She knows you like her like her," Nic said lightly. "She'll forgive you. But get going. Text me when you get there."

Parker laughed. "I will. I'll send you pictures of the launch."

"Good. Tell Emma I said hi."

With that, they ended the call and Parker calculated the miles back home. If the roads were clear, he'd be there in no time.

CHAPTER SEVENTEEN

THE WIND RUFFLED the blanket of snow and temporarily blurred the pier and the lake in the early morning light. The drive home had been slow—and difficult. But he'd made it. And in time to get set up for the launch that evening. He'd let Ty and Stacey know he was back, but first, he'd find Emma. He'd seen her car in the lot, partially covered by drifting snow, so she'd already arrived. Parker dropped his duffel in his cabin and went to check on the birds, where he'd probably find Emma.

He opened the door and stepped inside the dark cabin, his eyes adjusting to the dim light. The low hum of a portable heater was the only sound other than the wind outside. As soon as he could see, he recognized the top of Emma's head sticking out of the sleeping bag that took up the length of the bench. Her boots were on the floor near the table and her cane hung over the chair. His log was open on the counter, and both cages were covered. Trying not to make noise with his steps, he went farther inside. Emma turned her head on the small pillow, facing him now. It was almost nine o'clock. Late, he knew, for Emma to still be sleeping.

When she winced as she shifted her body, he guessed she wasn't resting all that comfortably on the wooden bench. He leaned over and lightly kissed her temple. When a little frown appeared, he kissed her cheek. That did it. Her eyes popped open and a second later a smile lit up her face.

"Hey, Em," he whispered. "It's Christmas Eve morning. Did you sleep here all night?"

She struggled to raise herself on the narrow bench. "I need to get out of the sleeping bag."

"I don't know how you got into it and had any rest on that narrow bench in the first place," he said, smiling.

She scratched her head. "It wasn't easy."

She winced as she maneuvered her body, but managed to unzip the bag so she could get to her feet. A little unsteady and stiff, but she was smiling. "Done. And to answer your question, yes, I stayed here. It's the crow. He's sick." She told him how she decided he had an infection, maybe salmonella.

"I read your notes, so I know that's fatal. If something bad happened, I wanted to be here." She rolled her eyes. "I know, that sounds ridiculous." She looked at him quizzically. "Wait a minute. Why are you here? What happened? Is Nicole with you?"

He shook his head. "No, no, you're not being ridiculous and Nic isn't with me. Everything's fine, but I'll tell you about it later." He'd also tell her about standing watch over a bird a time or two. Later. "I'll have a look." He put his hand on the cloth covering the crow's pen. "But prepare yourself."

She nodded at the cage. "Go ahead. I'm ready."

At the first exposure to light the crow used his loud voice to greet the day. Emma let out a gasp of relief. "Wow. He's on his perch, too."

Parker checked the feeder. Only a few chopped nuts and seeds were there. "He must have been hungry again. That means it was some other minor infection, if he's bounced back so soon."

"Good." She gave him a sidelong glance. "I almost forgot I'm mad at you for leaving so fast."

"I'm mad at me, too. And Nic wasn't happy

with me, either. Following her up to Vermont was a very bad idea." He told her about their talk, and how she ended up reassuring him. "She knows how much I love you, Em. She also wants to work things out with Jackie on her own without me trying to protect her or hovering."

Emma nodded along, but pulled on her boots and took the cloth off the owl's cage. Parker waited for her to react, but she kept herself busy with the birds.

"Emma? I'm really sorry for taking off like that."

"And I kick myself for suggesting it in the first place." She shrugged. "I was wrong and it seems you were, too."

"I didn't go because of anything you said. I lost sight of Nic being mature enough to sort out her own life." He moved closer to her and opened his arms. "I love you. I wanted to stay here with you all along. You must know that."

Emma stared at him, hesitating. But then she stepped into his arms and lifted her face for a kiss he was happy to give.

"When did the wind pick up?" Emma asked, as if noticing it for the first time.

"It was with me all the way back from Pennsylvania. I had to dodge some downed trees coming into town, and later, I'll clear some limbs and branches on our entry road."

"I wonder what it will mean for the launch."

"That's hours away."

Emma stepped back and looked down at her sweater and jeans. "I need to get home and clean myself up." She rubbed her palms together. "Now that I know the crow is on the mend I can hardly wait for tonight to see the pretty lights and the holiday crowd."

Parker's phone buzzed. "A text," he said, frowning at the screen, "from Mike. We've got trees down all over. He has a report that a large one is blocking one of the main access streets in town." He kept scrolling and frowning. "He says he's diverting the street crews to try to clear those spots, otherwise Stacey and Ty are saying there'll be no launch."

He looked at Emma, noting her determined face.

"I need to go check the other entry points, Em. Maybe Bill and Will can get in through the back of the sanctuary and bring their chain saws."

"You go. I'll finish up in here," Emma said.

Parker dug in his pockets and pulled out his hat and gloves. He shook his head. "Wish me luck."

On the way to the blocked road, Parker saw some relatively small branches blocking the driveway into the sanctuary. Those he could move himself and the bigger ones with his chain saw, but from there, it was tricky. He reached Bill Rivera, who said he and Will would find a way to work their way in. But on time? That's what worried Parker.

On his way back to the cabin, he met Mike coming up from the beach.

"Since we're trapped, I might as well be here." He waved his phone in the air. "I'm keeping track of everything by phone and text, anyway."

Parker filled him in on what he saw.

"We can check the boardwalk. See if it's still walkable. And the lights," Mike said.

Parker led the way and he and Mike tested the railings and cleared branches off the planking. Several trees in the woods were downed, but posed no threat. Where lights had loosened or tangled in the wind they straightened them out.

"I'll come back here before the launch starts," Mike offered, "and check this area again. The wind is still coming strong."

When they started back, they heard a voice behind them calling their names. It was Stacey, barely recognizable in a long down coat with a hood pulled tight.

"Hey, guys, I don't live far, so I walked over. If the worst happens and we have to cancel, I can get home easily enough."

"No canceling," Mike said, looking at his phone. "These guys are working hard. We'll clear everything no matter what it takes."

"That's bold," Parker said.

The three walked to the pier. The lake was frozen over so snow was blowing across the surface, looking like sand blowing over a dune. Emma joined them to find out the status, and then went off with Stacey to help set up the center.

Over the next few hours, Will and Bill worked with the town crew, and Mike and Parker cleared away and cut up smaller branches.

Finally, Mike got the word. The town trucks had opened every road, except two farm roads. "Looks like the show can go on."

"I never doubted it," Parker said.

Mike just shook his head. "We got lucky."

ABOUT AN HOUR before showtime, a steady stream of cars approached the sanctuary. Hardier folks, including many young families had left their cars on the dirt road behind the sanctuary and took the boardwalk route to the lake. The wind had died down, but snow flurries were adding a fresh dusting of snow. When the roads opened, Emma had hurried home to shower and change into fleece-lined pants and her down jacket, the same way most everyone was dressed that night. The toddlers and young kids could barely move in their puffy snowsuits.

"Look at all the people enjoying the woods," Ruby said when she and Jason arrived. "That boardwalk makes the sanctuary so special."

Emma reminded Ruby it had all started with her. "You proposed linking the trails from the covered bridge to the back of the sanctuary. The rest flowed from there."

Ruby laughed. "Hey, it took a village, my friend."

"There's Dad," Jason said, pointing to Mike, who was talking with Parker and Ty. The three men had their hats pulled down over their ears and the ends of their scarves blew around in the breeze as they pointed gloved fingers this way and that. Finalizing the logistics, Emma assumed. Mike and Parker left the raised podium set up on the pier and Ty was alone with a mic in his hand. Ty had pretended like nothing happened at the fair and Parker decided to let it go. Emma wasn't so forgiving, but she kept it to herself.

"It's the final countdown to the lights coming on," Ruby said, squeezing Jason's shoulder.

Emma glanced at the crowd gathered by the pier. "I'll bet we're already way over two hundred people. Ty and Stacey had set two hundred as the threshold for success. Anything over that is a bonus."

"Familiar faces," Ruby said, pointing to a cluster of people. "Maggie and Georgia and their families, Mrs. Cermak and her husband."

"And will you look at that," Ruby said, her mouth dropping open. "That's Jim and Ruth Kellerman. Wow. Parker managed to achieve what no one else could. He turned that stubborn old guy into a friendly face in the crowd." She paused. "Well, maybe not friendly, but at least civil."

"I call Parker the Jim whisperer. Must have been that crow he brought in," Emma said. "The mythical storyteller bird must have whispered magic words in his ear. Maybe softened his heart a little, huh?"

Suddenly, Ty's voice booming welcoming words over the loudspeaker quieted the crowd. "We're so glad you're sharing a little bit of the holiday with us." He ran down the long list of people and businesses to thank. Emma could have hugged Ty for including her name as only one among many who'd helped. She and the diner owner who donated the hot chocolate and the florist who made the wreath got equal billing. She liked it that way.

"It's almost dark now," Stacey said. "Who wants us to light up the woods?"

Jason's hand shot up. "I do." Then he joined in the chant started by some older kids behind them. "Lights, lights, lights."

The chanting stopped abruptly when the white fairy lights on the pier lit up behind Stacey, bringing the first exclamations from the crowd. Then, all two hundred plus people looked behind them and a collective *ah* rippled through the crowd in response to the intricate outline of lights wrapped around the boardwalk railings and snaking through the woods. Gusts of wind sent lights and tree branches swaying and changing the patterns. The boardwalk light show succeeded in showing the woods in constant motion. The lit-up buildings completed the wonderland image.

Emma let out a long sigh. "Kind of makes you believe wood sprites and fairies are flitting about, doesn't it?"

Jason quickly chimed in. "I don't believe in fairies."

"No?" Ruby landed a kiss on the top of his head. "I didn't know that."

"But I believe reindeer can fly. *Some* reindeer."

Emma and Ruby laughed, but Stacey's voice grabbed their attention.

"A day like this is a team effort, but I want to make sure we recognize Parker Davis, our director and a naturalist with years of experience. All the changes you see here came about because of a collective vision. Then we hired Parker to turn our vision into a reality. What a job he's done." She held the microphone out to Parker.

Ruby nudged Emma's side and flashed a beaming smile. "He's smart, sweet and about as hunky as they come. You really hit the jackpot."

Emma snorted. "You're right, as usual."

Parker promised to keep it short. "I hope you won't leave today without becoming a member of this facility. And I'm going to ask again and again that you help our board bring the five-year vision to life. With enough help we can make it happen in four years—or even three." He gestured to the office and invited everyone to stop in anytime.

"I'd like to speak a little personally now. When I arrived here with my daughter, I was eager to get the renovations started. We had great work crews, led by Bill Rivera and his son Will. That father-son team jumped in today to help our town's road crews clear the fallen trees and limbs blocking our roads. Mayor Mike helped, too, as usual. I've come to know a few of you and while you were helping to pull this event together, you also taught me the rich history of this land—and this lake."

Parker shook his head. "But that's not the half of it." He started chuckling and even without knowing why he was so jovial, pockets of people in the crowd laughed along with him. "Here's the thing, folks. I hoped I'd like it here, and I do. But I *never* imagined falling in love with a fantastic woman. As my daughter Nicole says, 'she's really cool.'"

Emma's hands covered her mouth and cheeks. But even as she couldn't hide her own laughter, the tingling behind her eyes started.

"The best part is," Parker said, "many of you know her. You've seen her generous heart in action. Her great photographs tell you exactly how much she loves Bluestone River. I've had a close-up view of her dedication to this sanctuary. As a matter of fact she's involved in treating our injured birds." He paused. Even Emma felt the anticipation build in the crowd. "And not long ago, I learned she likes to dance." He put his hand over his brow as if scouting to see where she was in the crowd. Finally, he pointed to her. "There she is. Emma O'Connell."

The applause—and cheering led by Ruby—was immediate and loud. Emma didn't know half the people clapping, but she played her part and turned in all directions and waved both hands.

"Come on up, Emma," Parker said, "and be part of the dedication. What we have here today wouldn't have been possible without you. I'm pretty sure most everyone knows that."

Taken by surprise, Emma felt her heart beat faster.

"Get moving, Em," Ruby encouraged,

touching her back. "For once you're going to let someone give you credit for what you do around here."

The people standing in front of her were friendly and quickly moved aside to make a path for her to get to the pier. Excited or not, she watched the ground with each step and Parker met her halfway. He kissed her cheek and she put her arm through his and went the rest of the way to the pier.

The dedication went quickly after that. Ty and Stacey rolled a large easel onto the pier.

Mike stepped forward and said, "I'm confident the three generations of Abbots who took care of this land long before I was born would be gratified to see what the sanctuary board and Bluestone River are doing today." He pulled off the cloth and said, "As of today, this spot is officially relaunched as the Hidden Lake Bird Sanctuary & Nature Center."

The logo showed the outline of a tree in black with six birds perched on the branches. "Let's spread the word about this treasure and make it grow." Mike stayed in place until the applause died down. When he yelled Merry Christmas the crowd began to break up. Most of the crowd headed into the woods to walk on the planking and see the lights from all angles.

Emma hung back when people approached Parker to introduce themselves and chat. But when he saw Ruth and Jim Kellerman, Parker said they should go say hello.

"Maybe you should go alone," she said. "I'm not one of Jim's favorite people."

He took hold of her hand. "Ah, it's Christmas. Give it a chance."

Emma rolled her eyes. "When you put it like that…"

Ruth and Jim sat on the benches set up near the office.

"Merry Christmas," Parker said when they reached the couple. "I'm glad you came. I hope you'll come visit the crow soon. Like I told you on the phone, Jim, I believe the crow will live at the sanctuary now. We only name the permanent birds. Maybe we should call him Jim."

Jim waved off that idea, but Ruth nodded. "I like that. For sure, we'll stop in. I'm delighted you saved his life."

"After what you did for the crow," Jim admitted, "I get what you're doing a little better now."

"Nice to see you," Emma said, directing

her remark to Ruth. She didn't want her presence to break the cordiality between Jim and Parker.

"Same here," Ruth said, getting to her feet. "We're going to become members, but right now we need to get home."

Jim held up his aluminum cane and nodded to Emma. "My bum knee is giving me fits, so I'm hobbling around with this. But I like your cane better. Maybe I should get a fancier one like that."

Emma smiled. "I do like to make a fashion statement, Jim. I think you should do the same."

Jim pointed to the pier, with the lights shining on the new logo. "You've done okay with your family's money, Emma. Your parents would be proud of you. Neil, too."

At the mention of Neil, Ruth started to pull Jim away, but Emma said, "I think you're right, Jim. I hope so. My parents and Neil loved Bluestone River as much as we do."

An hour later, it was over, the cleanup work done. With their arms around each other she and Parker walked to his cabin. "I'm not ready for the day to end," she said.

"No reason it has to," Parker said, taking her hand. "It all went so well, but I have to admit I missed Nic's presence. It's Christmas Eve. She would have enjoyed this so much."

"I think about her mulling over her career choices at the fair at Neville. She reminded me of you. I can only imagine how much you miss her tonight."

"I expect I'll talk to her tomorrow. She was kind of vague about her plans. Well, *their* plans."

When they sat at the table, Parker suddenly frowned and pointed to the corner by the couch. "There's a huge box I've never seen before sitting over there."

"Oh, really? What could it mean that it's wrapped in paper with snowmen all over it?" Emma smiled smugly. "Would you like to open your Christmas present now?"

He paused and stammered his answer. "Uh, sure. As long as you open yours, too."

"I will, but you first." Emma went to the corner and started dragging it, but Parker followed her and carried it to the table.

"How did you get it in here?"

"I have my ways. His name is Mike. I brought it with me when I came back after going home to change. He managed to slip in here when you weren't looking."

Parker ripped off the paper and opened the

box. He grinned as he lifted the carving of the goose. "A Guy Hammond original," he said, in a hushed tone. "It's incredible! Nearly life size." He ran his hand across the smooth wood and the carved texture of the wings.

"I know you admire his work, especially the detail. I could tell by the way you've looked at my canes."

Parker nodded. "True. He's exceptional. I'll keep this in here, at least for a while. Then maybe I'll showcase it in the center." His smile widened. "Maybe." Parker put the carving on the table and then pulled Emma to her feet. He cupped her face in his hands and kissed her once and then again. Finally, he let her go. "Now it's your turn. Sit back down."

Emma did as he asked, excitement bubbling inside her. He was back. They were back. The launch had been beautiful and filled with love and pride in the center, and in Bluestone River, too.

Parker took a tissue-wrapped package out of the closet and put it in front of her. "Get going. I can't wait for you to see what's inside."

She tore into the tissue that covered a large intricately cut crystal bowl.

"It's not a Hammond, but I thought of you when I saw it."

"Oh, Parker, it's beautiful. I love it." She pulled out a ball of tissue from inside the bowl and another box fell out. This one was a square carved jewelry box. Another Guy Hammond treasure. She lifted the lid and took in a breath. A tiny ring box was nestled in the velvet lining. She looked up at Parker.

"Will you please open it?" he whispered.

"Are you sure?" Emma asked.

"I am. I'm dying here waiting for you to tell me you are, too."

Emma lifted the lid and took in a breath. It was a diamond surrounded by a circle of deep red garnets. She held the box in her palm and stared at this ring that Parker gave to her in love. Nothing in her life so far had been as special as this moment.

"Will you marry me, Emma? Maybe here at the sanctuary? Or the bridge where we danced the first time?" Parker paused. "Too much, too soon to think about?"

Emma tapped her temple. "Give me a minute. My mind is racing. Not about my answer, that's a big fat yes. But the wonder of it."

Parker took the ring out of the box. "May I?"

"Oh, yes," she said as she lifted her hand.

He bent down and slipped the ring on her finger. She held out her hand and stared at it. "It's perfect."

When he straightened up, she stood and walked into his open arms. "So, we're engaged. Imagine that."

He kissed her and brushed his cheek across her hair. "Let's really seal the deal. Wanna dance?"

"I thought you'd never ask. But we need some music."

"I don't think so." He led her away from the table and began humming the opening bars of "White Christmas" as he circled his arm gently around her waist. "See? We can dance without music."

"With a voice like yours we can."

He took small steps across the floor, singing and humming. Then he stepped back and looked into her eyes and twirled her under his arm.

"I *love* this, Parker." Her voice was full of joy. "I can't believe how much I love you."

"I'm one lucky guy." He drew her into his arms again and started a new song.

Suddenly, the cabin door flew open and amidst a great gust of wind and blowing snow, a person emerged, dropping a duffel and an oversized backpack on the floor with a thud. As if in triumph, she threw back the hood of her jacket and smiled.

Nicole!

Emma stepped back while Parker hurried to Nic and enveloped her in a bear hug. "I'm so glad to see you. How did you get here? And so fast? You were home when I talked with you last night."

"A friend from school was coming this way, so we shared the driving. She'll pick me up after Christmas to go back, but that's not important now. I just couldn't miss Christmas with you, Dad."

Nic smiled at Emma. "Oops. I've interrupted something." Then she noticed the carving on the table. "That's gorgeous."

"Emma gave it to me for Christmas." Parker glanced back at Emma. "Uh, we have news."

"O…kay." Nic smiled broadly. Then she picked up her pack and her duffel. "I'll go dump these at my place. Then I'll come back and you can tell me about it."

"Sounds good, Nic," Parker said, shaking his head in amusement.

Nic flew out the door the same way she flew in. "She's like the wind herself," Emma said.

"Hey, at least we get to share our news and have a little celebration."

"So much to look forward to, Parker," Emma said, stretching her arms wide. "We'll have a wonderful winter." She lifted her face for a kiss.

He caressed her cheek and kissed her lightly. "I love you, Emma."

"Love you back," she said. "And in case I forget, Merry Christmas."

* * * * *

*Don't miss other Bluestone River
romances from author
Virginia McCullough,
available at www.Harlequin.com!*